THE SPIDER HEIST

JASON KASPER

SEVERN RIVER
PUBLISHING

Severn River Publishing
SevernRiverBooks.com

This is a work of fiction. Names, characters, businesses, places, events and incidents are either the products of the author's imagination or used in a fictitious manner. Any resemblance to actual persons, living or dead, or actual events is purely coincidental.

ISBN: 978-1-64875-490-6 (Paperback)

PRAISE FOR THE SPIDER HEIST

"*The Spider Heist* is a nonstop thrill ride, with intriguing characters and layers of mystery that the author carefully unravels right to the very last page. Blair is an instantly lovable heroine: smart, badass, brave and yet flawed enough to make her very relatable. Nothing in this captivating thriller is as it seems. My heart was in my throat until the very end, and once I reached the last word, all I wanted was more."

-**Lisa Regan**, USA Today and WSJ Bestselling Author

"Outstanding! Jason Kasper spins an intricate web of clues, second-guesses, and action around a cast of memorable characters that will keep readers hooked from the first page to the final twist. I dare you to try and put it down."

-**LynDee Walker**, Agatha Award-Nominated Author of the *Nichelle Clarke* Series

"I flew through *The Spider Heist*. It's packed with action, twists, and laughs. Kasper wields excitement like a hammer, and he bashes you over the head with it, again and again."

-**LT Vargus**, Co-Author of the *Violet Darger* Series

"Jason Kasper weaves a masterful page-turner with *The Spider Heist*, starring his irresistible new character, Blair Morgan. If you like action, intrigue, suspense, and thrills, read this book."

-**Jeff Carson**, Bestselling Author of the *David Wolf* Mystery Series

"*The Spider Heist* robbed me blind, stealing both time and sleep. Once I picked it up, this book sucked me in like few others have ever done. Kasper puts you front and center in one of the best heist stories I've ever come across."

-**Brian Shea**, Author of the *Boston Crime Thriller* Series and Former Detective

"*The Spider Heist* is a tour-de-force of high stakes thriller action, unexpected twists, and nail-biting suspense. An unforgettable roller coaster ride that leaves you guessing until the end."

-**Steven Konkoly**, USA Today Bestselling Author of the *Ryan Decker* Series

"Twists and turns with an incredibly likable heroine— I loved it." -**A.G. Riddle**, International Bestselling Author of *The Atlantis Gene*

To my readers—

Thank you for making this all possible

1

BLAIR

His hands wrapped around Blair Morgan's arms, and with a violent, forceful shove, he pushed her toward the void of sky ahead.

She skidded to a stop at the roof's edge. Dark clouds loomed overhead, almost low enough to touch. The vast, stormy sky trembled on the brink of rain, shuddering with the hammering chop of police and media helicopters.

Blair felt like her heart would explode, the delirious fear driving her to a psychological breaking point from which she could never return. Her red dress was torn, black hair tousled and blowing in the wind that whipped up the smell of Los Angeles—vehicle exhaust mixed with salty ocean.

How had this happened, she wondered in a fleeting moment of terror.

And then, unable to stop herself, she looked down.

An anguished shriek escaped her throat. The Century City skyscrapers speared upward, mirrored windows poised to reflect her fall toward streets that looked impossibly small. Police cars barricaded every intersection, their thin, piercing wails rising helplessly toward her.

She struggled away from the edge, glancing backward with a panicked, irrational hope that *this couldn't be happening*. But the man held her in place, his eyes fiery behind a black ski mask. His partner stepped in to block her escape and shouted, "SWAT team is crossing the 34th floor—they'll be on the roof in thirty seconds!"

The two men were outfitted in masks, gloves, and guns. Bags of cash were slung across their backs, a prize they wouldn't part with even in death.

Desperate and unable to flee, Blair searched the murky sky until she saw them: two black helicopters roaring toward the roof, bristling with FBI SWAT agents poised on the skids. They'd arrive even sooner than their teammates swarming up the stairwell below her, but all of them would be too late to save her.

No other rescue was coming. The remaining helicopters circled like vultures, witnesses to the chilling spectacle on the rooftop. Like it or not, Blair was going over the edge. The man behind her would see to that. As she gasped for breath, he placed the barrel of a pistol to her temple.

He shouted into her ear, a voice without sympathy.

"It's time to go, Blair."

She bit her lip, shuddering in his grasp.

And then Blair began to cry.

2

24 HOURS EARLIER

Blair topped off the man's mug from her carafe, then picked up the bill holder and slid it into her apron pocket.

"Thank you so much for coming in to see us today. Have a great morning, and we hope to see you back at Greaney's soon—"

"How about we meet up after your shift, girl?" The young Latino man jerked his chin up toward her as he slouched, throwing one arm over the back of his booth seat. "You know, get a coffee or somethin'."

Blair stopped in place, examining him. The lower half of his face covered in a neat goatee, the rest hidden under a blue Dodgers hat. He wore a black jacket over a hoodie, its zipper drawn low enough to expose the tattoo of a hawk with wings spread across his throat.

She hoisted the carafe. "I work at a brunch joint. Coffee's the one thing I'm never short on."

"What about happiness?"

She scrunched up her face in confusion. "What are you, some kind of life coach?"

"Naw, girl. I mean, isn't...isn't that how the jingle goes?" He broke into song. "'At Greaney's, we don't brew coffe-ee...we brew happin-e-ess?'"

"Yeah, well, that's because they couldn't think of a rhyme about their swing shift starting at three a.m."

His eyes gleamed at her, undaunted. "Ain't gonna scare me off, girl..."

3

"Though in all fairness, you do have a pretty good voice."

"...you play hard to get all you want."

"Cool, because I plan on keeping it up until you leave."

"What's the matter, you afraid to date a gangster? Gotta have a little courage, girl. Same thing as freedom."

Spoken like a guy who's never been to prison, Blair thought.

She tapped an index finger against the carafe, regarding him with an expression that she tried to contain at tolerance. "Take it from a girl who knows. *Freedom* is freedom, gangster. And as hard as it is for me to pass up on a romantic *and* an amateur philosopher, I'm going to give you a hard 'no.'"

"Come on, girl." He raised his eyebrows suggestively. "You haven't even seen my hard 'yes.'"

Blair froze, her pulse quickening as she considered her reaction. Throw the mug of scalding coffee in his face. Clock him over the head with the carafe.

Don't do it, you need this job. Don't do it, you need this job.

She curled her lips into a grim, plastic smile. "If you'll excuse me, sir, I have to go in the back and dry heave while trying to purge this entire interaction from my psyche. Have a nice day."

Blair turned and marched toward the last open check of her shift. Flustered over the wannabe gangbanger, she overshot her destination and had to double back to find the right table.

"Can I get you anything else today, sir?"

"I'd just like some more coffee, thanks."

She tilted the carafe into his mug, but her hand was still shaking with anger. The coffee flowed more quickly than she anticipated, spilling over the sleeve of his suit jacket.

"I'm sorry," she said, "let me—"

"It's fine," the man replied, gently dabbing a napkin on the stain. "I've got lots of suits."

Blair looked over to find her manager lurking near the kitchen entrance and watching her suspiciously. Had he seen this latest transgression? Probably. Casually sweeping forward to replace the carafe at its station, she heard him call to her.

"Can I talk to you, Blair?"

4

She glanced toward him, lifting her carafe. "Just a minute, Donald."

Then Blair took a step backward, turning too late to stop herself from colliding with a runner balancing a tray of plates on his way to the dining room.

The runner struggled to stop the inevitable, but the tray had already shifted to an unrecoverable angle. The plates slid off the edge in unison.

Porcelain and brunch entrees detonated against the floor, and Blair winced, afraid to look at the carnage at her feet.

There was a smattering of applause from the dining room.

"Oh." Blair's face and neck burned with embarrassment. "I am so, so sorry—"

"Blair," her manager called urgently, waving her over as several busboys rushed out of the kitchen to clean up the catastrophe.

"Guys, I am *so* sorry," Blair repeated. "Completely my fault. It won't happen again, I promise." Finding herself ignored, she spun to face her manager. Taking a breath, she composed herself, set down the carafe, and walked over with as much dignity as she could muster.

"Yes, Donald?"

"Blair, this isn't working out."

She took a resolute breath. "It was one mistake."

"Knocking that tray over, or hosing your customer with coffee ten seconds before that?"

She considered the question. "Okay, two mistakes."

"Relax. I'm not mad about either of those."

Blair gasped a relieved exhale until he continued speaking.

"It's the dozen screw-ups before them, all in your first week, that give me cause for concern. If the runners get sent to dining with another wrong order from you, they're going to start quitting in droves."

"I just started working here, Donald. I'm still learning."

He winced apologetically. "You just started here at Greaney's, yeah. But your application listed employment at two other restaurants, and I'm beginning to see why neither lasted very long."

Blair crossed her arms. "I've got rent due in a week—this is horrible timing. Can't you just keep me on a little while longer?"

"Look," he said in a conciliatory tone. "The whole rent-is-due routine is a long shot. At your next restaurant, try playing the gender card instead.

5

Maybe even sexual harassment. It should buy you an extra couple of weeks. Please clear out your locker and go. We'll mail your paycheck."

Blair spun on her heels and marched to the register, where she produced a bill for one bottomless cup of coffee. Ripping the receipt off the printer, she stuffed it in a bill folder and returned to the table with the man she'd splashed coffee on a minute earlier.

Blair put on her best forced smile. "My shift is ending, sir, so if you need anything else another member of the wait staff will be happy to get it for you."

"I understand."

She set his check on the table. "Thank you so much for coming in to see us today. Have a great morning, and we hope to see you back at Greaney's soon—"

"You just got fired, didn't you?"

She paused. "Yeah, pretty much."

He looked out the window, then to her. "There's a Cheritto's across the street. I'll get a table. Come find me."

He was handsome, with neatly parted sandy-blond hair. Deliberate stubble dusted a strong jaw, and jade eyes projected total confidence. He had a well-muscled physique that spoke to a pricey gym membership, and his impeccably tailored gray suit accentuated every angle of his chest and shoulders.

Blair knew his kind. They swarmed like bees across the streets of Southern California—young businessmen with new money to spare, trying to dress and act like celebrities. But this one had missed the mark on his watch, a beat-up vintage model instead of the ubiquitous Rolex.

"No offense," she began. "You definitely have a better sales pitch than the last customer who asked me out. But I'm having a bad day and a bad week and a horrible month and my worst year ever. So I'm not what you'd call 'emotionally available' at the moment."

"I wasn't asking you out. This is business. I believe we may have a solution to each other's problems."

Blair tilted her head. "Is that so? What 'problems' do you think I have, exactly?"

"Money, for one. You just got fired."

She laughed. "This is LA. There are a million restaurants, and I can get a job at ninety-nine percent of them."

"Oh, I know you can. Judging by the state of your shoes and the fact that you haven't been here long enough to have a nametag, you've probably done exactly that two or three times in the past month. I never had the hands to be a concert pianist, so I didn't try. You should play to your strengths. See you at Cheritto's."

"Yeah? Well don't hold your breath while you wait, because I'm not going."

He shelled a twenty-dollar bill out of his wallet and set it atop the check.

"That's entirely up to you. But if you don't, you'd violate the first rule of making money."

Blair folded her arms, waiting for him to continue. She didn't want to give this smug businessman the satisfaction of asking what that rule was.

And she didn't have to.

He casually slid out of his booth and buttoned his suit jacket before adding, "Know an opportunity when you see one."

Then he turned and breezed out of the restaurant, disappearing from her view and into the sunshine.

3

STERLING

Sterling took a sip of coffee and set the mug down as Blair wandered into Cheritto's and scanned the tables for him.

He raised a hand toward her.

She carried a backpack over one shoulder, and now wore a white blouse. Clearly they'd made her leave her uniform shirt behind.

As she approached, Sterling appraised her features one last time. Her black hair was thick and long with a velvety sheen—she was easy to dismiss as Asian but for the wide, exotic brown eyes that defied a single ethnicity. She had an athletic build, probably a runner, and was attractive even without makeup and with her hair pulled into a bun. He could have extended his offer to any number of slim brunettes, but witnessing this one's sudden firing was too good an opportunity to pass up.

She'd do perfectly.

"Thank you for coming," he said as she took a seat. "My name is Sterling."

"Blair."

He gestured to the mug in front of her. "I got you a coffee, Blair. Not as good as what they brew at Greaney's, but it'll do."

She didn't touch it. "What is this about?"

"I work for a finance startup."

"I doubt that." She glanced suspiciously at the watch visible under his

8

coffee-stained sleeve. "You're wearing a vintage Omega Seamaster that looks like you put it in a blender. Not the timepiece of choice for finance hotshots."

"This is from my father. I inherited it when he passed."

Blair lowered her eyes. "I'm sorry."

"It's okay. One of my potential partners is on the brink of leaving his job to join my startup. We want him, but he's been having a streak of bad luck that's affecting his decision to join my company. If he bails for good, it would hurt our bottom line."

"What does this have to do with me?"

"He and his wife recently separated. Since then, he's been stumbling bad in the dating scene. Great guy. Not a ladies' man."

"You want me to, what, go on a date with him?"

Sterling shook his head, as if the question was in poor taste. "Nothing that extreme. He'll be drinking at The Rojo Exchange in Beverly Hills tonight. I'd simply like you to run into him at the bar, have a couple drinks, chat him up, and boost his ego a little bit. Then make whatever excuse you'd like, and leave."

"You think a few drinks with a woman will restore his confidence?"

"Based on what I know about him, I think it'll restore just enough. I could be wrong, of course, but if I am that's no skin off your back. He's a trust-fund baby, born into the family business, with all the baggage that comes along with that. His ego doesn't react well when he doesn't get his way. He's been on a downhill slide—I just need someone to level him out before our meeting on Monday."

"What do I get out of this arrangement?"

"Two grand."

"Done," Blair blurted.

"Good. And I'll do you one better," he added. "I'll double the payment if you get him back to his house."

Blair pushed back her chair and stood. "I hope you find the girl you're looking for. You'll have better luck at Sunset Boulevard."

As she turned to leave, Sterling stopped her with the words, "That would be illegal." He continued speaking calmly to her backside. "I don't break the law myself, and I'd never ask anyone else to."

She spun to face him. "Oh, so you're a real model citizen, then."

He shrugged indifferently. "Second rule of making money: don't waste what you've got. And the quickest way to lose everything is to try and outwit the law. Once you've seen the men in blue jackets haul off a broker who got greedy, you don't forget it. But that's never going to be me, or anyone that works for me." He took a sip from his mug. "Your coffee is getting cold."

Blair sat back down, folding her hands in her lap without touching her drink.

"So what are you proposing?"

"My friend likes to show off. You'll barely be able to get a word in edge-wise, believe me. Give him a good Monday-morning story about his week-end. He brought home a beautiful woman, she turned out to be a prude and left by taxi. That's an extra two grand. Totally optional, of course. You choose to walk away at the bar? You're still coming out two grand ahead, plus the free cocktails."

Her voice took on a suddenly higher pitch. "I'll need to get some clothes if you expect me to fit in among rich people."

"I was just about to mention that. You've got plenty of time to go shop-ping before tonight, and I'll give you a three-hundred-dollar allowance—"

"Six hundred."

"Four hundred."

"Five."

"—a four-hundred-and-fifty-dollar allowance to get some evening wear that wouldn't appear out of place in Beverly Hills."

A waitress appeared beside the table with a notepad.

"Welcome to Cheritto's. Are we ready to order, or do we need a little more time to look at the menu?"

Sterling raised his eyebrows at Blair. She returned his gaze levelly, picked up the coffee mug in front of her, and took a sip.

4

BLAIR

As Blair sat at the bar of The Rojo Exchange, she couldn't escape one thought: the irony of her situation had gone from merely impressive to abjectly staggering.

She'd never had the money or inclination to frequent Beverly Hills, much less places like this. Blair had always been quite content with her middle-class work, colleagues, and somewhat complicated love life. She was used to post-work drinks at a beer garden in El Segundo, where rock and roll songs transitioned to the roar of jets taking off at nearby LAX.

Here in Beverly Hills, she sipped an "elevated" cocktail—it was whiskey, bitters, and vermouth, what was there to elevate?—beside an intricate oil portrait of a stoic monkey in a Prussian general's uniform.

The bar's chairs and accents were a macabre tone of red, adorned with hip postmodern art. Above it all, the pervasive smell of sticky-sweet cotton candy wafted off pink cocktails trading hands over the bar, followed by plates of caviar tapas.

Yes, Blair decided, the irony was almost too much to bear. She missed the friendship of her coworkers, in a strange way she missed her lover, and perhaps above all, she missed her job. She was now at what could optimistically be called a personal and professional low point, yet she was being doted on by a suitor—if such a term could be bestowed on the heavyset man with darting eyes now plying her with alcohol—in a bar that could best be described as "circus chic."

Gordon asked, "Another Manhattan?"

"Please." She threw back the rest of her drink. Then Blair set the glass down and saw him looking at her hungrily, greedily, before flagging down another round. She had chosen an inexpensive red dress with a slit up one leg, and black suede ankle boots with a low heel. But under Gordon's probing eyes, she suddenly wished she'd chosen something even more conservative.

She could see why Gordon wasn't successful with the ladies—he was narcissistic and a terrible conversationalist. Either one would be a deal breaker. The combination of both was the next closest thing to unbearable.

She noted the pale band of skin around his left ring finger and would have assumed under other circumstances that he was a serial philanderer. He'd been quick to insert details of his financial success that did little more than reveal a deep insecurity. He must have often relied upon money in the past to lure young women to bed. Blair had tried to act impressed, enthralled even, but that was becoming more difficult with each passing minute.

"—but it's no big deal," Gordon went on. Blair had missed the intro to that sentence, and didn't bother asking him to repeat himself. "I've been successful, sure, but being a member of the lucky sperm club doesn't hurt."

"I'm sorry—the *what*?"

"Family money. I come from a long bloodline of well-to-do."

And how proud they would be, Blair thought, if they knew your business partners were hiring you a starry-eyed admirer.

"But I want to do my own thing," Gordon went on. "Something bigger. Something independent, you know? You ever get that feeling?"

"All the time," she lied.

The tattooed, handlebar-mustached bartender appeared and Blair gratefully accepted the drink with a word of thanks.

"So?" Gordon asked her.

She'd tuned out again. "Sorry, what?"

"I said, do you want to finish this round and get out of here?"

Blair felt her chest tightening with dread. She desperately wanted to get out of there. Just not with him.

But Sterling had promised an extra two grand if she let Gordon take her home, and Blair couldn't turn down that mountain of cash. She'd play along for another half hour, she decided, then call a cab and get out of Dodge before Gordon started undressing.

"I'd like that."

Gordon nodded self-assuredly. "I could get us a room at The Peninsula."

Blair gave him a tight smile and wordlessly returned to her drink. Sterling had said the house, not a hotel.

"Okay, okay...the Waldorf."

She set her drink down and looked at him. "I don't want to go to a hotel, Gordon."

"Oh. Well, in that case"—he smirked—"you're in for a real treat."

"How's that?"

"You'll get the best view of LA you've ever seen, right from my balcony."

* * *

Blair sat low in the noisy, two-seat sports car that Gordon piloted through the winding Bel Air roads. The headlights shone across manicured lawns and iron gates guarding expansive Mediterranean homes. Between the tree-covered hills and red terracotta roofs, she caught glimpses of private tennis courts and illuminated pools casting an ethereal blue glow into the night.

"It's an Aston Martin," Gordon announced.

"What is?"

"This car."

"Oh. It's...very nice." Blair hadn't asked and didn't care, and was now accustomed to Gordon's hopscotching thoughts of financial self-promotion.

"Same thing James Bond drives."

"I knew it sounded familiar," she offered, trying to sound convincing. While she didn't know about cars, she did know that Gordon was no Bond.

"Been to Bel Air before?"

"No."

"Quite a few bigwigs from the entertainment industry live here, you know. Celebrities, directors. Singers too. Homes on my street start in the six-million-dollar range. That's the *cheap* ones."

"Wow," Blair droned.

He looked over. "And I don't live in a cheap one."

Blair nodded distantly, keeping her eyes forward. She could feel him watching her, desperately waiting for her to ask him how much his house cost so he could parry it with a cool, nonchalant response.

The silence was deafening. Gordon wasn't suited for two-way conversations, especially when they involved some degree of subtlety.

After a long pause, Gordon began chattering nervously and fumbling for his cell phone. She surreptitiously glanced at the screen as he thumbed open an app to disarm his entire home security system.

The reason was clear: he didn't want security camera footage of her in his car.

Maybe he was still married after all, Blair thought, or maybe this action was just a threadbare reflex from when he was.

Gordon pulled into the driveway of a tan home with a steepled black roof, its exterior beautifully illuminated with the soft glow of security lighting. As the garage door opened, Blair noted the house number, committing it to memory. Gordon pulled into an open spot next to a huge black Mercedes sedan, then closed the garage door before exiting the car—her second indication that he sought discretion.

Blair's heart was thumping now, her mind a tumultuous clash of emotions. She felt like she was being watched, and attributed this to a justified sense of moral guilt. A lifetime ago, she'd turned sixteen without so much as a kiss from a high school boy. Now she was entering a strange man's home on the premise of receiving cash in exchange; she had become a sellout at best.

After jiggling his keys in the lock, Gordon held the door open for her to enter the house.

Blair faked a smile as she stepped inside.

Her suede ankle boots clicked against walnut floorboards. The interior smelled like sandalwood, and a section of quartz wall held a flat screen above a long glass fireplace.

Gordon closed the door behind her, and the deadbolt latching shut sounded like a prison cell. Blair shuddered, then tried to hide her reaction behind feigned admiration.

"Wow," she said. "This is...incredible."

He picked up a remote from a side table, and the fireplace blazed to life.

Blair clutched her purse as she took in the dining area, where a baby grand piano was nestled into a glass corner with breathtaking views of the city lights.

"You weren't kidding about the view."

"That's nothing. Come on out to the balcony."

Blair tried to refuse, but he was already leading the way to a sliding glass door that screeched as he opened it.

"Sorry," he mumbled apologetically. "I need to get that fixed."

Although Blair's discomfort grew with each step, she tamped down her fear and tentatively followed him outside.

The hillside below the house dropped away sharply into a grove of trees, and the LA skyline glowed on the horizon. She placed a trembling hand on the edge of the glass rail, steadying herself. Even if she fell, she told herself, there was a lower balcony to catch her—a deck lined with chairs, and a long rectangular pool jutting over the sloping hill. Its shimmering blue water seemed to be suspended midair, and Blair felt herself growing queasy.

Gordon followed her gaze. "We can go for a swim if you'd like."

"No thank you."

"Come on, it'll be fun. I'll make us a couple of drinks and we can head down."

Blair's breathing accelerated as she considered what to say to him. The truth? How would that sound?

Gordon, I'm...terrified of heights. I don't like stepping onto anything with a fall beneath it. That pool looks like it's hanging over a valley of death. Just standing on this balcony is testing my limits. And I haven't had nearly enough drinks to offset my paralyzing fear of heights in the slightest, much less test the structural integrity of a pool that's probably propped up from the side of the hill with toothpicks.

Instead she managed a weak smile and said, "Let's go inside."

As they returned to the main level, Blair's pulse subsided, and she calmed down even further when he closed the sliding glass door with another rusty metallic shriek.

"Make yourself at home," Gordon said, moving to a bar cart in his kitchen.

She was fumbling for her phone when Gordon entered the living room holding a pair of glasses containing two fingers of dark amber liquid.

Seeing her withdraw the phone, he asked, "What's wrong?"

"Oh, nothing. I think I'll just go."

"Nonsense! Have a seat." He motioned to a pair of couches on either side of the fireplace.

"I'm serious. I have to be at work early tomorrow."

Undaunted, Gordon approached and handed her a glass.

"Come on. This is three hundred dollars a bottle."

Blair let out an involuntary nervous giggle that released some of the tension inside her.

"What? Most girls are impressed," he shot back defensively.

"No, it's..." Searching for a word, she came up with, "Endearing. In its own way."

His face fell, and Blair silently cursed her reaction—she was supposed to be building his confidence, and instead he looked like a scolded puppy.

"Okay." She tucked her purse under her arm, keeping the phone in hand. "You know what? One drink won't hurt." She accepted the glass, then unlocked her phone to call a cab. "Don't take me too seriously, Gordon," she offered. "I'm just some woman from the bar."

Gordon reached out and placed a hand on her arm.

"Oh, Gordon," Blair said, backing away from him. "That wasn't an invitation to...touch me."

His face grew angry.

"What's the matter with you?" he shouted. "I rack up a three-hundred-dollar bill at the hottest new bar in Beverly Hills, drive you in a car that you could *never* afford, and now you insult me in my own estate? What are you, some kind of lesbian?"

Before Blair could overcome her shock to formulate a response, something happened that made her momentarily disregard Gordon altogether.

For the third time that night, Blair heard the metallic screech of the sliding glass door to the balcony.

Gordon turned wild-eyed toward the noise before dropping his glass. It hit the walnut floor and shattered as he stumbled backward.

"Don't hurt me!" he cried.

Blair raised both arms in the air—one with the phone, one with the whiskey glass—and heard her purse hit the floor as she did so. She remained perfectly still. The last thing she wanted to do was make a sudden movement that could startle a desperate man with a gun.

But the short, thickly muscled man stepping into the living room, semi-automatic pistol in his gloved right hand, didn't appear desperate.

Instead he stood commandingly before them, letting them see the gun without pointing it at them. His face was concealed by a black ski mask, and the wire coil of a radio earpiece descended beneath his collar. Blair immediately understood that this was no chance robbery. The man wore a police-like tool belt with handcuffs, a radio, and, most shockingly, a taser mounted in a cross draw opposite his pistol holster.

Blair canted her eyes down non-confrontationally as adrenaline coursed through her body—did he know who she was?

Gordon stammered, "T-take w-whatever you want—just don't hurt me."

"Gordon." The man in black spoke with authority, but his voice remained quiet and relaxed. "Shut up. And sit down before you hurt yourself."

He had a Boston accent, Blair noted—he barely pronounced the "r" in "hurt yourself." His eyes were thin; she guessed an Asian or Pacific Islander.

Blair watched Gordon taking shaky, almost comically deliberate steps around the front of the couch, his hands raised straight over his head. When he was more or less centered over a cushion, he fell backward like a puppet with its strings cut.

The armed man touched the collar of his jacket and said quietly, "All right, come on in."

The glass door screeched open again, and a moment later two more men entered, both wearing ski masks and tool belts. One was very tall and lean, pushing six foot two, Blair guessed, and the other was average build. Neither spoke.

"You." The first man pointed to Blair. "What's your name?"

Relief rushed through her. They were here because of Gordon, not her. They didn't know who she was...but what would happen if they found out?

"Blair."

"Don't worry, no one's gonna hurt you."

Blair met his almond-shaped eyes. "Okay."

"Go ahead and drop that phone."

She let it go, and it clattered onto the floor.

"Now set your drink down."

Blair did.

He pointed behind her. "We're going that way. Be careful around the broken glass." He offered a hand to help her step over the shards of Gordon's scotch glass. Would you look at that, Blair thought incredulously. One hand on a gun, the other offering to help.

"I'll manage, thanks."

He lowered his hand and stepped back.

"Turn around, and head down that hallway behind you."

Blair complied, walking slowly down a short corridor flanked by doors. Her mind careened through possibilities, settling on only one answer: Gordon had access to something these men wanted.

"Stop right there."

Blair came to a halt, feeling her breath catch in her throat.

"Step inside that door on the right—slowly."

She entered a dark room, and the man felt for a light switch behind her. When he clicked it on, LED disk lights illuminated a space that she took to be a guest bedroom. A California king bed was flanked by enormous night-stands, and the back wall was almost entirely glass, with the narrow balcony beyond.

"You need to use the bathroom?" the man asked.

"No."

He walked around her to the nightstand, lifted a corner of it to test its weight, and let it fall back down with a thud.

"That'll work. Come over here." He waved the gun to indicate the bed.

Blair hesitated, and after a pause, he said, "Just sit on the bed. I'm going to handcuff you to the nightstand, and then you can have some privacy. Okay?"

Blair slowly walked to the mattress, eyes cast downward, and took a seat, nervously adjusting her dress around her thighs.

She surreptitiously glanced upward as the man holstered his pistol. It was a standard frame Glock, so probably chambered in 9mm or .40 cal. Not that it mattered at this point. He was maybe five foot seven, quite stocky. She guessed his weight at one-eighty-five, trying to retain as many mental snapshots as possible for the police report she'd soon be completing.

At least she hoped that she and Gordon would survive that long.

As the masked man knelt and procured a set of handcuffs, it occurred to her that he hadn't even considered the possibility of her attacking him. From where she sat, she could have driven a knee into his jaw, disorienting him enough for her to claim the upper hand, however briefly.

Don't be an idiot, she thought. There are two others and you're not over-powering everyone. Just survive.

A moment later, she regretted her inaction. The man took her left wrist in his gloved hands and affixed a handcuff around it.

The latching of the cuff against her skin made her stomach churn. All her emotional baggage was bad enough under normal circumstances; now, held captive by a team of armed criminals, her mind was spiraling out of control. Even if they weren't going to hurt her now, what if they started drinking Gordon's oh-so-exclusive single malt and changed their mind by sunrise?

The man attached the other side of the handcuff to the nightstand leg, then rose and took a few steps backward.

Fearing that he'd view her as a threat who could identify him later, she kept her eyes cast downward. The man didn't exit, but Blair didn't get the sense that he was there to enjoy the view.

She got her confirmation when he said, with mild regret, "We're really sorry about this. It'll all be over in the morning."

"What happens in the morning?"

Now the man's tone shifted from remorseful back to authoritative. Excited, even.

"In the morning, we rob Gordon's bank."

"What? His...bank?"

"That's right. I'm sorry to tell you this, sweetheart, but you went home with the wrong guy on the wrong night."

Blair felt a wave of disbelief. A bank robbery...it wasn't possible. Of course, there was precedent—during the Northern Bank robbery in Belfast, bank officials were held captive overnight. But families were used as hostages, and besides, that was for cash. That also happened in 2004, when bank security measures were a scarce fraction of what they were now. No one robbed banks anymore.

At least, she reminded herself, no *professionals* robbed banks anymore.

The man continued, "Just sit tight. I'll be back to check on you in a bit."

He exited the room, closing the door most of the way in a concession to privacy that was the best she could expect under the circumstances. She should have been slightly relieved that things hadn't been worse for her so far, but she was too busy fixating on his words.

In the morning, we rob Gordon's bank.

Blair listened to the masked man's steps receding down the hallway to the living room. She could make out the quiet murmur of voices, but little more. Gordon's voice was higher than the others, still panicky.

She gently tested the solid wood nightstand, finding it to weigh at least a hundred pounds. The bracket she was handcuffed to was affixed between the top shelf and floor base—she wasn't going to remove it, and she certainly wasn't going to drag the nightstand anywhere without being heard.

She mentally raced through what she could reasonably assume about the situation. She'd seen the men's tool belts, the handcuffs and tasers and radios, and taken them as marks of premeditation and careful planning. But now she realized they were the signs of rookies dressing up to play robber, of amateurs who thought they were gunslingers.

No one could rob a modern bank. Or perhaps, she thought, a better way of putting it was that *anyone* could rob a modern bank—they just couldn't get away with it. Silent alarms would be triggered across landlines and cellular signals, police would respond to the "two-eleven," the armed robbery call, and the SWAT team would mobilize at once. Everyone in the bank became hostages during the inevitable police response. And if the LAPD let the robbers leave alive, the situation would end in a high-speed chase, or a gunfight, or both. There was no conceivable outcome that wouldn't endanger the lives of dozens of civilians in a botched bank heist decades beyond its time.

As much as Blair didn't want to admit it, the situation wouldn't get any better than it was right now. Only two innocent lives were on the line: her and Gordon. If Blair could get help in time, she could stop this robbery before it endangered anyone else.

She had to prevent the robbery, and she was the only one who could.

And maybe, just maybe, this whole thing was an opportunity. The prospect was too coincidental to ignore. Maybe she ended up here for a greater purpose, and by foiling this heist, she could get her old life back. She knew there was a way, so long as she could provide her previous supervisor with the right incentive.

Don't think about that right now, she scolded herself. Just end this thing before it escalates any further.

She looked at her wrist and saw that her handcuffs were a run-of-the-mill set of Smith & Wesson Model 100. No surprises there. A quick glance inside a slot in the metal revealed the lock spring visible, confirming that the cuff was only single-locked. Even easier.

All she had to do was pop the cuffs, get out of the house, and run.

That last part, however, was a bit of an understatement. Her ankle boots had short, stout heels—far from ideal for running through steep wooded terrain in the dark. But it could have been worse. If she hadn't been trying to hide her left ankle, she probably would have worn heels tonight.

She considered her wider surroundings, recalling the views from Gordon's car. The winding hills held stately homes separated by small patches of steep forest. She'd just need to reach the nearest occupied dwelling and pound on the door until someone let her in or called the cops. She could explain the rest to the police—Gordon's address, three armed men and their physical descriptions, and, most importantly, the bank robbery plot. Patrol cops could barricade the house, LAPD SWAT would be on the way, and only one hostage would be caught in the middle versus ten or twenty inside the bank.

She'd have to move quickly. This was no team of master criminals, but if they had any modicum of resourcefulness they'd activate Gordon's security system from his phone if they hadn't already. That's what she would do in their position—and then monitor the video camera feed for any indication of police response.

As if on cue, an automated voice from a control unit blared somewhere in the living room.

"*System armed.*"

Blair glanced at the glass door behind her, scanning the perimeter and finding a sensor at the top right corner. A small white cube was attached to the head of the doorframe, paired to a matching bar on the door itself. That would be easy enough to defeat, particularly from inside.

There was only one thing left to do.

Using her free hand, she slid a bobby pin out of her hair and felt a tangle of bangs fall free across her forehead. She unfolded the bobby pin and then bit the plastic tip on the straight end. Some of these tips were easier to remove than others, and it took three painful yanks against her teeth to assure her that this wouldn't work.

She delicately pulled open the nightstand drawer. The wood was tightly engineered, and the narrow space between the drawer and surface of the nightstand should suffice. She inserted the straight section of the bobby pin and pushed the drawer shut, then yanked the bobby pin out, shearing off the plastic tip against the sharp corner.

Suddenly she heard footsteps approaching. Blair let the bobby pin fall inside the drawer and eased it shut, then adjusted her position on the bed to slump her shoulders and appear badly shaken. When someone pushed the door open, she forced herself not to look up.

As slow footsteps approached, Blair nearly panicked. *He's just noticed that a bobby pin is missing from my hair, and now I'm going to pay for it. He's going to pull open that drawer and find it, realize I know how to pick cuffs, and then I'm going to be properly restrained with no way out of it.*

The footsteps came to a stop before her, and Blair closed her eyes as something heavy thumped down on the nightstand. A knife? A gun? She opened her eyes to see what he'd set down.

It was a glass of water.

Blair heaved an exasperated sigh.

"Hungry?" the man asked. Thanks to the Boston accent, Blair didn't have to look up to know it was the same man who'd handcuffed her.

She shook her head.

"Plenty in the fridge," he went on. "Pizza, some leftover sushi. I've been known to make a not-unpalatable turkey sandwich. And your glass is still in the living room if you want—not like you need to stay sober through this. I'm a little jealous, if we're being honest."

"I just want to be alone."

"Okay," the man said. "I'll check on you later. Don't be scared to ask for anything; I want you to be comfortable. You get hungry, you need to use the bathroom, just holler for me."

"What do I call you?" Blair asked, cursing herself as the words left her mouth. It was a suspicious question, indicating that she was trying to gain information instead of being a silent, willing hostage. The man shifted his feet to face her.

"What do you call me? What do you *call* me?"

Blair held her breath.

"An outlaw," the man proclaimed. "A renegade. The man in black, masked mystery man, man of mystery. Man who's about to be rich. Just pick one."

Blair nodded, waiting for him to leave.

"I put your purse and phone on the dining table. Just so you know where to find it when the cops let you go tomorrow morning."

"Good," she replied. "I wouldn't want to end my first hostage experience twenty dollars and three tampons poorer than I started."

He gave a short laugh and walked out of the room, leaving the door open.

Blair waited for the sound of his footsteps to fade. Then she deftly opened the nightstand drawer, seeing a stack of comic books and locating her bobby pin. Recovering it with thumb and forefinger, she maneuvered the straight side of the pin halfway into the lock of the cuff on her wrist and then folded the tip into a 45-degree bend. Sliding the bobby pin further inside the lock, she bent it again, then pulled it out to examine the S-shaped curve, deciding that it would suit her needs.

She slid the bobby pin into the keyhole, maneuvering the bent section until she felt it catch against the handcuff housing. Applying slight pressure, she pressed the bobby pin counterclockwise. The cuff released suddenly, and Blair stopped it before it banged against the nightstand.

She was free.

Standing, she walked quickly across the rug, then gently stepped onto the walnut floor, easing the short heels of her boots down as quietly as she could. Upon reaching the sliding glass door to the balcony, she looked to the door sensor.

It was a simple two-piece reed switch, and she momentarily wished Gordon had a cheap magnet lying around. She would have greatly preferred to attach one of those to the receiver on the doorframe, biasing the reed switch within so she could open the door undetected.

Instead she'd have to physically move the white magnet bar on the door

—and if that piece moved more than an inch from the receiver, the alarm would sound as surely as if she'd yanked the door open.

Grasping the narrow plastic bar on the door itself, she twisted it sideways to break the adhesive backing. If she dropped that piece now, her escape attempt was over before it began. Blair painstakingly brought the bar in her fingers along the top edge of the receiver unit affixed to the doorframe, pressing the adhesive side down so the two sensors were attached.

She gingerly released her fingers from the assembly, feeling satisfied that the magnetic bar wouldn't fall. Unlocking the door, Blair tensed and began to slide it open on its rails.

No alarm sounded, but the door screeched. She jumped but didn't hear any footsteps running down the hall, only the faint chanting of crickets pouring through the open gap.

Blair slipped outside onto the narrow balcony, feeling the cool night air against her skin.

The glittering universe of Los Angeles was visible above the black treetops ahead of her. She left the sliding door open behind her, noting that a row of waist-high glass panels was the only thing keeping her from falling off the side onto an impossibly steep section of hill—probably a forty-foot drop. The sight made Blair nauseous with fear.

She looked left, seeing the balcony corner end in a steep drop down the hill and into the trees. It was still too far for her to jump, even if she were courageous enough to do so.

To her right, the balcony stretched to the living room occupied by Gordon and his captors. Beyond the living room windows, a staircase led down one level to the pool deck. If she could make it down there, she could easily slip past the pool and leap the rail onto a gently sloping section of hillside.

That was her only way out. She forced a deep breath to calm her hammering heart. She was no stranger to stress, she reminded herself; in a way, she'd been through worse than this. Granted, it had broken her at the time.

But now, unlike before, Blair had a chance of escape.

She began edging to the right, stopping before a full-length window and peering inside.

A masked man stepped up to the glass, and Blair threw herself against the wall.

This was it, her mind screamed in panic—she was about to get shot.

But nothing happened.

She waited for her pulse to subside, then peeked back around. The man was gone, the room beyond the glass empty.

Blair continued working her way around the house, moving as quietly as the click of her boots would allow.

She reached the living room, daring a peek into the full-length window she'd have to move past—Gordon was on the couch, head in hands, and two of the robbers were seated across from him, facing away from her. Now was her moment to pass them unnoticed, save one inconvenient variable.

Where was the third robber?

No time to waste. Without a moment's hesitation, she crossed the living room window on her way to the stairs.

Then Blair heard a sliding door screech open behind her, and her blood turned to ice.

"HEY!" a man yelled.

The two men in the living room bolted upright, seeing Blair fully exposed on the balcony.

She sprinted for the stairs leading to the pool deck, but a sliding door opened to her front, and the other two robbers spilled outside.

Skidding to a halt before they could grab her, she darted back the way she had come only to find the third robber running toward her along the balcony.

There was only one way to avoid capture, and it was what Blair feared most.

She spun to the waist-high glass rail behind her, planted both hands on its edge, and vaulted herself over the side and into oblivion.

Her stomach lurched into her throat. Blair felt like she was descending into hell. Already delirious with fear, she saw only flashing snapshots through the panic. The haze of city lights on the horizon. Black treetops rising to swallow her whole. A flash of teak wood panels below. Then Blair had the fleeting and exhilarating realization that she was about to hit the pool deck rather than soar off the side of the hill.

Her feet smashed onto the edge of a pool chair, and it flipped, sending her pirouetting to the deck. She hit hard on her right side, the impact knocking the wind out of her but leaving her unhurt—and alive.

With solid ground once again beneath her, Blair regained her composure and struggled to her feet. Above her, one of the robbers peered over the edge in disbelief. Blair ran between outdoor tables and chairs toward the pool, seeking the glass railing that separated the deck from a gentle slope beyond.

But as she neared the edge of the pool's glowing sapphire surface, a second robber came charging down the stairs to her front. Blair reflexively spun and grabbed a chair, then whirled back around and released it.

The chair sailed through the air, impacting the robber and knocking him backward. He hit the ground with a curse, flinging the chair off him and rising before Blair could possibly vault over him.

She heard a crash behind her—the other robber had leapt over the balcony, aiming for a pool chair to soften his landing.

There were only two robbers now—the third must have returned to keep watch over Gordon—but they blocked all ways out.

All but one.

Blair stepped to the edge of the pool and felt behind her for the glass railing that stopped near the water. A foot-wide barrier framed the water and extended fifteen feet beyond the rail, marking the section of pool suspended over the hillside.

Blair slipped past the rail, placing it between her and the two robbers now approaching cautiously, hands extended and empty as if to coax her back.

"Relax," one of them said. "Don't do anything crazy."

"Crazy?" she shouted back, her pulse soaring. She was terrified of the men, and more terrified still of the fall unfolding beneath her. "Coming from the only criminals in LA stupid enough to try a cowboy stickup at a modern bank?"

The shorter of the two men straightened and looked to the other. "You hear that?" he said to his partner. Based on his accent, this was the man who'd handcuffed her. "She called us cowboys."

The taller man tried to reason with her. "You go over the side, you'll break your legs."

"Probably better than getting shot in the face, no?"

"You're not... we're not... you don't understand. You're not getting hurt. No one's getting shot, see?"

He waved his open hands, and Blair was briefly struck by the fact that neither man had drawn his pistol. Of course they hadn't. Her screams wouldn't travel far in the Bel Air hills, but a gunshot would. They couldn't afford to shoot her.

"Just come on back." The taller man approached slowly, offering his hand.

Blair took one step backward on the concrete pool barrier and released her grip on the rail.

"Okay." The man stopped in place. "Just take it easy."

Blair took another step backward, shakily placing the short heel of one boot behind the other.

The taller man said, "You'll get hurt, you don't want to jump—"

"OF COURSE I DON'T WANT TO JUMP!" Blair shouted back. "DO YOU KNOW HOW MUCH I HATE HEIGHTS?"

The shorter one muttered to his partner, "I like her."

Blair felt a wave of sweat break out on her forehead as she began hyperventilating. But she took another step and, after a few racing breaths, spoke.

"If you walk into that bank tomorrow, innocent people are going to get killed. That heist is going bad whether you know it or not."

"No one is getting killed," the taller man said resolutely. "There won't be a shot fired, I promise you that."

Blair's face scrunched up in sarcastic rage. "Oh really, guy in a ski mask? You promise—bank robber's honor?"

The shorter man shrugged. "She's got us there, buddy."

Blair went to take another step backward but stopped when she realized there was nowhere else to go. She stood at the pool's farthest corner, the edge of the world.

One of the robbers was speaking to her urgently, but she couldn't make out any of the words. His partner was racing toward the rail by the shallow side of the hill next to the house, seeking a safe descent toward the slope she now hovered over.

Blair looked behind her at the Los Angeles skyline shimmering against a black night sky.

Taking a final sharp breath, she swallowed, flexed her hands into fists, and jumped.

The sudden void turned her mind into a terrified blitz of thoughts. How far would she fall? There was no pool chair to soften her landing this time. Would she break a femur on the hillside below?

And, above all:

When.

Will.

This.

End?

She pinched her eyes shut as she continued gaining speed, the rush of velocity growing from a whisper to a howl. She tried to keep her ankles and knees together. She tried not to scream. But she was still falling, regretting the decision to jump, regretting her attempt to escape in the first place. Regretting every one of the myriad life choices that had led her to this moment.

When it seemed that she couldn't go any faster, Blair's feet smashed into the earth.

She braced for the impact, but there wasn't one—there were dozens.

Her boots struck the soft hillside too steep to stand on, and as her body pin-wheeled down the slope, she let out an involuntary yelp of pain. She tried to protect her head as she absorbed impact after impact, each feeling like a sledgehammer made of dirt was smashing into her over and over, never in the same place twice.

Just as her body had stabilized into a stuntman barrel roll, the open hillside ended in a border of landscaping bricks.

Blair soared over the edge of the barrier and crashed in a snarl of brush and vines in the trees beyond.

She gasped one ragged breath after another—had that really just happened? This entire night was surreal, but her body's painful objections assured her that she wasn't dreaming. Everything ached, every part of her body and mind struggled to recover from the frantic disorientation of her fall.

Blair pushed herself up to a sitting position, trying to evaluate her situation. Nothing seemed broken, and that was a start—but before she could feel a fleeting moment of gratitude, she heard the robbers crashing down the hill after her.

Clambering to her feet, Blair pushed her way into the trees. Branches and vines clawed against her bare arms as she ran downhill, the darkness of the wooded slope a merciful reprieve from the masked men. She searched for any sign of homes and found the dim glow of security lights down the hill to her right. Negotiating the uneven ground as quickly as she could in her boots, she heard a rustling of brush behind her. One of the men was closing in—and Blair realized in an instant of dread that she wasn't going to outrun him. Even if she could somehow gain distance in a sudden burst of speed, the slightest misstep would cause her to trip.

So Blair did the unthinkable.

She stopped completely.

Perhaps stopping completely was an optimistic way to put it, she thought. In actuality, she grabbed the trunk of a large tree, skidding to a halt until she faced it in an awkward bear hug.

Then she took a step sideways, trying to keep the trunk between her and her pursuer. Placing her back against the rough bark, she tried to listen as her heart raced out of control.

For a second she heard nothing but her own labored breathing. Then a branch snapped, sending a shot of fear up her spine—one of the robbers wasn't more than ten feet away.

Blair gulped in air, then held her breath as the footsteps drew nearer.

Her pulse sounded deafening in her ears, her heart slamming along at a fever pitch.

The footsteps drew nearer, moving slowly and cautiously, then stopped on the other side of the tree trunk.

After her desperate escape, Blair's mind was screaming for air, and her lungs felt like they were on fire. But if she took a breath now, he'd hear it. So she waited, listening as he took another step downhill, and slid her body in the opposite direction to keep the tree between them. She could hear the man catching his breath as crickets gradually resumed their chorus around him.

Just as Blair couldn't possibly hold her breath any longer, the man whispered a curse and continued running downhill, headed for the light of the nearest home.

Blair gratefully expelled the stale contents of her lungs and then drew in breath after desperate breath, her pulse finally quieting. After listening to the silence for a moment, she altered her direction downhill to avoid her pursuer. In the hills of Bel Air, she knew she couldn't go far without hitting an extravagant home. Blair moved more cautiously now, painfully aware that one robber was still at large in the woods.

It only took her a minute to locate lights through the trees ahead, and as she approached, she gradually began to make out the source. This was a dream come true—she saw the backside of an impossibly massive home, all of it lit up like a Christmas tree. Any estate this large would have extensive cameras and security systems.

Now, she just had to make it there.

Suppressing the urge to run, she forced herself to move quietly, deliberately, lest she reveal her position before she was home free. She continued to descend the slope toward the edge of a backyard, where a stone path led to the house's rear entrance.

When the security lights from the massive home stung her eyes, Blair broke into a sprint.

She smashed through the remaining stretch of woods and over a landscaping barrier, then loped across the open lawn.

Suddenly she was tackled from behind, crashing to the ground with the weight of a body on top of her. She began screaming for help, her throat burning with effort, as she struggled against her attacker. Inside the house, a dog began barking wildly. As the assailant rolled her over and tried to cover her mouth, she saw that he was the taller of the two robbers she'd fled from. She fought him viciously, writhing and biting at his palm over her mouth. Then, making a claw with one hand, she raked at his eyes.

She failed to injure his eye, her fingertips gaining little purchase from jaw to eyebrow. But her attack succeeded in dislodging his ski mask, flipping it backward over his forehead.

In the lights of the house, his face was laid bare.

It was Sterling.

For a moment, Blair went limp with shock and shame. This entire event had been a setup, and she had been the pawn to get Gordon to disarm his home security for an overnight holdup. Sterling saw the recognition in her eyes and, feeling her go limp, relaxed his grip and sat up to explain.

But Blair's shock lasted only a moment, and when it faded, a violent surge of anger set in.

Exploiting the gap created when he sat up from their struggle, she threw a fist at his crotch.

Her knuckles achieved only glancing contact, but that was enough. She continued striking him in rapid succession—his stomach, throat, ribs, whatever she could reach—but the blow to his genitals was the kill shot. He slowly rolled sideways into the fetal position.

Blair leapt up and began kicking his ribs with the toe of her boot.

"Get up, you pussy!" she roared. The dog inside the house was going crazy, snarling and barking so loudly she could hear it clearly from the edge of the woods.

She swung her boot into Sterling's ribs again as he groaned, hands moving from crotch to ribs to defend himself.

Finally she went for the *coup de grâce*, a heel stomp into his temple to render him unconscious. She raised one knee in the air.

As she brought her boot down, a pair of hands grabbed her from behind and swung her sideways to the ground. She struck the grass and another man was atop her—the shorter one who fancied himself a comedian—and he maneuvered behind her as she screamed "RAPE!" at the top of her lungs.

His powerful arms put her in a chokehold, her esophagus trapped in the crook of his elbow as he applied just enough pressure to cut off her air supply. Her cry ended in a choking gurgle as he rose and dragged her backward into the darkness of the trees.

"Rape, Blair?" he hissed. "*Really?* I was going to make you a turkey sandwich. I thought we had something special."

Blair gurgled.

He sighed, releasing the pressure on her throat. "Get some air."

She drew a breath, then started to scream again until he lightly choked her for the second time.

"Not *that* much air," he whispered, releasing just enough pressure for her to breathe but not scream. "What did you do to my poor friend?"

It was an appropriate question. Sterling, reduced to a zombie-like state of prostration, was now pulling himself slowly across the lawn, trying to reach the woods before the dog's owner came outside to investigate.

Come on, Blair thought desperately, staring at the back of the house. Sterling had just reached the long shadow of a tree on the lawn when a door on the third floor swung open. A Doberman raced onto the terrace as his owner stood in the doorway. The man was in a bathrobe, toweling his hair with one hand.

Sterling froze in the tree's shadow, and Blair could hear the man behind her hold his breath. Blair tried to scream but had her air supply cut off again.

The homeowner approached his balcony railing, staring at the tree line for what seemed like an eternity as the Doberman continued to sound its alarm.

Blair willed him to trust his dog, to unleash the animal to determine the source of its fury.

Instead the man scolded the dog and ordered it back inside. He threw the towel over his shoulder, returning to the house and closing the door.

Blair felt her body sag in her captor's grasp.

Sterling rose to his feet and performed a shuffling, limping motion until he reached Blair and his friend.

"You know, Blair," the short robber remarked, sounding surprised, "you fight pretty well, for a girl."

Blair swung a heel backward into the man's shin, trying to rake downward as he hissed a curse and maneuvered away from her. "Easy, little filly, easy."

Sterling arranged his ski mask over his face, breathing heavily. "Let's go," he croaked.

5

STERLING

Sterling studied his face in the mirror of Gordon's bathroom.

He looked like a train wreck.

His sandy hair was matted from the ski mask, face still pale from the aftermath of Blair's punch to his testicles. Nausea from the same was just now beginning to fade, although he didn't feel much better for it.

He turned on the sink, then removed his gloves and splashed water over his face. Wiping his hands on his shirt, he donned his gloves and turned off the faucet, watching his eyes in the mirror and wondering what he was going to do next.

Sterling's world had shifted on its axis.

He'd seen plenty of things go wrong before. More often than not, the higher the payoff, the more unexpected obstacles he had to negotiate in its pursuit.

But he had never, *ever*, heard of so much going wrong as the result of a single person. And a waitress, at that. She was a miniscule but critical element of a much larger picture than he cared to fathom at the moment, and yet she'd almost thrown incalculable planning effort out the window by blowing his op.

For what? She should have been a perfect hostage, particularly when it became apparent that her captors intended no harm to her or Gordon.

But this woman had picked her cuffs, executed a daring escape, and, when cornered, leapt off the edge of a pool deck and risked injury or death to stop a bank robbery. Why?

A man's rangy form appeared in the mirror, and Sterling turned to face him.

Marco was the tallest of their trio, topping Sterling's height by a five-inch margin that required Sterling to look up in order to meet his eyes. Sterling dreaded talking to him at whispering range for this very reason, though this time, he could add Marco's reticence. On the scale of risk acceptance, Marco was firmly rooted as the most cautious of his team when it came to aborting a job.

Sterling's concern was that this time, Marco would be right.

Marco rolled up his mask to reveal sculpted cheeks above a cleft chin and shoulder-length hair pulled into a tight bun. He had the frame of a marathon runner but was probably the least athletic of the three—no matter, Sterling thought. Physical capabilities weren't why Marco was here.

Analyzing Sterling's pallor, Marco spoke in a low voice marked by a trace of Russian accent.

"What happened out there? Alec said he left you alone for five minutes and came back to find the hostage stomping your brains out on the lawn."

Sterling ignored the quip. "What did you find out about her?"

"Data stops after her graduation from Mary Washington. She's had some records buried, and that takes pull. She could be a hacker, or have some government connection. Maybe she was military."

"Have you started a database scrub yet?"

"Of course. But it's going to take time. There's something else, too."

Marco held up his cell phone. Sterling glanced at the screen before squeezing his eyes shut and releasing a frustrated breath.

Then he examined the screen again, more closely this time.

"Of course there's a flash flood warning as soon as we commit. In LA, of all places. What are the odds?"

"Doesn't matter what the odds are. The warning is for the entire San Fernando Valley."

"I see that."

"Then why aren't we on our way out of here already?"

Sterling smiled, stroking his hair back into place. "Chance of a flash flood might go away by morning. There's still time for a sunrise weather call—we can always bounce the op then."

"No, no, no. I could bounce the op in the morning. Alec, bless his simple little heart, could bounce the op in the morning. But you're in charge, and you don't have the discipline to call something off that close to hit time."

"The discipline?" Sterling felt his smile fading. "I'll be in the arena right alongside you and Alec."

Marco conceded, "You always are. But a willingness to immolate yourself isn't an excuse to put the team under further risk."

"I'm no loose cannon." Sterling stared at Marco fixedly, continuing in a low, firm voice, "You know that."

Marco almost laughed in his face. "Of course you're not a loose cannon, Sterling. You're something worse: a lion. You get hungrier the closer you get to a steak, and every minute you don't abort this thing reduces the chances that you will, regardless of how the situation develops. Coupled to that is the fact that you feed off risk like a leech off blood, and one of these days, it's going to burn you. You're playing against the law of averages."

"If I give the go, it's because we'll pull it off."

"Maybe we do." Marco gave a resigned shrug. "Maybe we don't. But rolling the dice like this isn't what got us to where we are."

Sterling cocked his head. "It's my op, Marco."

"Yeah, you keep telling yourself that. I'm not saying tomorrow is the day one or more of us gets killed, or worse yet, goes to prison. But if it's not, it won't be because of your decision-making. It'll be because of luck. Think about that when—and if—we make it out of this score. RTB, Sterling."

"We wanted rain for a reason. Not *this* much rain, but...still. Our getaway platforms are equipped for it."

Marco blinked rapidly. "It's getting to them that worries me."

Sterling nodded, looking at himself in the mirror as he made his decision.

"We're still on. For now. In the meantime, let me see what I can get out of Blair."

"Do you want me there for backup?"

"She got lucky." Sterling's eyes narrowed in anger before he reconsidered. "On second thought, just wait outside in the hallway."

Marco pulled his ski mask back down. "Let's do it."

Sterling and Marco exited Gordon's bathroom and master suite, then walked down the hallway. Marco stopped outside the door to the guest bedroom.

With a final pause of consideration, Sterling entered.

Blair was seated on the edge of the bed, both wrists handcuffed around the leg of the nightstand. The cuffs were double-locked, keyhole facing down. At that angle, she couldn't have opened the cuffs even if Alec had given her a key—or so Sterling hoped.

"Who are you, Blair?"

"I'll tell you all about my background when you tell me yours, Sterling."

She spat his name out with contempt, as though it were a hateful slur.

"I'm extremely curious why your records are sealed. Did you assassinate someone for the government? Are you in witness protection after informing on the mob?"

"Your first guess is closer than your second."

"Where did you learn to do what you just did?"

"I dunno." Then, quoting Alec, she said, "Guess I didn't do so bad...for a girl."

Sterling gave a tight-lipped smile before grimacing.

"I didn't want to do this, but I'm going to have to search you."

"Sounds like you want to get hit in the balls again."

"Don't make this harder than it has to be. I've still got a job to do, and I regret to say that you've already made me look bad once. I can't risk you doing it a second time."

Blair said nothing in response, and Sterling approached her.

He placed his hands on her head, feeling along her scalp and pocketing two more bobby pins in the process. Then he kneaded her black hair where it fell free past her bare shoulders, the exposed skin now marred with tiny cuts from her fall and flight through the woods. Sterling winced. This was supposed to be a slumber party for her. All she had to do was rest for the night, and get found by the cops in the morning. How had it all gone so wrong?

Trying to conceal his hesitation, Sterling quickly ran his palms down the backside of her dress. Then he did a front sweep, cupping under her breasts and sweeping down to her abdomen like a TSA agent.

"Satisfied?" she asked.

"I'll need to take your boots off."

"Don't do that," she said. Her voice sounded slightly desperate, though he couldn't fathom why.

"Well, now I'm definitely taking them off."

He noticed her shoulders slump, the fire of defiance vanishing from her eyes and giving way to defeat.

What was this about, he wondered. A scar? A tattoo?

He knelt before her. "This will just take a minute. Try and resist the urge to kick me in the face, okay?"

She didn't smile.

Sterling started with her right side, unzipping the ankle boot and sliding it off her foot. He felt along the inside of the boot, and then set it to the side.

Then he started with the left foot, unzipping the boot and pulling it off.

The loose suede of the boot caught at her ankle. Sterling looked up and saw she wouldn't meet his eyes.

He pulled the boot the rest of the way off, saw what was underneath, and stood.

"You're on parole?"

His eyes were fixed above her left foot, where a narrow ankle bracelet held a small black box in place.

She nodded.

Sterling felt horrified. He hadn't even considered the possibility of a waitress wearing a tracking device. How sloppy was he getting?

Blair must have registered the shock on his face, because she said, "Relax, it's not a continuous GPS. It's a radio-frequency transmitter that sends a signal to a receiving unit in my apartment. The receiving unit can only tell if I'm home or not. It's just to enforce curfew for supervised release."

"Why should I believe that?"

She gave him a disgusted look. "No offense, buddy, but if I was lucky enough to have cops follow my tracker around, I wouldn't have bothered trying to escape three armed men. And I could have made it back home in time for curfew if you hadn't kidnapped me. Now I'm in violation, so thanks for that."

"What are you on supervised release for?"

"None of your business."

He shrugged. "Fair enough. Well, let's get this thing off you."

Blair was taken aback. "Why do you care? I told you, it's not tracking me outside my apartment—"

"Speaking as a career criminal, I'm foundationally opposed to shackles."

"Well that's funny, because you people are the only ones to handcuff me as of late."

He gave a nod of respect. "You win this round, Blair. But be that as it may, there's no better excuse to get rid of that monitor than being a hostage, right? Just tell them I did it against your will."

"You can tell them yourself, when you get arrested tomorrow."

Rather than answer her, he produced a pocketknife and flipped it open. Manipulating the ankle bracelet with one hand, he slid the blade's flat metal side between her leg and the strap and began slicing. The plastic strap chopped more easily than he expected—the only real resistance was from a small wire in the middle that soon split against the blade.

"There." He folded the knife and pocketed it. "That's better. Would you like your boots back on, Blair?"

She nodded.

Sterling helped her back into the boots, zipping them up before grabbing the anklet and rising.

"I'll be right back."

He stepped outside, waving for Marco to follow him back to Gordon's master suite and out of earshot.

Sterling held up Blair's ankle bracelet without a word, and Marco's gray eyes fixated on it like a bloodhound trying to pick up a scent. He took the device, analyzing first the black box and then the sheared section of the strap, paying particular attention to a sliced copper wire that protruded slightly where Sterling had cut it.

Then Marco's eyes lost their fire, going dull with boredom.

"This doesn't matter," he said softly, handing the device back. "It's a radio-frequency transmitter, not a GPS. They probably installed a receiving unit at her place."

"That's what worries me."

"Why?"

"Because she used exactly the same words to describe it. That sound like your average parolee to you?"

"No, but her escape doesn't sound like your average waitress, either. You sure know how to pick them, Sterling. I already told you I'd bounce mission if it were my op. Well, this doesn't make me any less confident in my decision. And it's good to see you worried, but that woman should be the least of your concerns at present. Within reason, we can keep a human being in line. We can't control Mother Nature."

"Swap out with Alec. I need him to get to work in the closet."

Marco spun and departed, leaving Sterling to stare past the open doors to Gordon's walk-in closet at the now-startling irregularity within.

A rug in the closet was flipped askew at the corner, revealing the lacquered black finish of a floor safe they'd uncovered shortly after entering the house.

Beside the safe was the bag of equipment Alec had staged in eager anticipation. Sterling didn't have to wait long for him to appear. Less than thirty seconds after his presence had been requested, Alec came strolling into the master suite like a teenager reporting to pick up his prom date.

He immediately rolled his ski mask up from his face to expose a broad jaw and almond-shaped eyes.

"These masks are friggin' hot," he mumbled in his Boston accent. "You feeling any better after getting assaulted out there?"

"Yeah. Thanks for the save."

"You're very welcome. Now let's talk about the other thing."

"The box?"

"The forecast. You saw the weather. We ain't committed yet, boss. No one's made us—yet—and cops would write this off as amateurs getting spooked if we bailed now."

"That storm could change direction by the morning, take the worst of the rainfall away from us."

"Or it could get stronger," Alec said cautiously.

"All right, spit it out."

"We've had a hostage Houdini and almost been compromised already. If we get a flash flood tomorrow, it's a physical safety risk even *if* everything else in the heist goes according to plan. And I can count on one hand the number of times that's happened."

"One hand?" Sterling responded. "I can count it on three fingers. What's your read?"

"I'd bounce mission if it were my op. But it isn't."

"I'll make a final weather call in the morning. Did Gordon say anything about his floor safe in the closet?"

Alec rolled his eyes.

"Say anything? He wouldn't shut up about it. You know the routine. We'll never get it open, it's a Wellington Hydra. The most sophisticated residential safe that money can buy. Silent alarm, network independent, multi-wall construction, blah blah blah. All he knows is what the salesman told him."

Sterling glanced in the closet. "Is any of that true?"

"Well, yeah. I love Wellington. Just look at the thing—it's a beautiful box. These go for upwards of 50K, and they're worth every penny. EN 1143-1 rated, 1.6-inch steel bolts. I mean, the thing's got a fully redundant motor drive mechanism. And Gordon sprouted a pair of balls as soon as I told him we found it. He's refusing to open the thing, says we can shoot him in the head for all he cares."

"All right," Sterling conceded. "I'll put that to the test and get him to pop it for us."

Alec looked offended. "What are you, crazy? Just let me work on it."

"You sure?"

"Everyone gets to do their specialty in this job except me. This is my time to *shine*, pal."

Sterling extended a hand toward the closet. "You've got till sunrise. If you don't get it open by then, I can guarantee that Gordon will gladly enter his combination when there's a pistol in his mouth."

Alec was nodding, but Sterling could see that he wasn't listening anymore. He'd already reached into his pocket and produced the white earbuds for his music, inserting them as he strolled over to the safe.

Sterling watched with amusement as Alec knelt over the safe and unzipped his gear bag. When Alec was in any other aspect of a job, he treated the world like his own personal stand-up comedy stage. But when there was a safe to be opened, he treated the process more like a ballroom dance.

There were many words for what Alec was. In formal terms, he'd be considered a safe technician or an advanced locksmith. In informal terms, he'd be called a safecracker or a housebreaker.

But Alec far preferred the Prohibition-era criminal slang "box man."

To Alec, that meant getting through any safe, lock, or vault. And since there was an already near-endless list of security mechanisms in that ever-advancing industry, Alec relied on an equally dizzying array of techniques.

Sometimes, the methods were simple. Lock manipulation. Drilling. Scoping. Brute force. Alec would casually mention his ability to punch, peel, or bounce a safe into submission or, barring that, use nitroglycerin "jam shots" to blow the door off.

That was all basic stuff. More advanced jobs might require keypad skimmers, autodialing machines, or X-ray equipment. Alec talked about plasma cutters and thermal lances the way most guys talked about their power tools.

But for this job, Alec couldn't haul hundreds of pounds of safecracking gear into the house, nor could he let the neighbors hear a low-grade explosive detonation. Opening this floor safe with minimal equipment required the use of gels and scanning equipment to determine which buttons in the safe's keypad Gordon had pressed, and in what order, based on fingerprints and button wear. With measurements in that latter vector rated by the micrometer, the process of assimilating data, much less compiling and testing the hundreds of possible combinations, could take hours. Or it could fail altogether.

And in this phase of the job, unlike nearly every other heist they'd conducted to date, they had nothing but time, and a surefire solution if all else failed: the threat of violence against Gordon. Rather than be discouraged by his own irrelevance for this job, Alec had seized upon the anomaly as an opportunity to test himself in a new safecracking method that he'd only ever practiced before tonight, never employed on an actual job.

Sterling stood there, watching Alec set to work with graceful patience. After a few minutes, the novelty wore off, and Sterling went to check on Marco and Gordon. Cracking that safe was going to take a while, if it happened at all.

The following morning, Sterling stood in the master suite, watching the hills of Bel Air come alive with a subdued glow. The first rays of sunlight were filtering through a bank of gray clouds, gradually illuminating the treetops and roofs speckling a landscape that stretched all the way to the distant buildings of Los Angeles.

Even from a distance, the city appeared daunting; the clouds overhead, even more so. Sterling's planning for the weather had been meticulous. He'd wanted rain in the afternoon, which was no small feat in LA. From there it was a matter of monitoring the subtropical jet stream, waiting for a favorable forecast.

And he'd gotten that favorable forecast for today, all right—chance of rain rising to near certainty in the afternoon, when he'd need it most. But as soon as he'd committed to the plan by capturing Gordon, that prediction had taken an unexpected turn.

In LA, the odds of a flash flood were so outside the realm of probability that he hadn't even considered it. Getting into the bank was easy, but getting out? That could become difficult very, very quickly under the best of circumstances. If excessive rainfall struck at the wrong time, it would be impossible.

And what about the woman?

Sterling's eyes fell from the distant city skyline to the outdoor architecture of Gordon's home. He'd seen it in the daylight before—his reconnaissance had been extensive—but never like he observed it now.

What were formerly abstract facets of exterior design now became an obstacle course, a gauntlet that Blair had negotiated the previous night. His eyes followed the glass rail of the balcony to the pool jutting over the side of the hill. Blair could have remained in the bedroom, perfectly safe, until the cops recovered her in the morning. Instead she'd traversed the balcony, jumped onto the lower deck, thrown a chair at him, and edged her way to the corner of a suspended pool before leaping into the unknown. It had been an extremely daring and very nearly successful escape, one that few people would conceive of much less execute.

From his current vantage point, Sterling could barely make out a sliver of ground below the suspended pool; it would take a stuntman to hazard that jump, even in daylight. Blair had taken the leap blindly, out of a desire to save innocent people from becoming endangered in a bank holdup. He knew he could leverage her dedication in the day ahead.

And in the next second, Sterling decided that he would.

Behind him, Alec spoke in a near-gasp.

"*Sésame, ouvre-toi.*"

Sterling turned to see Alec open the door to the safe, then transition from a kneeling position to lying on the floor of the walk-in closet. He interlaced his fingers behind his head, releasing a beleaguered sigh in the next closest thing to an expression of post-coital bliss. Having gotten the safe open, he didn't even bother looking inside.

"Gordon got any cigarettes around here?"

Marco entered the room wearing a backpack. He walked into the closet, stepped over Alec, and impatiently knelt over the safe to snatch a hot-pink thumb drive from within.

Then, unslinging his backpack, he withdrew a tablet and inserted the thumb drive into a port adapter. He tapped the screen before turning to show Sterling the display.

"Not bad," Sterling said. "That's our game ball."

Marco yanked the pink thumb drive out, depositing it and the tablet into the backpack and zipping it up.

He looked behind him to where Alec was still stretched out on the floor, savoring his latest conquest.

"Alec, what are you doing? Get over here."

"So...unappreciated," Alec grunted as he rose and approached them.

Sterling observed the two men as they waited for him to speak. Alec's round face looked boyish, his eyes mischievous as always. He might disagree with Sterling, but he'd follow orders with a shrug and a laugh regardless—all the way to jail or the grave.

Marco had no such lightheartedness in his face. His sunken cheeks and severe eyes conveyed a look of resistance, one born out of wisdom. For Marco, the cosmos weren't a matter of chance. In his mind there was far less chaos than there were events that could be predicted through meticulous planning and analysis. And that was exactly why he was so very good at what he did.

Alec looked at his watch and said, "It's about that time, boss."

Marco wouldn't meet Sterling's eyes.

Sterling swallowed. "We're a 'go.'"

Nodding, Alec said, "What do we do about the girl?"

"You know what we have to do."

"What makes you think you can control her?"

"Her concern is for innocent people. When I convince her that they'll be better served by her cooperating instead of resisting, she'll cooperate. And she'll serve our needs far better than a stranger."

Alec looked skeptical. "You'd better be right about that."

"You saw that fall she took. I am right."

Marco cut in, his slight Russian accent now sharp with anger. "Concur about the girl. But not the weather."

Sterling took a breath. "The worst of the storm looks like it's swinging north of us. We'll get rain, not a flood."

"The meteorologists don't know that for sure; neither do you. I know there's not going to be water knee-deep in the streets. But if there's even slightly more rainfall than the infrastructure can accommodate, it could hose our escape. Literally and figuratively. And that's a risk we can't begin to mitigate. The most valuable take from any heist is your freedom afterward."

"He's got a point, boss," Alec chimed in. "RTB. Weather report is indecisive. Maybe a flash flood hits this afternoon...maybe it doesn't. If we were taking votes—"

"We're not taking votes," Sterling said. "We're going; that's final."

Alec nodded. "Okay, boss. Ready to go pull up our skirt?"

Marco didn't wait for Sterling to respond. He hoisted his backpack and tossed it to Sterling, then pulled down his mask and disappeared out the door.

Sterling shouldered the backpack and put a hand on Alec's shoulder. "Keep an eye on Blair."

Then he walked down the hall to the living room.

* * *

Gordon's night had been tumultuous.

It started out on a high note, what with being approached by a stunning

44

woman in the form of Blair. From there his luck had gotten even better—a willing return to his residence, a hopeful uptick ending when masked men burst through the door. Gordon had quickly imploded into panicked crying and blubbering, followed by an almost catatonic state during Blair's escape attempt. And when it became apparent no one would tell Gordon anything until sunrise, he'd not only slept for hours but had looked utterly content while doing so.

Sterling knew that Gordon's emotional rollercoaster would only get more sickening before it ended. As would his own. But, Sterling thought, it would end before sunset, hopefully with his team having completed what they had come to do, and not in prison or dead. Either way, Sterling was about to step over the last threshold of commitment to his plan—to give Gordon the details and instructions, and, in doing so, remove all possibility of retreat.

Sterling shook Gordon awake.

Gordon, for his part, looked bewildered at his surroundings. Blinking and sitting up, he observed his situation in a domino effect. First, that the sun was rising outside. Second, that his wrist was handcuffed to a leg of the coffee table. Third, that he was in last night's rumpled suit. Fourth, that a man in a black ski mask was taking a seat on the couch across from him while setting a backpack on the floor.

Gordon's bewildered expression indicated a harried recollection of the previous evening's festivities.

"Is the girl still here?" Gordon asked. "Or did you let her out again?"

The emotional rollercoaster continued, Sterling thought. Having awakened to find himself alive, Gordon had become contemptuous.

Sterling said nothing, instead giving him a hard stare and letting the tension build.

Gordon looked to the backpack and, uncertain of the contents, quickly backed down. "So what...what happens now?"

"Now we talk about your role in today's festivities," Sterling answered. "Which, as you may have guessed, involves a substantial, extra-legal withdrawal from your bank."

"I'm just the manager, you moron. It's a small bank, and—"

"Your family owns the company, and you run the command branch. I want you to think very hard before you lie to me, Gordon."

"Don't try to act like a master criminal," he replied with a tone of disgust, wiping his mouth with the back of his sleeve. "You couldn't even break into my home without me disarming the security for you."

"And I'm going to rob your bank the same way."

Gordon halted at that, looking from Sterling to the backpack.

"I can't disarm the security system. And any breach in the protocol will send a signal to the police."

"I know that, Gordon. That's why you're not going to disarm the system —you're going to ensure it goes off." Then Sterling leaned forward. "Your bank has great security. But there's nothing protecting your office phone line."

"So?"

Sterling withdrew a digital recorder from the backpack, held it up so Gordon could see it, and pressed play.

The audio that spilled out began as a landline dial tone, followed by the beeping cadence of someone dialing a number. The connection clicked through after one ring.

"*LAPD Administrative Support.*"

"*This is Gordon Schmidt, manager of Mayfield National Bank location zero-one, Geering Plaza, Century City. We're going to run a routine test of our silent alarm.*"

"*Wired or cellular?*"

"*Wired.*"

"*Confirmation code?*"

"*6198.*"

"*Okay, Mr. Schmidt, dispatch to your wired signal is suspended for the next ten minutes. Cellular will remain active.*"

"*I'll call back to confirm once—*"

Sterling clicked the recorder off.

"You test the system every month. You'll place that call from your desk landline at 8:55 this morning, right before you disable your security cameras."

Gordon looked unimpressed. "So you can tap a phone. Congratulations. As much as I'd like to be there when you get arrested—because you will get arrested, if you're not dead before then—I don't want to get killed in the process. So I'm obliged to tell you there's more to my bank's security than that."

"I'm glad you brought that up." Sterling reached into the backpack again. "Let's start with your cellular alarm."

He withdrew an olive drab block of metal, roughly the length and width of a shoebox but less than six inches thick. Eight stubby antennas of various lengths protruded, arrayed in two parallel rows across the top.

Gordon's eyes narrowed suspiciously. "What is that thing supposed to be?"

"It's a portable cellular jammer. You're going to carry it inside your briefcase, and you're going to do it while wearing these."

Sterling set two more objects on the table. One was ostensibly the button for a suit jacket, wired to a small transmitter unit. The other was a small radio earpiece.

"We'll be seeing and hearing everything you do. In case you get forgetful—or reluctant—we'll remind you of your proper instructions."

"Have you seen my bank? There's a glass wall between it and the building's main lobby. What good does it do to disable the alarms when people outside the bank will see you and call the cops?"

"It buys me one minute. Maybe two. That's the difference between getting away or not."

Gordon appeared increasingly agitated, and began shaking his head resolutely. "I can't get into the vault. Even if I wanted to help you, there's a time delay—"

Sterling cut him off. "Your time delay expires at 8:57 this morning, three minutes before your location opens for business. Once that deactivates, you and your teller manager, Jeane Jackson, can insert dual keys and enter your respective codes to open the main vault."

"The main vault doesn't have much cash. It's mainly file storage and safe deposit boxes."

"And the teller vaults. None of which I'm interested in."

"Then what do you want?"

"Your cash vault, Gordon. Which is inside the main vault, and contains yesterday's Brinks delivery of 3.8 million dollars."

"I can't get into the cash vault."

"No, that's a separate set of dual access keys and codes. Which you share with your cash vault teller, Becky Stilwell, who will be at work by the time you arrive."

"We're not scheduled to open the cash vault until distribution has arrived. If I ask her to open it, she'll be suspicious."

"You don't have to ask her. We will. Your bank opens at 9:00. It closes at 9:01, with us inside. You're going to let us into the back, ensure your staff complies, and we'll be gone by 9:07."

"What about the security guard? He's not just going to let you waltz in."

"Let me worry about Jon Suttle."

"Oh. You're not going to—"

"No one's getting hurt, Gordon. Everyone goes home to their families tonight. This is going to end well." Sterling lifted his head high, exuding calm. "Especially for you."

"What do you mean?" Gordon replied, his posture collapsing with the inquiry.

"Very few active bank managers have a robbery under their belt."

"So?"

"Even fewer of them remain composed, telling their employees to stay calm and taking control as soon as the robbers are gone. You've got that chance, and you know it ahead of time. And let's not forget how brave you were last night."

Gordon tugged at an earlobe. "Brave?"

"After this, my team and I are ghosts. There are no witnesses to your captivity, so the official story is whatever you say it is. You want to do the talk show circuit, interviews, whatever, you're doing so as a hero who survived a terrifying ordeal—and ensured his employees all came out of it alive. That kind of publicity could be very useful for someone looking to fund their startup."

"Sure." Gordon gave an ugly laugh. "What a favor you're doing me."

"I'm doing you more of a favor than you think."

"No, you're not." Gordon looked squarely at Sterling, his voice dripping with contempt. "You're a thug. An animal."

"I'm not so very different from you. And if you help me with this, we can both keep our secrets."

"Think you can blackmail me? I'll tell my wife about the other women right now. Look at the life I've provided." He gestured with his chin, indicating the house around them. "She's not going anywhere."

Sterling shot him a challenging nod in return. "You think I'd plan this job relying on infidelity for leverage? That'd be thin. Very thin. No, Gordon, I've got something much more substantial to hang over your head."

Sterling reached into the bag a final time, procuring a neatly stapled stack of paper and handing it across the table.

Gordon didn't take it at first. His face flushed, brow wrinkled, indicating that he could see at a glance that he was looking at some financial report. But his feigned disinterest solidified into anger as he considered the context of their conversation.

He snatched the packet from Sterling, his eyes racing across the first page, his face reddening as he flipped to the second. He examined the pages quickly, looking between the highlighted figures.

Sterling watched him carefully, waiting for the moment of recognition. Gordon knew he'd covered his tracks well, and he was trying to discern whether Sterling's team had identified the pattern in his financial figures. Because once that pattern was pointed out, it couldn't be ignored.

Gordon stopped flipping the pages as he scowled. "You can't prove this. Not without—"

"This?" Sterling held up the hot-pink thumb drive.

Gordon's eyes widened. The sight of the thumb drive almost seemed to make him angrier than the financial report he clutched in trembling hands.

Then he threw the papers atop the coffee table and crossed his arms in anger. But he said nothing.

Sterling continued. "Embezzling is just bank robbery in a suit and tie. So whatever high ground you think you hold over me, don't count morality among it. You've been skimming the family till for six months now. As long as you help me today, you can keep doing it. But believe me, Gordon. If I am not standing inside your cash vault by 9:03 this morning"—Sterling leveled an index finger at him—"there is nothing in the world that will keep you out of prison.

"And if you get any bright ideas about hindering my escape, know that I'm keeping this report—and your little pink secret—on my person all day long. If I get away, I shred the evidence and you never hear from me again.

No one ever knows what I took from your safe. But if I go down in the next few hours, so do you."

"This is not an admission of guilt," Gordon prefaced, "but in white collar crime, you idiot, no one gets hurt."

"No one gets hurt doing the job my way either. And don't blame me because your trust fund wasn't enough for you."

Gordon licked his lips.

"And stealing from my bank won't be enough for you. This isn't your first robbery, and it won't be your last." His eyes looked even more sunken than usual as he glared at Sterling, his voice ominous. "Because like it or not, you and I are both addicts."

6

BLAIR

The sun was rising now, its brightness subdued by a rare accumulation of rain clouds that swelled over the horizon.

Blair gazed out the window, watching the weather turn. The coming storm reflected her mood: sullen, withdrawn, her mind heavy with thoughts of how she'd ended up as a failed waitress in her twenties.

She'd still have her former job, her former life, had she not been so stupid, so naïve. She'd be doing a job she loved for ample pay, she'd still be going out with her colleagues in El Segundo, far from the mess of wealth and personalities she'd encountered in Beverly Hills and Bel Air since yesterday evening.

And if last night's escape attempt had been successful, she would have had a solid chance of reclaiming that former job. Okay, she conceded, maybe not a *solid* chance—but at least *a* chance. She'd have had some opportunity for redemption, having stopped a heist plot before it had endangered people on the sidewalks and streets of LA. But she'd failed to escape and thus remained what she was: an ex-waitress, among other things.

Blair heard people moving down the hallway, and looked to the bedroom door that had remained open since she'd been re-captured.

Gordon walked past her door, casting her a contempt-filled glare before continuing out of sight. Two of the masked robbers, the shortest and the tallest of the group, followed Gordon to another part of the house. Neither looked at her, and less than a minute later their third colleague entered her room.

Blair watched Sterling stop inside the doorway. He was unmasked, his sandy hair matted and his eyes bearing a look of concern that had been absent when they spoke last night.

"Good morning, Sterling."

"Good morning, Blair."

There it was, Blair thought. She could hear concern in his voice as well, and she matched the tone with his expression to conclude he was experiencing doubt about the upcoming robbery.

So much the better. Maybe she could talk him out of this before it was too late.

She asked innocently, "Where are they taking Gordon?"

"To shower and shave. Gordon's going to work today."

"So that's the plan? Use him to get you access inside the bank?"

"More or less."

She shook her head, sighing wearily.

Sterling said, "It's going to work, Blair. I promise you that."

"I'm not worried about it working. Any amateur can get into a bank. But the LAPD won't let you leave."

"They won't have a choice."

"You know this is going to go bad, Sterling. I can see it in your eyes; I can hear it in your voice. But it's not too late to stop this and walk away."

"You sure about that, Blair?"

"I'm the only one who's seen your face, and the cops don't have to know that. All they need to know is that I met Gordon in a bar last night. I don't have to give an accurate description of what you look like, or the size and build of your teammates. If you call off this heist, I'll protect all three of you. You have my word."

Sterling drew a long breath, watching the gray sky beyond the window. Although he seemed to be giving the matter serious consideration, his next words removed all doubt.

"I'm not calling off anything. My team is taking this bank down." Then he added, "And so are you."

Blair stammered, "I'm—what?"

"Your records are sealed, so I don't know what kind of training you've had. I can't trust leaving you unsupervised until this is over. Your escape attempt bought you a front-row seat to the heist."

"Well," Blair objected, "you can't trust that I'll play along with your little plan, either."

"Yes, I can. And here's how: I'm going to give you what you want most."

"Stopping the robbery?"

Sterling conceded, "Okay, then I'll give you what you want second most."

"And what's that?"

"Keeping innocent civilians safe."

Blair paused for a beat, letting the words sink in. What was he going to ask of her in return?

"I'm listening."

Sterling gave a satisfied nod. "This thing will be over in six minutes, door-to-door. And we're not going to hurt anyone, least of all you."

"If that's true, then why would I need to keep innocent civilians safe?"

He paused, as if considering how to phrase his response. Blair could see that he was hiding something significant, but she couldn't figure out what.

He began, "If this thing goes bad, if we get pinned down, I'll need a hostage. Not to hurt, just to use for police negotiations. To make sure my people get away clean. And if that hostage is you, then it doesn't have to be someone else. I can release all the bank employees."

"What about Gordon?"

"If we get trapped in the bank, I'll need to release Gordon to do my bidding."

"You'd have an easier time with any other hostage in the world. Why use me?"

"Because I saw you on the edge of that pool last night, Blair, and I think you're brave enough to do it."

"What do you mean, 'brave enough?'"

Sterling rubbed the back of his neck. "This heist is happening no matter what, but I'm not out to scare anyone any more than I absolutely have to. If something goes badly today, you're strong enough to bear the pressure."

Blair flipped her hair back. "It sounds like you're flirting with me."

"I'm not. And whether this all goes according to plan or not, I'll leave you in the bank when we go. Will you do it? Willingly, I mean. Will you cooperate and not give me any trouble?"

"So when the cops stop you in the bank"—she wetted her lips—"you release all the other hostages."

"*If* they stop us. And yes."

"And in return, I serve as your leverage with the cops."

He gave a shaky laugh. "Exactly."

"Just tell me one thing: why are you doing this? You seem like a sharp guy. I just can't picture you robbing a bank."

Sterling grinned. "Regular life gets a bit tedious, doesn't it? The nine-to-five. Just existing, day in and day out. No surprises, just staying on the greased rails of a twenty-year plan toward some pension."

"No one gets hurt doing that."

He waved a hand flippantly. "Safety and comfort are overrated. Out there in the world, it's their law. Where you can cross the street and when. Cameras, litigation, traffic tickets. Don't agree, I'll sue you. See you in court, my lawyer will fight for me. Man enough to use your fists? Throw a punch and the cops are on their way. Assault charges. Restriction, restriction, restriction." He clucked his tongue.

"But when we do a heist?" He shrugged slowly, dramatically. "That's our law. For the span of time and space that we plan the job, we're in control. Who sees what and when, what they can do about it—or can't. Want to sue? Good luck finding us. Same goes for prison time, which only counts if we get caught."

"Which," Blair pointed out, "has an abnormally high chance of occurring in the next hour or two."

"Yeah, so my timing on this speech could have been better. But still."

He went silent, watching her until she spoke.

"Okay." She nodded. "I'll play along as your lone hostage. But heaven help me, if you hurt one person before this is over—"

"I won't. None of us will. And you'll be perfectly safe, Blair. You have my word on that."

She watched him closely. Behind his eyes there remained some lingering sense of doubt, but his words sounded sincere.

And for a fleeting moment, Blair almost believed him.

7

STERLING

Sterling watched the traffic light turn green from the middle back seat of Gordon's Mercedes S-Class sedan. Alec made the left turn onto Santa Monica Boulevard, with Marco seated beside him in the passenger seat. The drive wasn't a long one—all told, they'd be arriving at their destination in the Century City district less than twenty minutes after leaving Gordon's garage.

But to Sterling, the trip seemed to span a veritable eternity.

Now, with just a few blocks to go to their destination, he breathed an audible sigh of relief. He was grateful for only one thing about this most awkward ride of his life—it was almost over.

Rather than wear their masks in LA traffic, they'd instead made Gordon and Blair don blacked-out sunglasses. And since Blair had already seen Sterling's face, he had drawn the unenviable task of sitting in the middle seat between them.

The S-Class backseat was spacious, but not that spacious. Gordon's bulk had nowhere to go, leaving Sterling mushed into his side as if he'd drawn the worst seat on an airline flight. This was made far worse by the stench of Gordon's wretched aftershave.

Blair's slender body left her plenty of room to shift away from Sterling, and she'd taken full advantage. Every bump or turn that caused them to come into physical contact had corresponded with her pulling away. He looked over at her now, her vision blinded as she faced straight ahead, expression tense.

Sterling watched Alec make the penultimate turn onto Century Park East. They were about to pass under the shadow of the five-hundred-foot tower of glass and steel whose ground-floor bank he'd be robbing within minutes, and the thought made his pulse soar with anticipation.

He looked up at Geering Plaza, seeing a monstrosity of mirrored windows rising into the gray clouds of a stormy sky. At that moment he wasn't sure what intimidated him more—the building's imposing height or the turbulent weather. Either could play a role in making or breaking his op today.

As they passed the building, Sterling glanced at the pedestrian entrance leading into the glass-walled lobby, where a young trio in business attire chatted as they entered.

Alec turned right into a ramp descending to the parking garage beneath the building and then stopped to nonchalantly pull a ticket from the dispenser. A yellow gate opened ahead of them, and they proceeded to the first sublevel.

They were less than a minute from parking, and Sterling briefly considered what Blair had said—that anyone could rob a bank, but getting away was another matter entirely. She wasn't wrong. In many cases, the getaway required more skill and cunning than the actual robbery; and today, given the weather, would probably be one of those cases.

Alec swung the Mercedes S-Class into a spot marked *RESERVED - 501*.

As soon as the car engine died, Marco spoke from the passenger seat.

"All right, Gordon, it's your time to shine. Say something."

"I hate you all." Gordon's tinny voice echoed from a tablet in Marco's lap. "And I hope the cops kill every last one of you today, because that's what you deserve—"

Marco interrupted, "Audio and video are good."

Alec looked over from the driver seat. "That's your cue, Gordo. Break a leg out there."

Sterling touched Gordon's arm. "Sunglasses stay on until you're out of the car. And relax—this'll be over before you can say 'corrupt bank official.'"

Gordon wasn't amused. He felt for his door handle, then opened it and stepped out of the car with his briefcase in hand. Slamming the car door, he spun in place and walked toward the elevator. Sterling slid into the empty seat, giving Blair some space.

Alec adjusted his radio earpiece and called out, "Police scanner is clean."

A long silence ensued before Marco said, "Man, I can still smell Gordon."

He was right, Sterling noted. The horrid aftershave scent lingered.

"Well whose fault is that?" Blair asked, looking over despite her obscured vision. "You're the one who supervised him shaving."

"I was there," Alec said defensively. "We couldn't smell it until he opened the bottle and started slapping it on."

"Well, you could have made him shower again."

"There wasn't time—"

"Hold up," Marco said. "He's entering the bank. Cellular alarm signal is dead. Time hack 8:52."

Sterling could hear Gordon's voice through the tablet speaker as he greeted his employees. Marco said, "Security guard and tellers on station."

Blair pursed her lips. "You guys can't honestly believe you'll stroll back to the parking garage and drift away in Gordon's car."

Alec gave Sterling an accusing glare. "You told her the plan?"

Sterling swallowed. "Blair, you'll remain in the bank when we leave. Nothing else concerns you."

"It concerns me when the police don't let you leave. Because they won't."

"You don't believe in us?" Alec asked her with mock concern. Then, to Sterling, he noted, "It sounds like she doesn't believe in us."

"Blair," Sterling said firmly, "when you see how we escape, it's going to seem obvious."

"If you say so."

"I say so."

Marco announced, "Gordon's calling LAPD to test the wired alarm. Time hack 8:55."

"Police scanner is still clean," Alec said.

Sterling checked the digital watch on his wrist. Its split-second accuracy required him to wear it on jobs, so he'd switched his father's less accurate, vintage Omega Seamaster to his right wrist until they got away clean.

Then he began to feel the peculiar emotion reserved for the final minutes before a job. On site, he'd be lost in the moment. Afterward, the getaway would preoccupy his mind. But the minutes before a heist brought with them a unique blend of anxiety, fear, and sheer excitement. It was a feeling born of having time to consider what could go wrong, and the perpetual question: will I make it out of the arena today? Will all of my teammates? Or will one of us end the day in jail, or the morgue?

Sterling would have preferred the morgue. If he was killed on the job, he'd have nothing to worry about. And neither would his teammates—no additional risk would be assumed to recover a body. Instead, the remaining members would focus on their own survival and escape.

But prison...Sterling didn't think he could take it. He didn't see how anyone could. He'd undertaken this career in part to experience the ultimate freedom, which he couldn't do without risking the ultimate tyrannies: imprisonment and death.

Marco said, "Wired alarm dispatch is disabled for ten minutes. Gordon's shutting off the cameras. Time hack 8:56."

"We leave in one minute," Sterling said, sounding more confident than he felt.

Alec began to whistle "It's Beginning to Look a Lot Like Christmas."

"Thirty seconds," Marco called.

"Scanner is clean," Alec responded, then kept whistling.

Sterling felt the back of his neck burning with anticipation. If anything went wrong, he'd have put Alec and Marco in the thick of it. Both had advised him against proceeding, and yet...here they were.

"Twenty seconds."

"Scanner is clean."

"Ten seconds."

"Main vault time delay is off. Time hack 8:57."

"All right," Sterling said, opening his car door. "Let's take it."

8

BLAIR

Blair removed her sunglasses, seeing at once that the opulent interior of Gordon's car was empty. The three men were already slamming their doors shut and disappearing from view, and by the time Blair exited to the concrete floor of a subterranean parking garage, they were all clustered around the open trunk.

She closed her door and turned to them. All were now wearing their masks, and were still clad in belts bearing pistol, handcuffs, taser, and radio. But rather than controlling her, they were each pulling something out of the trunk.

Blair couldn't make sense of it—each man was donning what looked to be a full black hiking pack. The crew looked to be leaving a bank robbery, not plunging into one. What could possibly be inside the packs?

She caught her reflection in the car window and realized she looked like a crazy person. Hair in disarray, and wearing a red dress with tears in it, bare shoulders laced with scratches from her escape attempt.

Sterling slammed the trunk and gestured for her to follow the other two robbers now striding toward the stairs.

"Ladies first," he said, and she obeyed.

They entered a cool concrete stairwell lit by fluorescent lights, and followed the flight of stairs upward to the main level.

Then the first two robbers abruptly halted outside a door marked

LOBBY, and one of them held up a gloved palm to her with a single whispered word: "Wait."

Wait for what? It had been easy to follow them out of the car and up the stairs, to maintain a distracted momentum. But now that they'd suddenly stopped, Blair's mind exploded with horrible thoughts.

You're about to be a hostage. That was the first announcement of mental panic. And despite Sterling's gentlemanly proclamations of her safety, Blair knew the truth. Whether Sterling believed what he said or not, these men would hurt her when cornered by the cops. These men would kill her. Criminals always talked a good game when things were going fine, but desperate people did desperate things. And these men were about to be incredibly desperate.

Because they weren't making it out. They'd get the cash they came for, and then the LAPD would swoop in and block their escape. Blair knew that much—why didn't they? It was maddening, it was terrifying, and Blair felt like she couldn't possibly move another step.

One of the robbers said, "Bank entrance is unlocked. Let's go."

Then he threw open the door and advanced into the building lobby with his partner.

Blair couldn't move. Her knees were locked, her body frozen in terror.

She felt Sterling put a hand on her arm, force her through the door, and move alongside her.

The scene in the building's lobby turned to a frantic blur of chaos.

Weekday life was in full swing—businessmen and women were crossing the lobby with coffees in hand between marble columns separating the pedestrian entrance and the elevators.

The first bystanders to see masked men rushing toward the bank entrance acted uncertain, as if this were a Hollywood film shoot or some poorly executed piece of street theater. She saw a woman fidgeting with her coffee as she watched, and a young bike messenger stopped to film the short procession with his phone. Then someone screamed, and the sound seemed to set the lobby aflame with panic. Pedestrians fled for cover, racing for the elevators, the stairs, the exits.

As Sterling clung to her arm and guided her toward the bank, Blair glanced toward the lobby windows. The scene beyond was surreal: seven lanes of traffic screeched to a halt as bystanders bolted across Century Park East.

She looked forward, seeing the first two robbers already entering through the bank's glass door.

Then she felt Sterling release her arm and race past her to follow his partners inside the bank.

9

STERLING

Sterling had intended to escort Blair inside, ensuring she didn't panic and flee.

But upon seeing the scene that unfolded as Alec and Marco entered, he couldn't care less if Blair ran or not.

Because this bank robbery, he realized, was almost over before it began.

Alec was moving to the teller stations to begin crowd control; that much was going according to plan.

Marco, however, was about to get himself shot.

Sterling knew from his reconnaissance that Jon Suttle, the bank's security guard on duty that day, was a large and physically capable man. Sterling also knew the security company's protocol in the event of an armed robbery: comply so the thieves exit the bank as quickly as possible.

But Jon Suttle wasn't merely large. He was a corn-fed, six-foot-eight, 275-pound monster. And he wasn't complying with anyone, least of all Marco.

Instead, his first reaction upon seeing the masked robbers entering his bank was to reach for his pistol.

Marco responded by leveling his taser at Suttle's chest and squeezing the trigger.

Two dart-like probes soared from Marco's taser and struck Suttle in the torso and thigh, trailing their conductive wires behind them.

A rapid-fire clicking sound erupted as Marco delivered a paralyzing electrical current through the conductive wires. The charge then flowed along the path of least resistance between the probes—in this case, Suttle's body from his chest to his upper leg. The huge security guard turned into a rigid, quaking plank, and then he fell.

But he spun sideways during his descent, snapping the thin conductive wires and breaking the connectivity.

And just like that, Suttle was back in the fight.

"Taser failure!" Marco shouted, his voice a little too high, as the massive guard leapt off the ground and went for his pistol again.

Sterling drew his taser and fired, and a new pair of dart-like probes speared into the guard's abdomen and thigh. The guard grunted loudly, his jaw clenching as his cheeks rippled in sync with the rhythmic pulse of the electric current. Sterling kept the trigger depressed, the eerie stream of clicking noises marking a flood of electricity flowing into the guard's body.

Suttle went into a state of paralysis, and as he fell, Marco closed on him to apply handcuffs. When the guard hit the ground, he suddenly sprang back to life. Sterling saw, to his horror, that the fall had snapped a wire—one probe remained in his gut with the broken, threadlike filament dangling freely. Without two points of connection for electricity to flow between, Suttle would be fully functional.

Sterling raced forward, leaping on the massive guard before he could rise. He jabbed the front of his taser into Suttle's upper back, directly between the shoulder blades, while keeping the trigger depressed.

And that did the trick—suddenly the circuit was completed, and electricity flowed freely between the remaining probe in Suttle's leg and the taser in contact with his spine. The technique was known as a drive stun, and Sterling had hoped he'd never have to employ it.

He kept the trigger pulled as Marco wrestled the guard's hands together and tightly handcuffed his wrists.

With this complete, Sterling and Marco struggled upward, still wearing their heavy packs, and took in the sight of shocked bank tellers at their stations, staring at them in horror, hands raised.

Alec was still in the corner, covering the bank tellers as he announced, "Well, that got off to a bad start. As you probably guessed, this is a robbery. Not much of one so far, but...a robbery."

Sterling tried to catch his breath as he detached the spent cartridge from his taser and reloaded with a second one stored in the grip. Taking in the bank's interior for the first time felt surreal—after the struggle with the security guard, he felt absurd to be standing in a clean, well-lit commercial space.

He announced, "Mrs. Stilwell, Mrs. Jackson, please report to the back. Time to open the vault."

Two of the tellers abandoned their stations. Behind him, Marco shouted, "Thirty seconds!"

Sterling glanced backward and, to his surprise, saw Blair.

He'd almost forgotten about her, but expected that the moment he released her arm, she'd have sprinted off to notify the authorities and embrace her newfound freedom.

Instead she'd entered the bank of her own volition, and now crossed the tile floor as she appraised the situation: the bound security guard, the frightened but unharmed tellers. Her eyes met Sterling's.

"Come with me," he said to her, proceeding toward the employees-only section of the bank. One door led to the back, and Gordon was holding it open for Alec.

Once Alec took control of the door, he kept it ajar with a shoulder while watching the tellers.

Sterling stepped past Alec toward a row of office doors ending in the circular steel vault door. Two tellers were standing in the hallway as instructed—a slender blonde who was already stifling tears, and an old woman who was practically sneering at him.

"Gordon," Sterling said, "get the main vault open with Mrs. Jackson."

Gordon approached the vault door, inserting a key and punching a four-digit code into a keypad. "Jeane," he said, "your key."

The young woman fumbled a lanyard from her neck, shakily handing it to Gordon. He inserted it into a second slot.

Marco shouted, "One minute!"

Gordon asked, "What's your code?"

The blonde was in near-hysterics.

"Four..." she sobbed. "Two..."

She was overcome by tears, and Gordon shouted at her.

"Come on, Jeane! Are you trying to get us all killed?"

She began sobbing harder. Marco approached and laid a hand on her shoulder.

"Jeane," Marco said, "you're doing great. Four, two..."

"Nine...seven."

Gordon punched in the code and cranked the handle. The massive vault door swung open.

The cavernous space within was lined with steel walls of safe deposit boxes and smaller rectangular vault doors.

"Mrs. Jackson," Sterling said, "please return to your station."

With a final gurgling sob, the blonde vanished through the teller access door.

"Mrs. Stilwell, please open the cash vault."

In contrast to Jeane, Becky Stilwell was a grizzled old woman who limped forward with an expression somewhere between boredom and contempt.

"Hold your horses," she rasped. "I'm not about to be intimidated by a gang of common thugs."

Sterling rolled his eyes as she ambled up to the keypad, typed her code, and inserted a key. After Gordon did the same, he turned the handle and opened the door to the cash vault.

Inside was the proverbial gold mine: great rectangular blocks of shrink-wrapped cash, stoic Benjamin Franklins gazing skyward beneath the clear plastic.

Marco rushed inside, slicing open the wrap and using handheld scanners to sweep the cash for exploding dye packs.

Sterling said, "Mrs. Stilwell, please return to your station. Your manager will escort you now." He shot Gordon an authoritative look.

"Right this way, Becky," Gordon said, walking the old woman out of the back room.

As Marco tossed the dye packs aside and withdrew folded waterproof duffel bags from his cargo pocket, Sterling looked to Alec, who stood at the end of the hall, still propping open the door to the teller area to ensure no one left the bank.

Then Alec shouted, "There's the two-eleven," referring to the police code for robbery. He touched his earpiece and called out a moment later, "First units responding are three minutes out."

Sterling checked his digital watch: bypassing the cellular and landline alarms had bought them exactly one minute and forty-nine seconds.

He jogged to the opposite end of the hall, replacing Alec in the doorway to the bank lobby. Alec ran to the vault, where Marco was tossing the first duffel bag full of cash onto the ground.

"Two minutes!" Marco called.

Sterling looked out toward the lobby. The tellers were still behind their booths, the massive security guard still handcuffed on the tile floor. He stared at Sterling, filing away his height, weight, visual description.

Eat your heart out, Sterling thought. Compared to what will happen very soon, I'm just getting warmed up.

Alec came trotting down the hallway, then dropped a full duffel bag at Sterling's feet. Sterling hoisted the heavy bag over his shoulder, adjusting the strap so the cash was beside the hiking pack he'd worn in from Gordon's car.

As Alec was running back toward the vault to liberate the next load of cash, Sterling turned to face the bank's entrance.

And realized he wasn't going anywhere.

Beyond the glass entryway, he saw a flash of movement behind a marble column in the lobby.

Sterling caught another flash of movement—this one a dark shape behind a separate column, as if someone was taking cover.

Then he saw a pistol emerge from behind each column, aiming toward the bank's entrance. Sterling ducked behind the corner, concealing himself behind the doorway.

"Police!" came the first shout from the lobby. "Drop your weapons!"

10

BLAIR

Blair felt her eyes pinch shut, and then forced them open.

This moment, she knew, was where the whole thing went bad.

Sterling shouted, "We got cops in the building lobby!"

"I don't know what happened," the short robber called back. "Police scanner had the first units three minutes away—"

"Shut up!" Sterling yelled. "Get the rest of the cash bagged. We're going to Plan B."

Blair wanted to scream in frustration. She'd thought their plan was idiotic *before* she knew the bank layout. Now that she was here, their idea seemed even worse.

When takeover robberies worked—before the advent of most modern security measures, that was—it was because the thieves could intimidate the staff into not activating the alarms, usually by physical force. The robbers would be gone before anyone called the police. And that was the only way anyone had time to reach a bank vault and escape with anything to show for it.

By contrast, this crew had gone to elaborate measures to disable the alarms and then done a more-or-less standard takeover robbery—but this bank, of course, wasn't an independent structure. This bank constituted only one element of a massive skyscraper's ground floor. The glass wall rendered it visible to the main lobby of the entire high rise, so these robbers were spotted immediately.

Sure, they'd bought themselves a little bit of time. One minute, maybe two. After all, the alternative was for an alarm to be activated immediately, resulting in police units being sent to a pinpoint location as quickly as dispatch could make the radio call.

Instead, they had to deal with eyewitnesses fleeing the range of their cellular jammer before calling police. It would take longer for dispatch to sift through multiple panicked calls and send units to the bank—but not that much longer. Certainly not enough for the robbers to escape before police response arrived.

And now Blair was about to bear the consequences of that oversight.

Sterling sounded panicked. "Gordon, get over here."

Gordon approached from the teller area, looking like he was about to have a nervous breakdown.

Sterling ripped the button camera out of Gordon's suit jacket.

"Give me your earpiece."

Gordon complied, and Sterling pocketed the earpiece along with the camera before speaking again.

"You're going to put your hands up, exit the bank, and turn yourself over to those officers. I've got your cell phone. Tell them I want a negotiator to call me on it."

"Okay."

"Say it back to me."

"You want a negotiator to call my cell number to speak with you."

"Go. Now."

Panting heavily, Gordon raised his hands in the air and turned to the door leading into the bank lobby.

"Don't shoot," he shouted without exposing himself. "Don't shoot."

Sterling sounded furious. "Clock's ticking, Gordon."

With a final breath, Gordon rounded the corner.

The police response was immediate.

"Keep your hands up!" they yelled. "Walk slowly toward us!"

Gordon vanished from the back hallway, and a moment later Blair could hear the officers' shouts spike in volume as the bank door opened and closed.

Sterling peeked around the corner, then ducked back into the hallway. "He's out."

By now the other two robbers had approached, both carrying a sack of cash in addition to their hiking packs.

The tall one said, "What now, boss?"

"Go turn off that cell jammer," Sterling ordered. "I'm going to negotiate our escape."

11

JIM

It was quarter after nine in the morning, and Jim looked like a man in a state of shock.

He was at his desk in professional attire, but his mind wasn't on work. Instead he sat with elbows propped on the desk, hands cupped tightly in front of his mouth, heart speeding along as if he were at a dead sprint.

This couldn't be happening.

But his intuition had told him so, and it was very rarely wrong.

Jim's icy blue eyes were fixated on his computer screen, the display flashing the streaming feed of the local news network.

BANK ROBBERY IN PROGRESS.

The media had already arrived and were now broadcasting from behind police barricades. Their backdrop was Century City, its streets filled with the flashing red lights of first responder vehicles.

"*...the SWAT team is pulling up now...*"

The camera angle shifted from the ground floor upward, slowly revealing the five-hundred-foot tower of mirrored glass that was Geering Plaza. Jim's face felt flushed, almost scalding.

"*...and as this eyewitness footage shows...*"

Between reporter comments, the screen flashed the same three-second video clip that it had been playing since the coverage began.

"*...the robbers appear to have brought a hostage* into *the bank...*"

He watched the clip over and over, trying to convince himself he was wrong. But he couldn't.

My God, Jim thought, it's really her.

The clip flashed from two armed men, dressed in black as they charged into a bank, to a third man gripping the arm of a beautiful woman.

She was in a red dress and ankle boots, as if out for a night on the town. But this was morning, and her black hair trailed over a rip in the dirt-stained dress, and cuts were visible on her exposed skin.

In the video's final moment, she glanced over at the camera filming her, eyes wild but lucid. Then the cameraman bolted for the building exit.

Jim ran both hands through his silver hair, feeling a tension headache beginning to spread.

This video could have only one explanation.

The door to his office opened, and a buxom redhead stepped inside.

"You've seen it?" she asked.

He nodded, keeping his eyes on the screen.

"Agree that it's her?"

He nodded again.

There was a gap of silence as the woman waited for some further comment. Then she said, "We're going to have to get ahead of this, sir."

Jim pressed his hands flat against the desk, leaning back in his chair and looking at her for the first time since she'd entered.

His face darkened. "You think?"

12

STERLING

Blair was practically yelling at Sterling.

"You said you'd release *all* the hostages. Not just Gordon."

"Have a little patience."

"Patience? I gave myself to you as a hostage. I don't need patience. That was our deal."

"Just give me a minute."

"I don't have a minute. You want to protect these people? Release them now, or God so help me I will—"

Without warning, the *Star Wars* theme song rang out between them.

"See?" Sterling held up Gordon's cell phone. "Was that so hard?"

He plugged a small microphone box into the phone. The phone recognized this new device as an external headset, and it served to alter Sterling's voice on the receiving end.

Then he answered the call. "Who's this?"

A man replied, "Sergeant Sean Hollis, LAPD. Who do I have the pleasure of speaking with?"

"The new owner of this bank. You should have let us leave."

"I don't control the initial response—but now that we're in this situation, I can help."

"Good," Sterling said. "I want a fully fueled helicopter landing on the roof of this building within one hour, with room to carry four people plus luggage, if you catch my drift. Any questions?"

"I'll see what I can do, but one hour is a bit—"

"There are hospitals all over LA. Plenty of them have helicopters parked and ready to go. You'll figure it out—or you won't."

"Let me get to work on that. But it'll be a lot easier for me to convince my bosses if you release the innocent people in that bank as a show of good faith."

"You want innocent people?"

"I don't think either of us wants to see anyone get hurt in this."

"You know what? You're right."

"So how about releasing them?"

"The police officers in the lobby are making me nervous. I want them gone now."

"That I can handle—if you'll return the favor."

"Once those cops are gone, I'll send some hostages out of the building. Do not shoot—none of them are my people."

"That sounds good. Let's both make it happen."

Sterling felt his grip tighten on the phone. "I'm going to repeat that so there's no confusion: none of the people exiting this building are robbers. So do not shoot them, you understand?"

Hollis paused. "I understand completely."

"Good. Now get my helicopter."

Sterling hung up the phone, then turned to see Blair glaring at him.

"What?" he asked.

"What was that supposed to be?"

"Exactly what it sounded like," he said, quite unapologetically. "I just agreed to send hostages."

"You said you'll send out 'some' hostages."

"Well, I couldn't include you, now could I? If I say 'all hostages,' and then tell him I'm still holding you, then it's not a good look for my integrity going forward."

"You had better be sending out every civilian in this bank."

"That's what I meant. Now I need you to go wait in the vault."

Blair clenched her teeth. "The vault? Why?"

Sterling huffed a sigh. "Because," he explained patiently, "you're about to be my only hostage. As soon as LAPD SWAT positively identifies where you are in the bank, they can raid it. And shoot me and my friends in the face. Okay? And since SWAT is about to be jamming snake cameras in every air vent on the ground floor, I need you in the one place they can't see. That happens to be the vault."

"Tactical cable cameras," she corrected him.

"Sure. Whatever. I don't know who you are or why you know so much about cameras. Or probation tracking devices. Or vintage watches. And right now, I don't care. I just need you to go wait in the vault."

"I'll wait wherever you want—as soon as you let these people go."

"You said you'd cooperate. Am I going to have to handcuff you, too?"

Blair leaned forward. "That didn't help you last night. You got beat up by a 'girl' once. Don't make it happen a second time today."

He turned his eyes toward movement in the building lobby. Blair watched as the two LAPD officers rose from behind their marble columns, lowered their pistols, and jogged to the building exit.

Sterling met Blair's eyes, her expression inscrutable.

The *Star Wars* theme song began playing from Gordon's phone again.

From down the hall, Alec yelled, "You can put that thing on vibrate, you know."

Sterling ripped the phone out of his pocket and answered it.

"Good morning, Sergeant Hollis...I watched the officers depart, thank you. Yes, I agree you made good on your promise."

Blair's upper lip curled. Then she cupped one hand and drove her opposite fist into it slowly, ominously, in the universal symbol for beating. Sterling felt his eyes crinkle into a smile.

"Prepare to receive your hostages. I'll be sending them out shortly."

He hung up.

"Well?" Blair said.

Sterling looked down the hall to where Alec was jumping up and down, waving a hand excitedly as if to say, "Pick me, pick me." Sterling gave him a thumbs up.

Alec raced to the rear of the teller stations in such an aggressive burst of speed that Blair looked afraid he was going to draw his gun. He saw her body tense as Alec stopped behind the tellers.

"Ladies and gentlemen," he shouted in his Boston accent. The tellers jumped, looking to him in fear, and then Alec assumed a courteous, methodical tone as he continued, "Welcome to the Century City district of Los Angeles, California. Local time is 9:32 a.m. and the temperature is a balmy 63 degrees Fahrenheit."

Sterling held up his wrist and tapped his digital watch—*hurry up*, he indicated. He noticed Blair staring at his opposite wrist and realized she was looking at the vintage Omega Seamaster. No matter, he thought. She'd already seen it yesterday. So why did she look lost in thought?

He was quickly distracted by Alec's discourse.

"For your safety and comfort when exiting the building, please keep your hands up until the LAPD instructs you otherwise, indicating you have been presumed a hostage and not a bank robber in disguise."

Sterling waved his fingers back and forth across his neck, signaling to Alec that he better kill this speech quickly.

Instead, Alec's voice took on a stern, overemphasized tone—almost condescending, and spoken for the benefit of the lone security guard.

"If you require departure assistance, such as being handcuffed on the floor as a result of resisting a numerically superior, mostly nonviolent force, your fellow bank employees will be pleased to assist you as they exit."

Finally Sterling leveled a pointed finger and cocked thumb at Alec, pantomiming shooting him with a gun. Alec returned to a courteous tone, though he began speaking faster as a concession.

"On behalf of the entire crew, I'd like to thank you for joining us in this botched takeover robbery. We realize you have the choice of countless maladjusted felons to serve your hostage-taking needs, and thank you for choosing our merry band of criminal misfits. Have a wonderful Century City day."

No one moved. The bank fell completely silent, the tellers staring at them in wide-eyed confusion.

Sterling shouted, "You can go now. All of you. Kindly collect Mr. Suttle on your way out. Keep your hands up when leaving the building, and take all instructions from the fine officers of the LAPD."

From the floor, the security guard rolled onto his side and then sat up.

"Let's go!" Sterling said to the tellers. "Hurry up and get out."

The tellers scrambled into action, filing out of their booths and toward the bank door. Two of them helped the guard to his feet.

The elderly cash vault teller stopped her limping gait halfway across the tile floor and turned slowly toward the robbers. "May God have mercy on you. If any of you survive this, I hope you find the Lord. And that you can start over and build a meaningful life."

Alec answered, "We'll start sending out resumes tomorrow. You were my favorite hostage, Mrs. Stilwell!"

She gave a frustrated grunt and resumed limping toward the door.

Then they were gone—all the tellers and the security guard, turning toward the building exit before walking past the marble columns and out of sight.

Sterling looked to Blair.

"Happy?"

She nodded. "Thank you."

"You're welcome. Now please, wait in the vault. And pull the door closed—not all the way, just enough that they can't see you in there. When they, you know"—he waved a finger toward a ceiling vent above them— "start watching us."

Blair bowed her head gracefully, casting a final glance at Sterling's vintage watch. Then she turned and walked down the hall toward the open vault door.

Sterling watched her step inside before pulling the door partially shut behind her.

Then he whirled around and strode to Gordon's office, where he cranked the handle open and entered.

Marco looked up at him, unmasked.

His tactical gloves had been replaced with disposable blue nitrile gloves, and he was hurriedly stuffing his pack with the black jacket that he'd just removed. Beneath it was a collared, short-sleeve uniform shirt with patches on both shoulders. Marco's chest bore a badge with a round, six-pointed star bisected by a snake-and-staff symbol and the words *EMER-GENCY MEDICAL TECHNICIAN*.

Sterling looked to the television mounted on the wall, where muted news footage showed the bank tellers—and one handcuffed security guard

—descending the building steps at a distance, all under the escort of LAPD officers. The procession disappeared behind patrol cars blocking the view, and the camera zoomed out to reveal it was filming from behind a police barricade half a block away.

"You good?" Sterling asked.

"I'm always good," Marco replied, closing his pack. "Hurry up and pop the balloon. Weather's going to turn on us."

Sterling looked back to the television, where a female reporter was speaking into a microphone with one finger on her earpiece.

"All right," Sterling agreed. "I'm on my way."

Sterling stepped out of the office and closed the door. He glanced back to the vault, where Alec was lovingly examining the door's solid construction, considering the myriad ways in which he could penetrate it given the equipment and time. Sterling snapped his fingers.

Alec looked up and gave him a nod; Blair was still inside the vault.

Sterling returned the nod, jerking a thumb toward the building lobby.

For the second time that day, Alec began whistling "It's Beginning to Look a Lot Like Christmas."

Taking a breath to steady his nerves, Sterling walked through the customer area of the bank to the glass door, now closed, before gripping the handle and pulling it halfway open.

Then he listened, hearing no movement outside. He scanned the marble columns, seeing that the building lobby was completely empty.

Stepping outside the bank, he could make out the whirling red lights of patrol cars outside. The building had been cordoned by local police but not yet encircled by a massive, coordinated response by authorities. That part, he knew, was on the way at this very minute.

Sterling began walking toward the elevators. He heard shouting outside and looked over to see a few intrepid LAPD officers outside the building doors, yelling at him to put his hands up.

Sterling complied, and then continued walking. He stopped before the elevators, lowering one gloved hand to the fire alarm on the wall beside him.

Sliding two fingers over the white T-shaped handle, he pulled it down.

The quiet lobby exploded with a shrill siren, strobe lights on the walls flashing amid the noise. The building elevators began gliding down to ground level, their descent marked by ticking red numbers.

Sterling raised both hands above his head for the benefit of the officers outside. Then he crossed the lobby and walked back into the bank, locking the door behind him.

13

BLAIR

Blair gazed across the brushed stainless steel façade in the main vault, looking at the rows of safe deposit boxes that had gone untouched. She walked past the teller vaults and some loose cash, none of which interested her. If she was going to be killed as the robbers' last remaining hostage— and there was a very good chance she would—she wanted to understand this heist.

Because right now, she couldn't.

She stepped into the cash vault, stopping just inside the open door.

And there it was, she thought. The aftermath of this robbery— shredded plastic and discarded packets of cash in a concrete cube, the space as hollow as the blind greed that drove these men. She reached down and picked up one of the abandoned stacks, spreading the hundred-dollar bills down the middle. A flexible square object was embedded in a cutout within: a small incendiary device known as a dye pack. The bank's door frames contained radio transmitters that would detect the passing of any active dye packs, initiating a ten-second timer before they exploded in a red cloud and rendered any stolen money useless.

So this crew of robbers had been able to quickly scan for dye packs. That much wasn't extraordinary, if you know what you're looking for. They'd done a few things right so far, but not nearly enough. Their manipulation of the alarms had been clever, but ultimately futile.

Suddenly a shrill, piercing wail split the muted silence of the vault. Blair recognized the fire alarm at once, though it took a mounting escalation of thoughts to realize the significance.

Because the fatal flaw to their plan—robbing a bank on the ground floor of a building with a large number of people—provided something that no takeover robbery of an independent bank location could.

People.

A limited number of police were outside, she knew. More on the way with each passing minute, yes, but how many would it take to contain the deluge of hundreds of office workers? None could be presumed innocent at first glance. The police would have to screen every individual before releasing them, lest the robbers escape in the melee.

Was that their plan? It couldn't be—it was too risky, and it relied upon too much luck. Then again, they were robbing a bank in the first place, which, in the modern era, was as good as locking yourself in a prison cell. What was the sense behind anything these guys had done? Methodical one minute, cavalier the next—the Boston robber's speech to release the hostages had sounded like something out of an improv comedy practice.

She thought of Sterling tapping his watch in an attempt to end the sermon, and that made her recall that he'd worn a watch on both wrists. His left arm now bore a digital watch, but the one he'd had on at Greaney's the previous morning was now on his right.

Her mind fixated on that thought once more, bringing with it a cascade of recent snapshot memories.

She thought back to seeing them use tasers on the security guard, who was in the process of drawing a lethal firearm. Even a cop would be hard-pressed to exercise that level of restraint under the circumstances. So these ruthless cowboys weren't so ruthless after all...but that in itself presented a dilemma of logic. They'd shown a level of restraint limited to real professionals...but no real professionals would run into a bank like this.

She thought back further, to what Sterling said during her escape attempt the night before, as she stood on the edge of Gordon's pool. He had just stood there, gun in holster.

You're not... we're not... you don't understand.

You're not getting hurt.

No one's getting shot, see?

She thought about the impossibility of escaping this situation, and yet Sterling's sociopathic confidence that they could—and would.

And then she thought back further, to the previous day, when she'd sat across the table from Sterling.

You're wearing a vintage Omega Seamaster that looks like you put it in a blender. Not the timepiece of choice for finance hotshots.

And that thought had evoked a second memory, long since forgotten. One ridiculed and dismissed by a great many people, and to an extent, by Blair herself.

Until today.

Things got strange after that. Blair looked from the dye packs on the ground, to the concrete walls around her, to the partially open vault door. She thought about how Sterling had been eager to release hostages—what sense did that make? He could've bought more time with more hostages, not less. Releasing the people in the building would temporarily overwhelm the barricades outside, but it would exponentially increase the LAPD's ability to order a SWAT raid immediately afterward.

Taken individually, none of these factors made sense.

Taken together, they pointed to one almost incontrovertible truth.

And suddenly, Blair Morgan no longer felt afraid.

14

STERLING

Sterling had given a few glances around the corner and toward the front of the bank, watching the deluge of people flooding through the building lobby and onto the street. The sheer volume of evacuees was overwhelming the police's ability to contain or process them; Sterling could have taken off his mask and had a decent chance of waltzing through the crowd and down the sidewalk.

As the last people left the building, the fire alarm shut off.

And then Gordon's phone rang again.

Sterling picked it up before the ringtone could annoy him for long. "Mayfield National Bank," he said into the voice distortion box, "Century City branch."

"This is Sergeant Hollis again."

"Sergeant Hollis." Sterling stepped inside Gordon's office. "How have you been since our last call?"

"Busy," Hollis answered. "When you said you were going to release some innocent people as a show of good faith, I wasn't expecting the whole building."

The news footage continued on Gordon's muted television screen, now showing a massive crowd pouring onto the street as the LAPD officers struggled to corral them.

Marco, by now, was long gone.

"You wanted innocent people. I must have given you five hundred."

"And I assure you that every one of them is going to a containment area until we confirm their identities and place of employment."

"That's not my problem."

"What I mean, sir, is that if you sent anyone from your crew out with those employees, we're going to catch them."

"I told you, none of my people were coming out. Not yet. I'm a man of my word, Sergeant Hollis. Now let's see if you're the same. Where's my helicopter?"

"The hospitals have refused to give up their only life flight assets, and as police we can't legally commandeer them."

"That sounds suspiciously like an excuse."

"No excuse, just a small delay. We commissioned a civilian charter flight instead. LAX is working the airspace de-confliction for their flight plan to Century City now. A bit of red tape, but we'll get it worked out soon."

"I'm glad to hear that, because you're running out of time."

"Let's talk about the remaining hostage."

"What's to talk about? She's coming with us onto the helicopter, and we'll release her once we're safe. Not before."

"That's not quite what I mean, sir."

"Then what do you mean?"

There was a pause as the negotiator steeled himself. For no reason he could quantify, Sterling began to feel unsettled.

Finally, Hollis spoke.

"Sir, we know that it's Blair Morgan inside the bank. Do you think I could speak to her?"

Sterling hung up the phone.

He planted a hand on Gordon's desk, steadying himself, his eyes darting around the office.

If Blair wouldn't tell him who she was, then he'd have to find out on his own.

He located a remote and turned on the volume for Gordon's television. The screen was still filled with news coverage of the bank robbery in progress, and a female reporter spoke into her microphone against a backdrop of police barricades.

"*...the fire alarm has just stopped, and it appears that no further civilians are exiting the building...*"

Sterling flipped between news stations, looking for any mention of Blair's name.

"*...early reports indicate that only one hostage remains inside the bank...*"

He changed the channel to a male anchor.

"*...what the robbers are demanding remains to be seen...*"

Changing the station, he found a still shot of an impromptu podium on the steps of a building. Before it, a throng of reporters stood in patient vigil. A reporter's voice droned over the footage.

"*...awaiting a press conference from the FBI. The speaker is reported to be Assistant Special Agent in Charge Jacobson, who our sources confirm is currently heading the federal task force responsible for identifying the thieves believed to be behind over a dozen sophisticated robberies across Southern California...*"

Sterling felt his neck begin to burn.

"*...these much-publicized heists have yielded an estimated twenty-one million over the past three years, and investigators believe they are the work of a very large and possibly international cast of thieves now operating in the US. As of yet, it's unclear what connection, if any, exists between these burglaries and the bank robbery in progress...*"

He burst out of the office and walked down the hall to the vault, pushing Alec to the side. Blair stood inside, facing him as if she'd been waiting for him to arrive. She was smiling.

"You." Sterling pointed. "Come with me."

Blair nodded and exited the vault as ordered.

Sterling waved her into Gordon's office, past the two waterproof duffel bags of cash and two hiking packs all lined up neatly along the hallway. Sterling knew she was noting the absence of the third set of bags—along with Marco.

When she stepped into the office, she asked, "Did your third guy leave with the crowd?"

Sterling rolled his ski mask off his face. "Nah. He's no quitter."

"Okay. What did you want to see me about?"

"The negotiator wanted to speak with you. I want to know why."

She glanced at the TV, where the image was flipping from the empty podium to a newsroom where a retired-detective-turned-talking-head was filling airtime before the press conference began.

"Well, Shirley, as far as I'm concerned there is no connection. The only pattern investigators have found connecting the previous string of heists is their nonviolent execution, occurring after-hours and targeting large hauls of cash or jewels..."

"Interesting story," Blair noted. "What do you think of your coverage?"

"I'm not concerned with publicity. Why did the negotiator want to speak with you?"

"...while deplorable, none of those high-stakes burglaries have involved the use of guns or hostages, and given the success of this criminal network in recent years, it's unlikely they're getting desperate..."

"He's got a point," Blair said, evading the question. "You know, you thought of almost everything. Just one tiny kink in your plan."

"What's that?"

"...the one wild card here is the young woman seen entering the bank. Calls continue to flood into police, but her identity has yet to be publicly established..."

Blair responded firmly. "You picked the wrong hostage."

"How do you figure?"

He saw her looking at his right wrist again.

"What?" he demanded.

Blair met his eyes. "I know you guys are the crew behind most, if not all, of those other heists. You're the ones that federal task force is trying to find."

Sterling laughed.

"I'm flattered, but there are probably dozens of people working those jobs. And if we could pull off their scores, we wouldn't need to steal anymore."

"Neither do they. That's what makes them so interesting."

"They don't rob banks."

"And that's what makes this situation so interesting. What are you after? We both know it's not the cash in these bags. The world may believe that, but I know who you are. There's another reason you're doing this, and it hinges on everyone thinking you're *not* capable of any high-end robberies. But...you are."

Sterling now had an empty feeling in the pit of his stomach. "That's funny, I seem to recall you saying more or less the exact opposite last night."

"Well, kind of a lot's changed since then. And you and I both know they're not sending a helicopter to meet your demands. So how do you plan on getting out?"

He didn't answer.

"That's the other part I can't figure out. But"—she cracked her knuckles —"I doubt anyone but me suspects you're part of a sophisticated heist crew."

"The news would seem to indicate otherwise."

Blair gave a polite smile. "You'll see what all that's about in a minute. You should start thinking about your getaway plan—you'll need to execute it a lot sooner than you think."

"What's that supposed to mean?" Sterling asked, his voice nearly a whisper.

"I saw your taser routine. You guys may not be willing to resort to violence, but the police are. And to them, you're just a bunch of gun-toting thugs."

"I'm counting on it. Now tell me who you are."

"*We're now going live to a press conference that authorities say will shed light on this situation...*"

Blair gazed dispassionately at the screen. "Here's where you find out."

15

JIM

Jim straightened his tie in the mirror, his ghostly blue eyes holding a perpetual air of determination. He projected authority, an aura matched by his full head of silver hair. Some men resisted going gray in their forties; Jim had embraced it. Against his tanned face and perfect white teeth, it made him look distinguished. Stately.

He caught himself twisting his wedding ring, an involuntary nervous action that he forced himself to stop. Then he picked up his binder from the table before him and turned to push open the door.

Stepping into the humid air outside, he saw the podium waiting like an altar.

Beyond it was an even larger crowd of reporters than he expected, interspersed with video cameras filming live. Camera flashes erupted as he stepped up to the microphone.

The reporters began shouting at once. He heard the inquiry of whether there was any connection with the previous string of heists shouted in every possible variation of wording.

Jim set down his binder on the podium and flipped it open to his notes. Then he adjusted his microphone to speak, and held up a hand for the reporters to quiet.

He glanced at the microphone, feeling as if it stared at him more intently than the crowd of gawking reporters. Jim very suddenly felt the urge to start twisting his wedding ring again.

But instead he set both hands on top of the podium, cleared his throat once, and spoke confidently.

"This morning finds street terrorists holding our city hostage," he began. "Common thugs have taken over Geering Plaza in Century City. There has been much speculation about the identity of the unmasked woman sighted entering the bank this morning."

He paused to collect his thoughts.

"I can now confirm that we have identified this individual as Ms. Blair Morgan"—he looked up at the crowd—"a woman formerly employed by the FBI."

Jim paused for dramatic effect amid an uproar among the reporters. He held up a palm, waiting for them to fall silent before he continued.

"As of one year ago, Ms. Morgan was a special agent. She was assigned to the federal task force responsible for apprehending the network of thieves conducting sophisticated robberies across Southern California. That task force was, at the time of her assignment and continuing to the present day, commanded by myself.

"My task force employs representatives from the FBI, California Highway Patrol, LAPD, and the Department of the Treasury. These honorable men and women are working tirelessly to bring this gang of thieves to justice, using all available resources to end this string of robberies.

"Ms. Morgan was assigned to us after extensive training and operations with a specialized FBI unit known as the Tactical Operations Section, or TacOps. These agents specialize in what are known as covert entries: essentially, legal break-ins to install court-authorized surveillance devices. They are government-trained experts in defeating locks, security cameras, and alarm systems. As a TacOps agent, Ms. Morgan was the closest legal equivalent to a professional burglar.

"In accordance with her extensive specialty training, Ms. Morgan managed our efforts in establishing and supervising surveillance of suspected members and support networks for this band of thieves. As part of these duties, she routinely rotated in as a member of a surveillance team.

"Now I'll note here that assignment to a federal task force of any kind requires the highest level of individual and moral accountability. Any member of these high-profile teams can be called upon to testify in court as a critical witness to a case of national interest; in order for their testimony to remain unimpeachable, their administrative jackets must be on par with the finest professionals in law enforcement.

"When Ms. Morgan was assigned to the task force, her record and her performance were stellar." He frowned, reaching to turn the page of his notes as his hand fumbled for purchase against the paper. "But as we made progress in the case against the criminal network, Ms. Morgan chose to place results over the rule of law. Her integrity became compromised. She falsified a report, stating that she personally observed something that didn't occur, in order to gain a search warrant that she believed was the missing piece of the task force investigation.

"It was later established by surveillance footage and geophysical mapping that Ms. Morgan could not possibly have seen what she claimed in her report. She was immediately indicted and pled guilty. Her sentence was reduced in exchange for a forfeiture of future service in any public office, and she was recently released after completing a nine-month prison sentence. And last night she violated the terms of her supervised release by failing to return home within the hours of curfew.

"The regrettable events of this morning indicate that Ms. Morgan has taken her skill in defeating various security systems, extensive knowledge of law enforcement procedures, and possibly contacts made in prison, and attempted to ply them for personal gain. While the identities of her co-conspirators are as of yet unknown, it seems that Ms. Morgan is trying to replicate the illegal successes of the criminals she once hunted by assisting, if not leading, her own team of thieves. But unlike the heist network that has been operating for the past three years, Ms. Morgan and the men she accompanied into the bank do not rely on technical skills to steal.

"Instead, these vicious criminals resort to violence, brandishing weapons to terrify innocent people into submission. Ms. Morgan's efforts to apply her law enforcement experience to build her own heist crew have failed. And now, we will end her reign of terror as suddenly as it began.

"We are asking anyone with knowledge of Ms. Blair Morgan's where-abouts or activities between her release and this morning's robbery to please come forward with information. Any detail, no matter how small, could help us to bring this dangerous standoff to the safest possible conclusion."

He swallowed, then spoke his final line with particular emphasis.

"And Ms. Morgan, if you are watching this, know that turning yourself in to authorities is the only golden ticket you have left."

Jim closed his binder, a gesture that ignited pandemonium in the crowd. This was already turning into a spectacle, a media firestorm with Jim reflecting off the center of every camera lens.

And for the first time in a career that he fully intended to stretch upward into politics, Jim didn't want the attention.

16

BLAIR

Blair watched Jim exit the stage without taking questions—of course he wasn't taking questions. He'd had his media event, and now he was headed here to the bank. And she knew exactly why.

Her head was throbbing. She rubbed her temples and felt suddenly dizzy, pinching her eyebrows together to clear her head.

Sterling said, "Any traffic on the assault?"

She tried to speak, but felt like her heart was beating in her throat. Finally Blair looked at Sterling with blurred vision and managed, "Any traffic on—what?"

He held up a finger to silence her, and Blair realized he was transmitting to one of the other robbers via a throat mic and earpiece.

"All right," he continued, "we're going to displace to an alternate location."

Then Sterling returned her stare and said, "We're out of here."

"Where are we going?"

He gave a short laugh, but it had an edge that made her uneasy. "'We?' I'm taking my partner and moving. *You* are going to wait right here. I guess now we know why your records were sealed after Mary Washington. I'm impressed you were TacOps—jealous, even, because you could've helped us plan this heist better than we did. But our relationship ends here."

The short robber entered Gordon's office, tapping his ear to indicate something he'd heard over their team radio.

"So, ah...just heard." He looked to Blair. "TacOps. I'm jealous. If you could've helped us plan this—"

Sterling cut him off. "Enough. You and I need to get out of here, now."

"Not necessarily. Just call the negotiator. See if we can get a few of those hostages back."

Blair looked to Sterling. His body was tense, practically quivering with suppressed rage. But she had to tell him the truth.

"I can't wait here."

"You can, and you will. Or leave the building and turn yourself in to the cops; I don't care. But our arrangement ends here. You've lost all your bargaining ability."

"My bargaining ability?" Blair shot back, raising her voice. "I didn't ask to be dragged into this! But now that I'm in it, you can't leave me here in the bank."

Sterling set a hand upon his belt, a Western gunslinger ready to draw. "I've got a taser and a set of handcuffs that says I can."

"You haven't made it out of this building yet. I can help."

Sterling's eyes were half-lidded, his voice deep. "Of course you can help —you've done a bang-up job so far. But between your escape last night and you turning out to be an ex-fed, we'll take our chances from here on out."

"I know what the FBI is going to do."

"So do I."

"You might know their tactics and procedures. But that's not going to help you today."

"Yes, it will."

Blair felt her toes curl within her boots. "I know things, Sterling. This is no longer a by-the-numbers hostage standoff. You heard that press conference. Did you notice how it ended with the line about the 'golden ticket?' That wasn't a metaphor; it was a message. For me."

"Meaning what, exactly?"

"The part that concerns you? It's going to affect your escape, if it hasn't already. I'll explain everything. But not here." Then she raised her hands in emphatic submission. "Look, you can tase or handcuff me anywhere else in the building just as easily. And if you want to, I won't fight it. But I guarantee by the time I tell you what I know, you won't. So let's get out of this bank before SWAT kicks in that door and kills us all."

The short robber nodded. "She makes a convincing argument."

"All right," Sterling said. He placed a hand on his throat. "Are the elevators good to go?"

Blair shook her head. "How should I know?"

Sterling pointed a finger at his ear, indicating he was on the radio.

"Good," he said, presumably to the third robber. "We're coming up before they raid the bank."

Sterling and his partner donned their hiking packs and the bags of bank cash.

"What are in the packs you guys carried in here?" Blair asked as they hoisted everything onto their backs.

The Boston robber answered, "If you have to ask, you don't need to know."

They quickly moved out of the bank into the building lobby, past the marble columns and officers shouting at them to put their hands up.

As they reached the elevator bank, the short robber produced a key that he inserted and turned in a wall slot labeled *Fire Service*. The elevator doors whirred open.

"*Sésame, ouvre-toi*," he said, raising an eyebrow to Blair.

They boarded the elevator, and he inserted the key into an interior fire service key slot, this time turning it two clicks clockwise before removing it.

Then he held the door close button and said to Blair, with a satisfied grin, "That meant 'Open Sesame.' In French."

"Whatever," Blair muttered.

Seeing that she wasn't impressed, he added, "I say it when I crack a safe, too. Real suave-like, you know?"

Blair hung her head in momentary resignation, and the elevator doors closed in front of her.

17

JIM

Jim slid into the driver seat of his SUV, slamming the door shut with more force than he intended.

Despite his nervousness, he'd pulled off the press conference well. The footage would play back as a Bureau victory. Now came the hard part: bringing this bank standoff to the safest possible conclusion for the residents of LA.

He pulled out of his parking space and drove through the streets of El Segundo. His destination wasn't far from the task force headquarters, but Jim drove a circuitous route to make sure no enterprising reporters were following him.

Once he was certain his tail was clear, he piloted his SUV off the street and through a small parking lot, slowing as he approached a vehicle entrance in the adjacent brick building. A surveillance camera guarded the passage, along with twin signs on either side that read: *VIDEO SURVEILLANCE IN EFFECT. ALL TRESPASSERS WILL BE PROSECUTED TO THE FULLEST EXTENT OF THE LAW.*

Jim drove in regardless, knowing full well that the camera was inoperative and the signs were installed to keep the kids and spray painters out. Meanwhile the contract to sell the building had fallen through three times in the past year, so the space within remained unoccupied.

His automatic headlights activated as he entered the tunnel, weaving around a curve to a small interior parking garage. The six executive parking spaces were empty, as they always were before he arrived, and he carefully pulled into a slot. Then he gave a cursory glance to the small pedestrian entrance. That was empty too, and Jim knew from a previous scouting expedition that it led down a short path with access into the vacant building as well as the outdoor parking lot. That exterior outlet was similarly marked by an identical video camera and signs prohibiting entry—which, Jim thought, had apparently achieved the desired effect. He'd been here many times, all undisturbed.

That made this site unique in the area; maybe, he thought, even in all of LA. Or very nearly so, at least. No one came or went, and even if someone wanted to track Jim's location by hacking his phone, there was no cell or GPS signal here. With only one way in by vehicle and one by foot, Jim would see any entrants immediately. All these factors made the hidden parking garage perfect for necessities better conducted out of the public eye, and this was one of them.

Killing the engine, Jim removed his seatbelt. He checked his cell phone and saw there was no reception, a habitual confirmation to verify what he already knew. Nothing would disturb him now. He'd only been here once since Blair's departure from the task force, and it was to deposit the item he now came here to recover.

Stepping out of the SUV, he approached a metal grate for water runoff situated against one wall. He knelt to lift the heavy grate and set it to the side, then held his tie against his chest with one hand while reaching into the space. It took some probing against a filthy, muck-strewn surface before he felt the smooth plastic of a waterproof bag. He lifted it out of the space, clutching the heavy bag in one hand as he checked his backside and hurriedly replaced the metal grate. Then he reentered his SUV, closing the door and unzipping the bag to recover the contents.

It was a snub-nosed .38 revolver.

The pistol was secured in an ankle holster, and Jim hurriedly affixed the Velcro strap of the holster above his left foot. Then he adjusted his pant leg over the revolver, feeling a bittersweet wave of sentimentality.

He wouldn't get to take a shot that day—he should be so lucky—but he could trail the SWAT assault. And there was one thing he could offer the assaulters, whether they wanted it or not. Sometimes, he knew, the wheels of justice required a little grease to continue turning.

Jim wondered if this new generation of agents even knew what a "throw-down piece" was. In the modern age of political correctness, he doubted it. Even when Jim was a new special agent assigned to New York, the practice was little more than a hushed reference among a very selective group of people.

The sad truth of law enforcement was that there were an infinite number of ways you could be forced to take a perfectly legitimate kill shot, all too many of them in low-light conditions requiring a split-second decision. There were also, Jim knew, an equally infinite number of ways an investigation could second-guess your decision in the aftermath. On the street, you lived or died. In the air-conditioned offices where investigators judged your actions, it was all about organizational reputation and media fallout.

The throw-down piece was simply a matter of insurance, and cheap insurance at that. The requirements were simple: concealable and untraceable. Any number of junk guns with serial numbers filed off would do the trick, and raise no eyebrows in an evidence room. Criminals used such weapons all the time. And if you *had* to take that shot, and in the aftermath found that the suspect had wielded something nonlethal, you had to protect yourself. A throw-down piece relieved you from guilt, and protected your career, your family, and your organization.

Jim remembered a class at the academy where he'd learned the twenty-one-foot rule. Two students participated: one playing an agent, wearing a dummy gun in a duty holster. The other playing a suspect, armed with a fake knife. They were spaced exactly twenty-one feet apart. On the blow of an instructor's whistle, the mock suspect charged the mock agent. The latter didn't have to do much—just draw their dummy gun and point it at the suspect in time to say "bang" before their opposition reached them with the dummy knife.

To the investigators judging a shooting after the fact, and to the public at large, twenty-one feet would seem like a lot. It certainly did to Jim the first time he was taught the rule. But out of his entire academy class, not a single person had drawn their gun in time to theoretically shoot the suspect before being theoretically stabbed. Actually, he thought with a rueful grin, that wasn't exactly true: they had a competitive pistol shooter in their ranks, a young kid from Connecticut who'd done the amateur circuit. He'd just barely managed to get a shot off, but still not in time to avoid getting struck by his assailant.

Jim had remembered that ever since. In the theory of law enforcement shootings that could remotely be deemed questionable, a tie should go to the shooter. In reality, that was up for debate, and the debaters held your entire world in their hands. Not just yours; your family's as well. When you're going against the worst scum that the human race is capable of producing, who do you care more about—the suspect or your wife?

A throw-down piece was, if he was being honest, a last resort. But if in the course of raiding Geering Plaza an unarmed robber should be shot, Jim could deposit the throw-down piece as he passed the body. Or, more likely, he could "recover" the gun himself after the shooting. After all, suspects died in a variety of positions, and the weapons they held could often slide in all sorts of directions.

Jim started his SUV, shifting to reverse and placing his right hand against the passenger seat headrest, looking over his shoulder. His SUV had a backup camera, sure, but muscle memory was a tough thing to overcome; he never relied on the screen.

Looking behind him, he caught a glimpse of the backseat. Long ago his world had become a constant reminder of Blair, and this truck was just another trigger.

How many times had they made love in the backseat, right here in this garage?

He could think of at least three occasions, all of them when there wasn't enough time for a lunchtime or after-hours rendezvous at their usual hotel but they couldn't resist each other long enough to wait.

With a wry smile, Jim shook his head at the phrasing of *making love*. What he and Blair had done to each other, particularly on the few occasions they shared in this hidden garage, was far less romantic than the term suggested. But what choice did Jim have? His wife was, well...his wife. There were no exploits of conquest there, sexually or otherwise. And when Blair arrived at the task force, they were drawn to one another with magnetic intensity.

Blair was enraptured by Jim's power and authority, he knew, and he in turn had found himself unable to ignore her beauty, her wit, and her runner's body. Jim had never before had an affair, and to do so with a subordinate was an insanely risky proposition. That long-running indiscretion was bad enough, but to make things worse, the emotionality involved had further clouded Jim's professional judgment. Now that Blair had chosen to turn to a life of crime, this thing was going to end one of two ways.

Focusing his gaze on the concrete wall beyond his rear window, Jim reversed his SUV out of the parking spot. Putting the vehicle in drive, he accelerated out of the tunnel, heading toward the foiled bank robbery in Geering Plaza.

18

STERLING

Sterling, Alec, and Blair took the elevator to the 30th floor, and then advanced two flights on the stairwell so the police couldn't pinpoint their location.

As they reached the 32nd floor, Blair asked, "Will you guys really be going to the roof?"

Sterling led the way down the hall. "Not until we have an ETA on the helicopter. Until then, we'll hole up somewhere close."

"Can you leave me on the roof when you go?"

"We could. But we're not going to."

Alec added in a conciliatory tone, "Blair, it's a five-hundred-foot fall from the roof—you'll be safer in the building."

Blair said nothing.

Sterling made his way through an office lobby, seeking an inconspicuous place to wait for the helicopter's arrival time. Depending on what Marco transmitted about the police response, they might need to reach the roof in a hurry.

They made their way into a conference room. The trio collectively examined the cabinet immediately inside the door, which held a Jaeger-LeCoultre Atmos desk clock. Immediately to its side was a framed picture of a heavyset man shaking hands with the US President from two administrations prior.

Sterling set his bags down and advanced past an oak conference table to a wall of windows, looking down over buildings to the forested residential foothills beyond. Were it not for the gloomy gray clouds blocking visibility beyond that, the horizon would have been delineated by the hilltops of Bel Air and Beverly Glen.

Alec set his bags down, then joined Sterling at the window.

"Quite a view," he said to Blair. "Check it out."

"I'm fine right over here on solid ground, thanks."

"Says the woman who did an Evel Knievel leap to her death off the pool last night."

"It's funny what two armed men can accomplish in persuading me to momentarily overcome my fear of heights."

"Friends," Alec chided. "What two *friends* can accomplish. Because what are friends, Blair? Friends are people who expand our comfort zones—"

"Enough," Sterling snapped, turning from the window to face Blair. "You've got the head of an FBI task force calling you out in a live press conference, and apparently you used to work for him. You conveniently kept that fact from us. Now is your one and only chance to come clean on what affects my escape before we never see each other again, so talk."

He saw Blair's shoulders hunch before she spoke. "It has to do with why I was convicted."

"I don't care why you were convicted. No offense. Get to the point."

She paused, then took a seat at the conference table and folded her hands atop the polished oak surface.

"If I don't tell you the whole story, you're not going to believe me. And if you don't believe me, you're not going to let me go to the roof. So just hear me out."

Sterling couldn't fathom why a woman purporting to be so scared of heights was asking to go to the roof. He nodded to Alec, and they both took a seat across from Blair.

Finally she asked, "Does the name Matt Korb ring a bell?"

"No," Sterling said flatly. "Go on."

"He's a diamond salesman the task force suspected of fencing stolen jewels from some of the heists. We had his storage facility under surveillance for three months, waiting for him to slip up and give us enough cause for a search warrant."

"Let me guess: he didn't slip up."

"No, he didn't. There was a physical line of sight to a narrow dead zone for our surveillance cameras. So I reported that I personally saw him adjusting his jacket, and that beneath it was a weapon in plain view. Since I reported it within the dead zone, there'd be no camera footage to contradict my report—and with the corroboration of criminal activity, we'd get our search warrant. Since that would take at least a week, it didn't matter if we found a gun during our raid or not."

Sterling nodded. "Then how'd you get caught?"

"We conducted our search of his facility, and found nothing. I thought it was over. But Korb's legal team filed a motion in defense. I don't know where they found these people—they had access to technology enabling them to build three-dimensional terrain models using LIDAR data, showing with scientific certainty that the camera dead zone would've given me only 2.5 seconds to witness the presence of a weapon."

Alec shrugged. "2.5 seconds is long enough to see a gun. So?"

"They also acquired footage from a hidden security camera of an adjacent building. It showed 3.7 seconds of Korb's movement from the time of my report, including our surveillance dead zone. Their model contained three-inch-resolution imagery, and the still frames showed that Korb's jacket remained untouched and no weapon was visible, nor could it have been, as per my report."

"You remember these details pretty clearly."

"I had a lot of time to relive it in prison."

"Well," Sterling announced, "that is tragic, and I'm sorry for the pain you've endured. But that's got nothing to do with our escape, so unless there's anything else, we're done here."

At this, Blair's eyes began to tear up.

Then she said, "I wasn't finished."

19

JIM

Jim stopped his SUV, flashing his credentials at the patrol officer manning the perimeter. The officer nodded and moved one end of the yellow road barricade, allowing Jim to drive past.

He parked within the perimeter, then stepped out of his SUV to assess the scene.

Jim already knew the basic layout, of course—which bank had been robbed, and the particulars of an extensive and growing police perimeter. But every crime scene had a particular feel to it, and Jim liked to feed his intuition the way a hunter went on high alert before reaching their tree stand.

The Mayfield National Bank sign was visible on the ground level, with the entrance just off the sidewalk. He scanned upward thirty-six stories of sheer glass heights to the building's pinnacle, where the police and media helicopters lazily circled beneath the cloud cover, trying to get their footage before the sky burst into a torrential downpour. The chop of helicopter rotors echoed down a canyon of buildings to reach the swarm of people standing outside.

The streets around Geering Plaza, of course, were pandemonium.

Jim's own time on an FBI SWAT team gave him a profound lack of envy for the first responders here. Processing anyone leaving a hostage site wasn't a simple process. Everyone was a potential threat until a search confirmed they had no weapons. Then identities had to be checked and confirmed to make sure no robbers had attempted to flee among the crowd. The log of civilians processed then became evidence against which the police would scan for possible accomplices, with an inside source being the nexus of many high-yield armed robberies.

And instead of processing a small group of hostages, the fire alarm had triggered a flood of hundreds outside into the street. He could see the impromptu cordon area, a swarming mass of bodies herded into the street to await individual processing. They either were or soon would be hungry, thirsty, and in need of a restroom, none of which were needs that the police could handle at present.

Glad it's not me working the cordon, Jim thought. Instead he proceeded toward the joint command vehicle, a hulking white block of a truck whose rear entrance was guarded by a single patrol officer.

Jim flashed his credentials, and the patrol officer opened the door for him.

The truck was a mobile outpost for command and control of emergency incidents. Every interior wall was filled with screens and radio equipment to manage multiple police elements. Jim approached a broad-shouldered man in a regulation LAPD uniform who was sketching out assault options with a fit LAPD SWAT commander in black fatigues.

"Commander Wells," Jim called, "that won't be necessary."

The heavyset man turned, revealing a ruddy face and graying mustache that drooped into a frown at the sight of Jim.

"ASAC Jacobson," Wells replied, "did you get lost on your way to the media? News cameras are all outside. You'll be more comfortable there."

Jim was miffed by the comment, but kept his poker face intact. After all, Wells was only pissed because he knew what was about to happen.

"FBI SWAT will be executing the assault."

"LAPD SWAT still has emergency launch authority."

"Sure, for the next five minutes until my people get here."

"We're perfectly capable of carrying out this operation."

"Bank robbery is federal, and we reserve the right to claim jurisdiction. And being that a former special agent is involved..."

"I saw your little press conference. The bank hostages they released said your woman was unarmed and issued no orders other than demanding their release."

"Oh, you mean she didn't announce her intentions to people sent out of the building to be eyewitnesses to her innocence? I wouldn't have guessed that."

"Then let's see if I can guess something: you've already found a reason to personally accompany the assault."

Jim shrugged noncommittally. "If there should be a standoff during the assault, I have prior history with the subject—"

"I'm sure you do, Jim."

Jim's face went cold—a dead-eyed, appraising stare that made Wells regret the words. But Jim knew that any emotionally charged response would ignite a rumor he'd never be able to quell, so he controlled his reaction. "We'll be sending one team for the ground assault. Two helicopters will drop a second team on the roof to clear top-down. LAPD SWAT can trail the ground team inside, then conduct search and clear once FBI SWAT has moved upstairs to the next floor. If you want to be of use beyond that, Commander Wells, I suggest you prepare to process the crime scene."

Wells looked incredulous. "You say this like you've already got your timeline. When exactly do you think you're assaulting?"

Jim shook his left wrist free of his shirt cuff, checking his Rolex. "I'm waiting on my SWAT commander. He should be here any—"

There was a double knock at the door. Jim turned and opened it, revealing a young man in his thirties wearing olive drab camouflage fatigues and tactical boots. He was clean-shaven, with close-cropped auburn hair and a full face beset by dull green eyes.

Jim knew exactly who he was.

The man spoke in an Alabama accent. "Sir, Senior Special Agent Vance. FBI SWAT commander. My men are on scene, prepping next door for emergency assault."

"Let's have a word outside, Vance."

Jim said nothing else to Wells as he exited the joint command vehicle and followed the young man onto the street. He reminded himself to pretend that Vance was making a first impression.

But Jim knew all about Senior Special Agent Clint Vance, and he couldn't have asked for a better SWAT commander for what he needed to happen.

Vance had been a sergeant in the 82nd Airborne, with multiple overseas tours. He was no stranger to firefights before he joined the FBI, and in SWAT, Vance had quickly made a name for himself as highly competent—and aggressive. In the gray areas of law enforcement, which is to say perceived risk to life with seconds or less to make a shoot or no-shoot decision, there were guys you could trust to back your official version of events, and guys you couldn't. Vance was definitely in the former camp.

Before his press conference, Jim had called his mentor to ask his guidance in settling "the Blair problem."

His mentor answered immediately.

As usual, Jim had to provide remarkably little explanation—his mentor, as usual, had anticipated the inquiry and run his personal background check, then told Jim that Vance was, quote, as "gangster as it gets with a badge."

And now, here they were, Jim and Vance, standing on the street adjacent to the besieged high rise.

Jim began, "I need to speak with you candidly."

"Of course, sir."

"And drop the protocol," Jim said. "I'm talking to you man to man, one pipe-hitter to another."

Vance squinted as he tried to gauge whether Jim was for real or trying to play a part. Some conversations occurred "off the books," and Jim's language indicated he was headed in that direction.

"I'm listening," Vance said tentatively.

"Blair Morgan."

"The woman in red."

Jim nodded.

"What do you need, sir?"

Jim nodded again, pleased that Vance had picked up his connotation. This second nod was virtually identical to the first. But the eye contact—and the solemnity of the nod—said something else altogether.

Clint smiled, and then shrugged. "Consider it done."

"Can I, Vance? How many Boy Scouts on your team?"

"Not enough to rule the vote."

"And how would you—or rather, your career—suggest getting around your Boy Scouts, Senior Special Agent Vance?"

Vance thought for a moment, and then smiled again. He was looking forward to this. "I'll ask you for comments at the end of my mission brief."

"And?"

"Bad guys wore hiking packs into their heist. Kindly point out the possibility of explosives. Then let me have a private word with my team."

Jim was skeptical—that seemed a matter of chance to the point of being flimsy. "You think that's enough?"

"I've told them enough stories from the sandbox. Our IED protocol is pretty tight. As long as there aren't cameras rolling, consider her a CONUS kill."

Now it was Jim's turn to smile. He hadn't heard that term used outside the military—after all, for police, every possible kill occurred in the continental United States, or CONUS.

For Vance, it was a joke. He'd killed people overseas, sure, but the prospect of shooting someone in the US, whether a home intruder or robbery suspect, was another matter altogether. And the fact that Vance joked about that to someone so superior in rank was another indication that Jim could count on him.

Jim asked, "Your boys packing a throw-down piece?"

Vance winced. "There's a couple guys I wouldn't trust to see that go down without reporting it. It's way outside our team SOP." He was referring to Standard Operating Procedure, or their team-internal protocol.

"Relax," Jim said. "You put her down, and I'll make sure there's a piece in vicinity."

Vance's expression morphed into one of appreciation bordering on awe. What Jim was discussing was exceedingly rare among even local police departments. In the ranks of a modern-day federal agency, it was unheard of.

But Jim was no ordinary ASAC, and judging by the slow smile forming across his face, Vance was no ordinary SWAT commander.

"How long do your men need to initiate?"

"Ten minutes before we'll be at full kit, ready to bang. Our other element can be skids-down on the roof as early as twenty minutes from now."

"Good." Jim checked his Rolex. "Continue planning for an emergency assault."

Then he lowered his wrist and stared hard at Vance. "And then plan on assaulting in twenty minutes."

20

STERLING

Sterling sat still at the oak conference table, his lips pursed in thought. He tried not to appear overly doubtful, but that was becoming more difficult as Blair continued speaking.

She went on, "There's a reason I couldn't turn myself in after the building evacuation. You saw the news footage—the cameras are too far away to see everything. If I took a step out the front door now, some sniper would put a .308 round through my heart. If I stay in the bank, I'll be killed in the SWAT assault. And either way, a throw-down piece will conveniently be recovered from my body."

Sterling felt his eyes narrow. "Why do you say that?"

"Because Jim wants me dead."

"Who is Jim?"

"Jim," Blair repeated. "ASAC Jacobson. The guy who just gave that press conference—"

Alec asked, "That dapper fellow?"

"Yes, that one. And he's going to do everything he can to make sure I don't leave this scene alive, whether I'm innocent or not."

"Stop being naïve," Sterling dismissed her. "Cops don't execute people. You should know that: you are one."

"Was one."

"So no one's going to kill you."

Blair touched her forehead. "What is so hard for you to understand? I know things about Jim."

Sterling cocked his head, incredulous. "What does that mean—you know things?"

"It means I could burn his career to the ground," Blair replied, her voice rushed. "And now that he thinks I'm a robber, he's afraid I will."

"I don't mean to sound callous, but this still has nothing to do with our getaway."

Her fists were tight now, fingernails biting into her palms. "It has every-thing to do with it. Let me spell it out for both of you. I don't care if you chalk it up to emotions, premonition, or psychic powers. Take your pick—just *trust me*. Here's what will happen outside this building. The FBI is claiming jurisdiction from LAPD. And that guy who just gave the press conference—"

Alec said cheerily, "That dapper fellow."

"—didn't make that speech for posterity. He removed me as a hostage in the public eye. That means when I'm killed—which, again, he's going to do everything in his considerable power to do—there won't be any public outrage. And he'll initiate an assault on this building as soon as he can."

"The FBI isn't that ruthless."

"No, not the FBI. Just Jim. But anyone who can do his bidding trusts him completely."

"How can you be so sure?"

"Because I was one of them."

Sterling frowned, trying to temper his disbelief. "One man can't alter the course of a multi-agency hostage response."

"Now who's being naïve, Sterling? With that press conference, he already has. Jim is concerned with power. And political maneuvering. He'll crush anything that gets in the way of that."

"And what secrets, exactly, do you know about Jim that he'd kill you to protect?"

Her mouth opened, then closed, before she answered. "I already told you how I lied to incriminate Matt Korb and get the search warrant."

"Yes."

"Jim is the one who asked me to do it."

Sterling examined her a moment. "Okay, so he's a bent cop...why did you agree to lie for him?"

"Because we were having an affair."

Sterling's breath hitched. If everything she was saying was true—no, he thought, if even *half* of it was true—then his decision to involve her had put her into the worst possible nightmare scenario. He rubbed his forearm, remaining silent so she'd continue. Her voice sounded hollow now as she gazed out the window.

"At the time, the task force was long on funding and short on results. We were in danger of getting shut down. And if that happened, Jim would have been passed over for promotion and transferred to a second-tier office on the east coast. He said he was going to leave his wife for me, but the proceedings could have taken a year or more. The Korb warrant was supposed to keep Jim and me together, here in LA—"

Gordon's phone erupted with the *Star Wars* theme song.

Alec called above it, "Can we talk about changing that ringtone?"

Sterling answered the call, speaking into the voice distortion box.

"You're running out of time," he began. "Where's my ride out of here?"

Sergeant Hollis answered, "Good news, sir. I've got an ETA."

"Let's hear it."

"Your helicopter will reach the rooftop in twenty minutes. They're finishing the preflight inspection now."

"Is that a fact?"

"Barring any mechanical issues, the pilot has assured us he'll arrive by then."

"What if it starts raining?"

"Given the circumstances, air traffic control has authorized... let me see what they called it... 'Special VFR Clearance.' As long as the cloud ceiling remains higher than the roof of your building, he'll land there."

"And what helicopter will our esteemed pilot be flying today?"

"Sikorsky S-92A. Twin-engine, medium-lift, and it'll be fully fueled on takeoff. Depending on what altitude he flies at, the pilot says he'll be able to take you up to six hundred miles."

"I want pilot and co-pilot, and no one else on board. No surprises, Sergeant Hollis."

"There won't be any, you have my word. I'll keep you posted on any updates to the ETA once he takes off."

"Well I'd like to believe you. But as it so happens, I just saw a very interesting press conference by an FBI agent named Jacobson."

"I'm sorry about that..."

"You know Blair volunteered to replace the hostages, right? She put her own life on the line to spare any risk to others. And that's going to become very apparent in the immediate future."

"Sir, I don't doubt you. The honest truth is—"

"Oh," Sterling scoffed, "the truth? Let's hear it. Because according to the press conference I just watched, truth isn't weighing into the equation at all, much less by the staggering degree that you're claiming."

When Hollis spoke again, it sounded like he was smiling.

"You remember my introduction, sir? Sergeant Sean Hollis, *LAPD*?"

"Yeah."

"I was going to say, the honest truth is that the LAPD can't control what the FBI says, on the air or off. But you're dealing with me, sir, so I encourage you to have faith. Together, we've both accomplished what we said we would. I got the police officers out of the building lobby, and you released all but one of the hostages. Am I right or wrong?"

"You're right."

"I'd go so far as to say that you and I are seeing this situation eye-to-eye, and I have no doubt that after your helicopter arrives in"—he paused— "eighteen minutes, you'll drop off the last remaining hostage at a place of your choosing. As long as she and the pilots are safe, I wish you the best. Because that's where the LAPD's involvement ends."

Sterling gave a tight smile. "Thanks for your help, Sergeant Hollis. Now please make sure my helicopter is here on time."

Then he ended the call, detached the voice distortion box from the phone, and dialed a number from memory. It rang twice before the call connected.

"I've got Blair on speaker," Sterling warned, "so watch what you say."

Marco replied, "Understood."

"What did you get? The negotiator said that—"

"Yeah, yeah, I heard it. They want you on the roof seventeen minutes from now."

"Why?"

Marco answered, "Because that's when FBI SWAT is doing their 'simo'—a simultaneous ground and rooftop assault. They're clearing toward the middle."

"Ground *and* rooftop? You sure?"

"Positive. When the agents breach ground floor, two helos are dropping another team on the roof. FBI SWAT is leading the charge, with LAPD SWAT backfilling the main clearance from the ground up."

Sterling shook his head. "Why don't they just send in the National Guard?"

"Cal Guard's actually been notified that—"

"Forget it. I don't want to know. If we show ourselves on the roof now, you think they'll advance their ground assault ahead of schedule?"

Blair began nodding her vote in the time it took for Marco to consider the question.

Finally he answered, "Honestly, yeah, I do. When you go topside, they'll have visual identification of two out of the three robbers. They'll send in the FBI ground team, knowing that the helos are bringing in the other half of their assault element. It's going to rain within the hour—flash flood warning is still in effect. The cops are racing us, and we're racing the weather."

Sterling looked outside, toward the rain clouds spanning the entire sky.

"Got it," he replied. "How much longer do you need for your end?"

"Three minutes."

"Good. We're heading up to the roof early—no need to delay this any longer."

"Want me to stage the party favor?"

"Definitely. Stand by for our call."

"Done. Hope you know what you're doing."

"You know I don't. Stand by anyway."

"Got it. RTB."

"Yeah. Thanks for the vote of confidence." He disconnected and looked to Blair and Alec.

Blair gave a curt nod. "I need you to take me to the roof."

"You think," Sterling said with an unfocused gaze, "that's the one place you can't get shot."

"There are media helicopters broadcasting live. I *know* it's the one place I can't get shot. And even if I'm wrong, it doesn't affect you. That's the least you can do for involving me."

Alec said, "You must really be convinced your old boss is gunning for you—you're even more scared of taking a bullet than you are of heights."

"Only slightly. But yes."

Sterling propped a cheek on his fist and announced, "All right, Blair. You can come with us to the roof, and stay there when we leave."

"When you leave?" she said dryly.

"Yup."

"From the roof."

"Yeah," Alec blurted. "From the roof. I thought he was making that pretty clear."

She gave them a condescending smile. "We all know there's no helicopter coming. So how are you leaving?"

Sterling didn't answer her question. Instead, he replied, "They want to land a team on the roof? They can go right ahead. But you're the only one who will be left up there to see it."

"So you'll leave...how? On the helicopter that's not showing up?"

Sterling sighed. "Yeah. On our phantom helicopter. Off to that non-extradition country in the sky—the final resting place for people like us."

Alec snapped, "People of our ilk! Come on, Sterling. So few chances to use the word 'ilk' in our lifetime, and you just passed up a massive one. Statistically speaking, the best you'll ever get."

"Sorry," Sterling conceded, restating, "For people of our ilk."

Alec said, "So there's an army of shooters coming to tear this building apart from top to bottom." He tapped his watch. "How far you wanna push the timing of our escape?"

Sterling knew what he meant. He also knew another thing Blair didn't: the further they pressed their luck in the next few minutes, the better off they'd be for the next few hours.

And judging by the response of law enforcement, and Mother Nature herself, they were going to need all the luck they could get.

"All the way, buddy," Sterling answered. "We're going to push it all the way."

21

JIM

Jim wrapped the Velcro straps around his ribs, connecting with the armored plates suspended on his chest and back. He smiled to himself as he listened to Vance's Alabaman drawl as he briefed his men using the building blueprints tacked to the wall behind him. This team was clearly good: Jim could tell from the brevity of the commander's brief and the composed posture of the nodding team members. They were confident in their abilities, as they should be.

Most FBI field offices cultivated a SWAT team from their special agents, usually a part-time duty in addition to the agents' full-time jobs. But the "Big Four"—New York, Chicago, DC, and, of course, LA—had a full-time SWAT team. For these teams, raiding buildings and executing high-risk warrants was a way of life. Jim had served on the New York team and found it the pinnacle of his FBI service. Even the FBI's elite Hostage Rescue Team couldn't hold a candle to the Big Four teams; as a national asset, the Hostage Rescue Team was rarely deployed before local organizations resolved crises on their own. Walk down their corridors, he recalled, and you'd see plaques denoting prestigious training exercises with military special operations units. Walk down the hallways of his old SWAT building and you'd find the walls equally filled, not with training plaques but framed news articles from their raids in the city.

Seeing the LA SWAT team made him nostalgic for those days, a touch envious to reclaim an earlier time in his career. But those days were over; Jim's career had taken a different path when he was up for promotion, anointed by the well-connected mentor that had been looking out for him ever since.

No matter, he thought while donning his navy blue FBI windbreaker over the vest. He'd get a taste of his former life today—the rush of storming through the breach point, the heart-stopping explosions of flash bang grenades, and the shouting of federal agents announcing themselves to the criminals inside.

And these LA boys had shown up prepared to play—with plate carriers bearing rows of magazines, radios, and flash bang grenades worn over olive drab fatigues. He glanced enviously at their weapons, which were a bit better than what he'd used in his day. Their compact M4 assault rifles were decked out with the entire trimming: infrared lasers, taclights, holographic reflex sights for close quarters shooting. The only indication that they weren't a special military unit was a single patch on their chests reading *FBI* in large black letters.

Vance swung his hand to a photograph of Blair tacked below the blue-prints, continuing to speak in his Alabama drawl. "Blair Morgan is known to be in the bank, presumably playing hostage to a minimum of three confirmed robbers. LAPD is still processing everyone who evacuated after the fire alarm, so we can't rule out additional employees hiding in the building.

"Primary objective is the neutralization of minimum four suspects: three men and the woman. Secondary objective is deliberate and full clear-ance of all thirty-six floors, which is LAPD's primary mission—after we've proceeded past a given floor with priority jurisdiction. LAPD SWAT will be backfilling behind us, so we'll have freedom of movement to pursue suspects wherever they go in the building.

"Two helicopters with Red Team are spinning up now. When we execute the ground-level assault, they'll be touching down on the roof to begin their clearance from the top down. There's only one stairway in the building, so once we have that isolated from top and bottom, there's nowhere for the suspects to go."

Then Vance looked to Jim. "Sir, you have anything to add?"

The team turned to Jim. He suddenly felt ridiculous in his blue jacket and body armor over shirt and tie, but this was what rank did to a man.

Jim nodded. "Some of you who don't know me are worried that an ASAC is trailing the assault." He looked across their faces as they struggled to contain a visible reaction to this comment.

Then he continued, "Don't be. I spent four years on SWAT at the New York field office, and I know the judgment calls that have to be made on the ground. And I promise you this: I have your back. Your version of events is the only version of events. Make no mistake, gentlemen, this is a historic raid for the Bureau. Your careers will reflect your participation, and I'm going to personally take a vested interest in the future promotions of each and every one of you here today."

Jim saw a few heads bobbing in subtle nods, so he continued, "One additional note on Blair Morgan. Do not forget that she's a former FBI Special Agent. She knows our tactics, techniques, and procedures, and you can bet your bottom dollar that she's trained her team well. They'll respond to your assault accordingly. Consider every one of these suspects, *especially* Blair, to be armed and highly dangerous.

"We know from this morning's video that the suspects carried in hiking packs. And whatever's inside, they're not filled with sugar cookies. Based on Blair Morgan's level of training and inside knowledge of task force, as well as her previous self-locating near the hostages, it is reasonable to conclude that the packs contain medium weapons or explosives as a last resort. And based on my personal knowledge of Blair, she's not letting herself get taken alive.

"Once you've got the crew boxed in, their goal will be to take out as many cops as possible. So choose your shots carefully, gentlemen, because these people are the reptiles of the reptiles. They will not hesitate to kill every one of you if you don't take them out first—so whatever happens inside this building, know that you're dealing with true monsters today."

22

BLAIR

The elevator continued its ascent to the top floor as the short robber droned on.

"Now there's no question that the movie *Dumb and Dumber* is the greatest artistic achievement of our species. But without the impromptu lines during filming, it would have been top three at best. Probably behind the pyramids."

Blair asked, "There a point to this?"

"I'm just saying"—he raised his voice—"it's good to have a plan, but it takes some improvisation to achieve true greatness. That's why our getaway is a bit...well, flexible. Even if we tried to explain it to you, you wouldn't understand the artistic process."

The elevator came to a stop at the 36th floor, but the doors didn't open until the short robber pressed and held the corresponding button. Once they did, he re-inserted the key into the fire service slot and clicked it ninety degrees counterclockwise to the *Hold* setting. The doors remained open, the elevator frozen in place. Sterling unceremoniously dropped Gordon's phone on the elevator floor and slipped out.

The two robbers strolled down the hall as Blair tried to catch up, looking back at the frozen elevator and trying to comprehend their plan.

"What if the negotiator calls?" she asked.

The short robber answered, "We won't need phones where we're going."

"Or the elevator," Sterling added.

"Or that."

The phone began ringing as they walked away, playing Gordon's *Star Wars* ringtone. The two men didn't break stride, so Blair didn't, either.

Sterling asked, "So what did Jim mean when he referred to your 'golden ticket' in his press conference? Was it a threat?"

"More like a promise, and not one I trust. He was saying that I could turn myself in and have the best legal defense available, or get killed. Between me and Jim, 'golden ticket' meant being represented by Wycroft."

"Wycroft?" Sterling asked incredulously. "As in, *Damian Horne Wycroft?*"

"Yes."

"Well, I wouldn't believe that either. Unless Jim won the lottery and can pay a quarter-million retainer every month."

"Oh, Jim can summon Wycroft all right. It'd be pro bono representation in public, and I have no idea what would occur behind the scenes to make that possible."

Sterling scratched his jaw. "Explain."

"Jim's got powerful connections. One in particular that he only ever referred to as his 'mentor.' But Jim got advance notice of everything from that source—who the OPR was investigating and when, the particulars of any political maneuvering that affected the Bureau. That's how Jim knew the task force was in danger of having its funding pulled."

"If you're so confident that Jim can get Wycroft to represent you, then why did you say you don't trust his promise?"

Blair felt numb as she replied, "Because he could have played that card when I was indicted for lying about Korb. In fact, Jim promised he would, if I got caught. That was part of the arrangement."

Sterling cringed. "But when push came to shove, he hung you out to dry."

"Yes."

Then the short robber said, "There's one thing I don't understand—if Jim told you to lie in your surveillance report, why didn't you take him down with you?"

"I'm not a rat. The only reason I'm telling you people is because you're career criminals."

He nodded solemnly. "That's right, Blair, we are. Hardened career criminals. Edgy and tough. Forged in the pressure of high-stakes heists. But still," he went on as they walked, "surely you could have reported Jim? Maybe cut a deal?"

Blair felt her nostrils flaring. "*Maybe* cut a deal? OPR was breathing down my neck to give them information on Jim. They were dying to get my testimony, even after I'd been sent to prison."

"So why not take it? Other than not being a rat."

"My fate is tied with Jim's."

Sterling perked up at this. "You've got more dirt on Jim than the one event?"

Blair nodded.

"You have proof?" his partner asked.

Blair felt her stomach harden. "Of course I do—I was raised in the surveillance world, remember? The evidence is stashed away, nice and safe. But he doesn't know that I have it. Otherwise...well, I might have been clipped already."

"Clipped?"

"Smoked."

"Smoked?"

"Murdered," she said testily. "But my evidence cuts both ways. It incriminates Jim for admission of the crimes, and me for not reporting him. So if I tried to take him down, he could have lengthened my sentence by testifying that I was an accessory all along. So I took my bid on the chin, and nine months later walked out of prison."

The man stroked his throat. "And into my dreams."

"Whatever," Blair groaned. "You know, last night I was obsessed with stopping this heist before it endangered civilians. Today, seeing how domesticated you people are, I'm more bothered by my former colleagues. Everyone in the task force turned their back on me the second I was accused of falsifying a report. Now Jim's leading the publicity charge to discredit me further, just in case they can't kill me first."

"Yeah," the short robber agreed, "we are pretty awesome, aren't we?"

"I just want to say, now that I know who you guys are"—she shrugged—"best of luck with your careers. Your secret's safe with me."

"Secret? You don't even know my name. And, well, I don't really care if you turn in Sterling. Just means I'll get promoted."

"I could know your name if I wanted to."

"No, you couldn't."

Blair touched his arm suggestively. "Even if I agreed to go on a date with you?"

"Alec," the short robber blurted. "So where are we going? I really love the coffee at Greaney's, but if you'd prefer cocktails we can—wait, I see what you just did there."

"Alec," Blair repeated. "Well, now your name, *and* your other secret, are safe with me."

He cocked his head. "What other secret?"

Sterling took a right, following a new hallway around the corner. "She thinks we've been doing all those California heists."

"What heists?"

"You know, the network of thieves that's been all over the news."

"I thought they suspected some gang with dozens of operators involved."

"They do," Blair said, "but I always thought it was a much smaller crew. My theory was six people or less, radically changing their MO with each job so if they got caught—or when the statute of limitations ran out on one job at a time—they couldn't be tied to everything they'd ever done. But none of the jobs have ever involved violence. And seeing you guys using a taser on a would-be hero is what we in the law enforcement racket call an 'indicator.' So is Sterling's watch."

Alec gave an impatient huff. "What's wrong with Sterling's watch?"

"June last year. The Shea Jewelry Emporium heist. There was a delay between shutting down the security system electric and cutting the auxiliary power. There was a half second of film, practically a still shot. It showed a masked robber—about Sterling's height and weight. Couldn't tell much else, except one thing."

"Giant balls?"

Blair ignored him. "His watch slipped out between the sleeve and cuff of his right wrist. Half the dial was visible. That frame was enhanced and studied by dozens of detectives across the state. They consulted every watch guru they could find. And the best guess that came back was some kind of vintage Omega Seamaster."

Alec pointed to the Omega. "He bought that one at a pawn shop in North Hollywood two weeks ago. Laurel Canyon and Archwood. I was there."

Blair didn't miss a beat. "Laurel Canyon and Archwood was the site of the '97 North Hollywood bank robbery."

"It was?" Alec stammered. "Well, there's a pawn shop there now."

Sterling said, "Either way, your watch theory doesn't sound like it'd stand up in court."

"That's what everyone said." Blair felt a jittery sense of excitement as the memories of her old job rushed back. "Most people dismissed it. The rest assumed the thief was left-handed, because the watch was on his right wrist. I'd forgotten about that detail...until I saw the watch on your right wrist today."

He clutched at the strap on his bag of cash. "If we were good enough to pull off the Shea Emporium job, why would we bother with strong-arming a bank?"

"You wouldn't. You wouldn't need to do any of this—using me to get Gordon to deactivate his home security, or even Gordon disarming the bank alarm. You have ample skills to do both yourself."

Sterling lifted his chin at her. "You're not doing a very good job of proving your theory. I'd expect better from a former detective."

"Special Agent. And I specialized in covert entries, not detective work."

"Whatever. You're the cop. How do you reconcile everything you're saying?"

Blair walked in silence for a moment.

Then she said, "I think you want to appear less sophisticated than you are. You want the world to think you're thugs. I can't figure out why. But I'm guessing it has something to do with whatever you're really after today— which, I would imagine, has nothing to do with the bank. And everything to do with the absence of your third friend."

"Swing and a miss," Alec said.

"But what concerns me more is your getaway. If you know there's not a helicopter coming, then why are we headed to the roof?"

Sterling replied in a mocking tone. "There *is* a helicopter coming. Sergeant Hollis assured me of it. Why would the police lie?"

They stopped before a heavy door marked *AUTHORIZED PERSONNEL ONLY*, and Alec pushed it open to reveal a sparse utility hallway.

Blair followed them through the doorway. "You wouldn't have started this heist without a way out—but for the life of me, I can't imagine what that is."

"Compliments to the chef," Alec said, turning right and leading them up a short flight of stairs.

"So when this is all over," Sterling asked, "what are you going to tell the cops?"

"Nothing that will help them find you. Nothing about your third member being gone this whole time. And nothing about your watch, or potential connections with those other heists. I'll say you guys seemed like amateurs, rogue gunslingers. And to you two, I'll say this: good luck with your getaway. Keep frustrating the task force. I'll be cheering you on from the sidelines."

Blair looked forward, and abruptly stopped in place.

The stairs ended at a steel door marked by a yellow sign with bold red lettering that spelled *ROOF ACCESS*. Those words alone caused a knot of fear to well up in the pit of her stomach.

Because at age seven, Blair had tried to fly.

After tying a towel around her neck to serve as a cape, she'd climbed to the roof of her garage to begin her superhero training in earnest. Standing fearlessly at the edge—she'd debated putting a pillow below just in case the cape didn't work, then decided that half-measures wouldn't do—Blair leapt.

The attempt had cost her a broken leg and an entire summer spent at home, reading books with her cast propped up on pillows. Her superhero career was permanently over.

But ever since, her fear of heights transcended all rationality. It was manageable in most indoor spaces, though she still preferred not to stand beside elevated windows. But once that door to the roof was opened, she knew, her knees would turn to jelly and the fear would encapsulate her thoughts almost to the point of blurring her vision.

Sterling moved to push the door open, and Blair shouted, "Wait!"

"What?"

"I'll go back down. Turn myself in."

Alec said, "You're so worried about the feds shooting you, that might not be such a good idea."

Blair tried to swallow away the lump in her throat. "I can't deal with heights. Okay?"

"You did okay with them last night," Sterling reminded her. "I wouldn't have jumped off that pool deck—but you did. And here"—he nodded to the door—"all you have to do is not jump. Cry all you want, as long as you're crying in front of the media choppers. Because if what you say about Jim is true, then the roof is your safest bet."

Blair tried stalling for time. "All right, guys, come clean with me—what happens on the roof?"

"What happens on the roof?" Alec was excited now, bouncing from foot to foot. "What *doesn't* happen on the roof? Sterling and I wave our arms, we shout at one another, we look like we're having a good fight and give SWAT the confidence to launch their ground raid."

"Why would you want them to speed things up?"

This time it was Sterling who spoke, sounding troubled.

"Because we need to beat the storm."

Blair could see that he was deadly serious, though she had no idea why. And the urgency in his eyes told her that they couldn't wait any longer.

"All right," she gasped, nodding before she could change her mind. "All right, let's go."

Sterling pulled his mask over his face and then pushed open the door.

Blair followed them outside, and in one swirling moment regretted the decision more than anything else in her life.

Ahead of her were the dark clouds of a stormy sky, swollen and ready to burst. As she stood atop the terrifying pinnacle looking east toward downtown Los Angeles, a sideways glance revealed the rooftops of skyscrapers around her. Blair's thumping heartbeat was drowned out by the rotors of helicopters swooping toward them.

She looked up to see media and police choppers edging closer, cameras trained on the roof. Sterling and Alec strode out onto the rooftop, ostensibly searching the sky for a getaway helicopter that would never come.

Blair took a few shaky steps onto the windswept roof, a lump of fear forming in her throat. The ground felt like it would crumble beneath her at any moment—the concrete seemed wobbly, insecure.

"Hold up," Sterling shouted, listening to his earpiece. After pausing a beat, he announced, "We did it. They're moving to breach the ground floor now."

"Who is?" Blair asked.

"Your friends—FBI SWAT." He listened for a moment longer, then looked up. "Looks like you were right, Blair. Jim is coming in with them, and he's got a shotgun."

23

JIM

The explosive charge detonated with a *BOOM* that sucked the air from Jim's lungs. The blast faded to a deep echo in the building lobby and was followed by the clattering of glass fragments onto the floor.

The lead shooters chased the blast by chucking a pair of flash bangs into the now-empty doorframe. The concussion grenades blasted with a deafening roar and a blinding flash of light, and then the formation of FBI SWAT officers poured into the breach.

The media would consider the explosive charge and concussion grenades to be overkill, but the team couldn't take any chances. Blair was on the roof with two robbers, but a third man was still at large in the building. And, in their worst-case scenario, he was waiting near the front door with an assault rifle, ready to shoot SWAT officers as they entered the lobby.

Jim followed the line of men funneling into the shattered doorway. He felt ridiculous trailing the fully-equipped FBI SWAT shooters—but the 12-gauge shotgun in his hands helped alleviate that feeling. Jim had loaded the powerful shotgun not with scattershot but slugs; they were essentially lead cylinders that could punch a quarter-sized hole through wood or metal and do much worse to flesh and bone.

As he ran into the lobby, his eyes and nostrils stung with the fumes from the demolition charge and stun grenades cooking off in a confined space.

His shoes crunched on fragments of glass as he followed the row of FBI SWAT shooters swinging their barrels in every direction amid shouts of "*FBI! Don't move! FBI! Don't move!*"

Footsteps clattered into the lobby behind him, and Jim cast a backward glance at the flood of LAPD SWAT officers pouring into the void. They were clad in black kit, and looked like robot storm troopers. Jim had even seen a female officer in their stack, and she wasn't being relegated to the trail of their formation like he was. What was the world coming to?

But solid close quarters combat principles were solid for a reason, and Jim ascertained at a moment's glance that he didn't have to worry about some robber jumping out and shooting him from behind. The LAPD SWAT officers were flowing into the building like water down a drain, stuffing their rifle barrels into every uncleared space.

Which was good, he thought, because Vance's boys were headed straight for the stairwell.

In the guessing game of three known targets on the roof versus one possible target in the building's other thirty-six floors, FBI SWAT was playing the odds. The lead men reached the stairwell and began racing up, intent on making as much vertical progress as they could before those three robbers re-entered the building. Their disappearance from aerial surveillance would force a deliberate, floor-by-floor clearance upward, soon to be assisted by the two helicopters ferrying Red Team toward the rooftop to begin clearing from the top down.

But to Jim's surprise, his twin radio earpieces broadcast that the three suspects hadn't gone anywhere.

Instead, the speaker monitoring at Mission Command transmitted, "*Three suspects remain on the roof, appear to be arguing.*"

Jim couldn't believe Blair hadn't darted inside at the first sign of a breach. Hopefully her crew was falling apart, because remaining on the roof meant they'd be sitting ducks for Vance's men.

Unless...

A disturbing thought occurred to Jim.

What if Blair was deliberately waiting on the roof? If she wanted to be taken alive, that was her best bet. Even Vance couldn't gun down someone in cold blood with the cameras rolling. If Blair was banking on that, then it meant she was willing to go back to prison—and that, Jim feared, meant her only consolation would be exposing him in some effort to reduce her sentence.

Would she do that? She hadn't the first time, though Jim knew that was merely good luck on his part. He'd never threatened her; he'd been prepared to, sure, but she didn't even give him the chance. She just...went silent, and took the rap.

Jim entered the stairwell behind the last FBI shooter and began moving up, certain that at any moment Blair and her fellow thieves would disappear from the roof.

But as he took the steps two at a time, he heard Mission Command's next transmission clearly. *"Three suspects are still on the roof. ETA for Red Team helos, six minutes."*

Unable to fathom Blair's logic, Jim continued racing upward, moving as quickly as he could but still losing ground to the FBI SWAT officers in front of him.

24

BLAIR

Alec touched his earpiece and then announced, "FBI SWAT is headed up the stairwell now. LAPD SWAT is moving behind them."

Blair's mind was troubled with the memory of Jim's betrayal, a memory now compounded by the fact that he was *personally coming for her*.

This information had come at a very strange time: namely, as she stood on the windy roof of a Century City skyscraper that had a SWAT team charging up its stairs. But through the delirious fear born out of altitude, a rush of emotion flooded into Blair. The thought of her downfall triggered regret, anger, and, now that she'd come clean with Sterling and Alec, a strange sense of pride.

Every step of her life and career had been of her own volition, often against the advice of people who wanted the best for her. Everyone at Mary Washington thought she'd change her mind about the FBI before graduation, but she'd forged ahead. Everyone in her FBI class had told her that TacOps was a career dead-end, but that was her passion. And her success as a covert entry specialist earned her a spot on the prestigious task force assigned to stop the ongoing series of heists.

And that's where she'd met Jim.

She'd been seduced by the allure of his power, his confidence. He'd led her down a path, and she'd followed willingly—though it had ended in a far darker place than she ever could have imagined. In prison, she'd been truly broken for the first time in her life.

Now, his presence on the raid meant only one thing: he wanted to make sure Blair was killed. Ordering it wasn't enough. He wanted to see her body and make sure the job was finished. How would he react if she was arrested on live TV, if she remained standing on the terrifying pinnacle of this building with news helicopters filming as SWAT officers handcuffed her?

If she was captured alive here, Jim would bury her.

Jim, the Bureau, and any other powers that be would throw the book at Blair. She didn't have the money to sustain a lengthy legal defense, so a public defender would represent her, and they'd be crushed beneath the churning machinery of every local and federal institution that could get a piece of the action. Blair's only bargaining chip was her evidence against Jim—for the Korb report, and other things—and while it was enough to take him down, they'd never let her walk away. Not after this.

And Blair would go to prison. *Back* to prison, she corrected herself. She could survive the time—couldn't she?—but the previous days had taught her that a different kind of prison waited outside the bars of her cell.

Jim wasn't to blame for what happened to her—she alone bore responsibility for her actions then.

And she alone bore responsibility for her actions now.

Blair spun to face Sterling, squaring off against him beneath the murky gray sky.

"I'm going with you," she announced.

A beat of silence between them.

"Come again?" Alec asked.

Blair kept her eyes on Sterling's. "You put me in this situation. Now you can get me out of it."

"Leaving you on the roof," Sterling replied, "*is* getting you out of it."

Alec announced, "SWAT team just crossed the 4th floor."

Blair suddenly felt as dizzy as she had during Jim's press conference. "I couldn't get a decent job before this. What's going to happen to me after? Jim just proclaimed me a criminal mastermind before an investigation had a chance to begin. My face is all over the news; I won't even be able to find work as a waitress."

Holding a fist to his mouth, Alec muttered, "Not that it worked out so well for you before."

Sterling glanced about uneasily, his response delayed. "Blair, you don't even know us."

"Yes, I do. You're professionals. I spent over a year hunting the people who committed those heists—and now I've found you. No one knows where you go, and if they did they'd have arrested you already. You can take me with you, and after putting me through this, you better do it."

"Are you serious?"

"I've never been so serious about anything in my life."

Alec said, "SWAT team is passing the 9th floor."

Sterling assumed a cautionary tone. "Blair, there's still our getaway...it's going to be fast, and it's going to be dangerous. If you don't like heights, then you're not going to make it. And staying on this roof is your best chance of staying out of prison."

"I know that."

"If you value your freedom, I'd stay here."

"I'm not free out there. Not anymore."

"Blair, if you're sure this is what you want..."

"No!" Alec shouted. "This cannot happen!"

Sterling looked at him. "Why not?"

"We're on TV—people could think she's one of us! Consider our reputation, man. There's never been a woman on a heist crew."

"What?"

"Look at all the great heist movies—*The Killing*, *Rififi*, *White Heat*, regular *Heat*—there's never a woman on the team! It messes with the whole"—he waved his hands in front of his face—"you know, dynamic. Also, the SWAT team is on the 13th floor—I know your math is rusty, but they're almost halfway here."

"All right, Blair," Sterling said. "You want to come with us, I'll take you. For now."

She took a breath, meeting his eyes levelly. "I'm in."

He drew his pistol from the holster. "But just in case we get caught on the way out, I need you to act like a hostage until this is over."

"How convenient," she said, her eyes dropping to the pistol in his hand. "If this getaway involves taking one step closer to that edge, you're going to have to treat me like one."

25

JIM

Jim crossed the 13th floor, his legs exhausted from the climb. His shotgun, formerly hoisted at the ready, was now carried at waist-level from sheer fatigue. Granted, Jim was carrying less gear than any of the SWAT shooters —but he was also the oldest.

The FBI SWAT team thundered up the stairs above him.

Vance transmitted over the radio, "*Blue Team crossing Level 15.*"

"*Copy. LAPD SWAT has cleared Levels 1 and 2, now proceeding to Level 3 for deliberate clearance. Three suspects remain on roof.*"

Why would they still be waiting on the roof? By now it was clear to them that there was no helicopter coming. Waiting in plain view of police choppers defied comprehension; but then again, so did all of this.

What was Blair thinking?

A *bank robbery*, of all things. In this day and age of modern security measures and police response time, it was a suicidal move even for her. Given her experience studying the methods of successful heists, she should have known this would be a hatchet job from the beginning. Blair had her photo and fingerprints on file from federal service. There was nowhere she could disappear to. She must have lost her mind in prison.

And whose fault would that be? The desperate wave of shame and guilt washed over him, so powerful that his only recourse had been to suppress it altogether. To not think of it, to play the party line that one of his agents had experienced an unfortunate lapse in integrity. It wasn't unheard of, though the timing—at the apex of political pressure for task force results—had nearly caused his funding to be pulled several times over.

Jim had been placed in charge of the task force as one in a continued series of "kingmaker" moves, climbing a ladder to greater positions of power. But command of the task force came at great risk: this time, his mentor hadn't waited until a case was nearly closed and then assigned his protégé so Jim could take the career credit.

With the inception of the task force, everything was built from the ground up with Jim at the helm. The entire effort was open-ended, aimed against a highly proficient network of heist crews that defied all laws of probability in slipping up or getting captured. This time, his mentor had said, Jim would rise to the occasion—or he wouldn't.

So when pressure had come down on all sides to shut down the task force, what could Jim do? There was always one answer to that question: whatever it takes.

His manipulation of Blair hadn't been ill-intended. He'd hoped for everything he told her—a search warrant, decisive evidence, progress in the case, and continued funding. As for leaving his wife to be with Blair...well, maybe but maybe not. That much depended on which way the political tides were turning above him, and whether he could sustain his career track amid a potentially messy separation. Publicly leaping into bed with a prior subordinate would be an iffy prospect, but he'd seen superiors get away with worse from time to time, provided they had the right support.

And Jim's mentor had all the support he needed, right down to a one-time pass with Wycroft, a criminal defense attorney of such power and resources—and unspoken connections with judges—that his pro bono representation practically amounted to a get-out-of-jail-free card. And with the words "pro bono" in the media, Wycroft could then receive the requisite amount of funding from Jim's mentor. There would be no cap on the payment his mentor could provide; there never was.

Jim hit the next landing, crossing the 16th floor. If he were any less fit, he'd have been gasping for air on a lower level by now. But the SWAT shooters above him continued hauling up the stairs—their physical prowess was incredible. They were now minutes away from cornering Blair and two other henchmen, and the odds of Blair getting killed in the crossfire were good. That would, regrettably, be the best possible conclusion of the incident.

If she was captured...Jim could envision it already. Why she'd kept quiet about his involvement in her false statement was beyond him. Even if she was in love, his rebuke of her should have tipped her over the edge. He could've used Wycroft to prevent her from going to prison. But in the end, with OPR breathing down his neck, Jim had decided to save that one-time pass for himself.

Jim crossed the 18th floor, flexing his grip on the shotgun. Heaving another breath, he charged up the next flight to remain close to the last of Vance's men.

He needed so badly for this to be over, one way or another. Everything since the day Blair got caught had been a turbulent mix of relief and guilt, of having narrowly missed being hit by a bullet that instead struck your mistress in the heart. Jim had told himself every lie in the book. That he couldn't have saved Blair, that if he hadn't given her the instruction she would have thought it up on her own and gotten caught anyway. But none of it was true. The fault was his and his alone, and in the end, suppressing the memories was his only recourse. He'd relied on sheer denial, right up until this morning when Blair appeared on his news feed.

He crossed the 20th floor—sixteen more to go. But he felt a growing sense of unease about the tactical situation. Why would Blair and her two fellow robbers still be on the roof? It was as if they were trying to lure the SWAT shooters toward them, but that didn't make sense either—unless they planned on surrendering alive, or actually wanted to die in a rooftop shootout. If the latter, the firefight would be very quick and nearly one-way, particularly with the FBI SWAT helicopters inbound. Those boys hanging off the chopper skids could take out three rooftop shooters in a matter of seconds.

Blair knew that a SWAT assault was proceeding upward into the building, and at a minimum she would suspect the imminent arrival of air-based SWAT elements landing on the roof.

If he were in that situation, he'd re-enter the building and force a meticulous floor-by-floor, room-by-room deliberate clearance that could take hours.

So why didn't she?

Despite the hostage negotiator's insistence that all the robbers asked for was a helicopter, Jim didn't buy it for one second. Blair would remain on the roof for only one reason—if she had a legitimate means of escape.

But what was it?

He realized then that rather than seeking capture or death, the three robbers on the roof had a third option.

What if they had their own helicopter coming in?

Had that been the getaway plan all along?

It couldn't be, Jim told himself—that would be far beyond Blair's finances. But it was the only explanation, unless they wanted to survive in custody or die on the rooftop.

Jim transmitted over the tactical frequency.

"Mission Control, advise Police Air to watch for possible suspect heli-copter approach. If a bird touches down to pick them up, I want it followed to the ends of the earth."

"*Copy—no one's entering the airspace. Red Team helicopters are ninety seconds out.*"

Was there something else? What else *could* there be? The entire block around the building was surrounded. Short of a zip line or a lateral rope reaching some distant rooftop, there was no way out.

"You're sure the elevators haven't moved?"

"*We're sure. They're still locked in place. One remains at the top floor; the others are at the ground level. Will advise if that changes.*"

Jim crossed the 27th floor. The lead SWAT shooters would be reaching the roof in just over a minute—and there'd be no hope left for Blair.

26

BLAIR

Alec shouted, "SWAT team is on the 28th floor—ninety seconds left!"

Blair's mind reeled. The shooters storming up the stairwell weren't the only imminent danger—she saw the tipoff that death was also coming from above.

The media and police helicopters that had been drifting overhead tipped their hand. Almost in unison, they increased their altitude until their rotors were almost churning across the thick blanket of gray clouds. Blair knew what that meant: they were acting on orders, clearing a restricted altitude for aircraft with priority clearance.

She caught a glimpse of them moments later in the sky to the southwest: a pair of black helicopters flying in formation, slipping in and out of sight between buildings. The pilots were trying to keep as many high rises between them and the target rooftop as they could, delaying their visual exposure to the rooftop bandits for as long as possible.

Only now they were so close that the pilots were running out of options to remain unseen.

"Eighty seconds left!" Alec shouted.

And if the teams aboard those helicopters didn't shoot or arrest them, then the shooters storming up the stairwell would.

Blair saw Sterling watching the sky to the southwest as well—he'd seen them too.

And yet he did nothing.

She told him, "Those aren't news choppers, Sterling. Whatever your exit plan is, now's the time."

He didn't answer at first, and that pause made Blair infinitely more scared. It was clear by now that Sterling didn't have some personal helicopter coming to spirit them away—and even if one magically appeared, it was too late.

Every second was one step closer to death or capture, another flash of time they wouldn't get back.

And Blair's fear of heights was amplified further by the fear of capture, the knowledge of what awaited. It wouldn't be like the previous night. The handcuffs that the cops put on wouldn't come off until she was inside a cell, and the next time she'd see Sterling and Alec would be in some unwinnable and highly publicized court proceeding.

Alec yelled, "Seventy seconds!"

Sterling grabbed her arm with his free hand and stared forcefully into her eyes.

"The cameras are on us. I've got to make this look convincing. You're now my hostage, understood?"

She nodded. "I'm ready when you are."

She searched his eyes for some indication that he wasn't going to abandon her, that he had a way out. Had he been toying with her this entire time? What possible way was there out of this mess?

Without releasing her arm, Sterling holstered his pistol and dragged her toward the edge of the roof. Alec followed, and the two men began stripping off their haul in unison.

First they unslung their bags of cash, dropping them at their feet. Then they each removed their black hiking packs.

Alec hastily grabbed his bag of cash and strapped it across his back, then repeated the process with Sterling's bag. Why wasn't Sterling carrying his cash anymore?

"Sixty seconds!"

It didn't matter—either way, those hiking packs were apparently staying on the roof along with whatever was inside them.

Or so she thought.

The truth became apparent a moment later, when Sterling and Alec knelt to open the pack flaps and pulled out identical items.

At first the items they held looked woefully insubstantial, some assemblage of nylon webbing with sturdy metal clips attached. Still kneeling, they routed the nylon around metal brackets on the roof.

She hadn't even noticed the brackets, both inconspicuous stainless steel loops bolted into the roof's concrete surface. Blair guessed they were anchor points to tether maintenance workers operating close to the rooftop edge, where a safety lanyard protected against a gust of wind or sudden slip.

Either way, the brackets looked purpose-built to whatever Sterling and Alec were doing, routing sections of the nylon webbing through adjacent loops.

Their gloved hands moved together, an almost choreographed mimicry of one another. She'd seen something like this before—some documentary, something she had to turn off when it made her skin crawl.

"Oh, no..." Blair murmured, any further words stuck in her throat.

"Fifty seconds!"

Her worst fear was confirmed a second later, when both men pulled something new out of their packs and secured it to the assembly they'd already rigged.

This new object brought with it the realization of what had filled their hiking packs this whole time. The helicopters wouldn't be able to see it—not yet—but Blair could.

It was a length of rope.

27

JIM

Jim continued running up the stairs, embarrassed to be losing ground to Vance's last shooter. Screw it, he thought; if these guys could run up a building at his age, they could judge him. Until then, he was holding his own.

Then came the radio transmission that changed the course of the mission—immediately for Jim, and then, half a minute later, for every officer on the scene.

"*This is Eagle Three. All units, be advised: suspects have moved toward edge of roof, dropped their hiking packs. They're kneeling over the packs now, and Mission Command, you may want to initiate IED protocol...*"

Jim released one hand from his shotgun and grabbed the stairwell rail, stopping himself with a jolt.

"Vance," he transmitted breathlessly, "take your team back downstairs."

Jim didn't wait for a response. Instead he reversed direction himself, leaping down the stairs three at a time.

Vance's reply was firm. "*Negative. My team will manage its own IED protocol.*"

Jim was already checking the door at the next landing: it was unlocked. Abandoning it, Jim continued downstairs as he replied.

"It's not an IED! Don't you get it—they're not staying on the roof. Start heading back down." Jim paused to consider the implications of what he was about to say next, then chose to do it anyway. "That's an order."

"I have tactical command. We're moving topside."

By then Jim was testing the next door down: unlocked. He continued plunging down the stairs. Forget Vance. He would realize his error soon enough—but until then, Jim was on his own.

Then he heard a fragment of radio traffic from Mission Command.

"...Red Team helicopters will be wheels-down in forty seconds, and—standby."

Here it is, Jim thought. Here's where everyone else realized what he did half a minute ago. Finding another unlocked door, he spun and darted down the next flight of stairs.

"Suspects have dumped rope from their packs—I say again, rope. Now they're... they're casting ropes off the side of the building, all units prepare for possible rappel—"

No kidding, Jim thought. He abandoned another unlocked door and raced down to the next floor.

Whatever Blair had planned, Vance's team would be too late to stop it.

It was up to Jim now.

28

BLAIR

Blair looked down in horror.

The ropes were a checkered red-and-blue pattern, and scarcely larger than finger-width. No way were they strong enough to hold...well, anything. Certainly not Alec and his twin bags of cash. Not even Sterling, even though he no longer carried anything on his back.

And then Blair realized why Alec had donned both bags of stolen cash while Sterling remained unburdened.

Sterling's burden wouldn't be cash.

It would be *her*.

Blair went incoherent with fear. This couldn't work. It mustn't. She was unwilling to go back now, yet unable to move.

"Those aren't going to hold—we can't—you can't..." she stammered.

Sterling and Alec pulled metal clips from behind their belts. They must have worn climbing harnesses beneath their pants, Blair thought—which was confirmed when they routed the rope through the metal in an arranged hitch that would allow it to slide through.

"Forty seconds!"

They upended their hiking packs, dumping two huge coils of rope onto the roof. One end was attached to the anchor point in the roof and routed through their harnesses.

The rope then disappeared into the remaining coil that, to Blair's horror, they now cast off the edge of the building.

Then Sterling grabbed Blair and pushed her toward the void of sky where the ropes disappeared. She tried to fight him, skidding to a stop at the roof's edge. Police and media helicopters now swarmed overhead, trying to angle for a good view.

Blair stared down the five-hundred-foot drop to the pavement lined with emergency vehicles. *This couldn't be happening.* She struggled backward, held in place by Sterling's iron grip and Alec stepping in to block her escape.

"SWAT team is crossing the 34th floor—they'll be on the roof in thirty seconds!"

She looked around wildly for anything that could stop this. She found the two SWAT helicopters approaching at full throttle, but they were too far out to stop what was about to happen. Blair drew in ragged breaths of air as Sterling placed the barrel of his pistol to her temple.

He shouted into her ear, a voice without sympathy.

"It's time to go, Blair."

She bit her lip, shuddering in his grasp.

And then Blair began to cry.

Sterling holstered his pistol and said, "Don't choke me, or we both die."

Then he pulled Blair to his back, placing one of her arms over his shoulder and the other under his arm. Her hands locked around each other over his chest, tensing into a fierce white-knuckle grip. Her sweaty palms were smeared together, her legs feeling wooden and immovable. She clung to Sterling's back like a shipwreck survivor to the only floating scrap in a vast ocean—he was her only chance of survival, of escaping, of starting over. She didn't know how or where; she just knew she couldn't go back.

Before she could steel herself for what was about to happen, Sterling stepped backward and she was over the edge—and with a sudden gasp, she saw nothing below her but a terminal fall.

Her feet were dangling free until Sterling and Alec lowered themselves into L-shaped positions over the edge, their legs parallel to the ground. Blair crushed Sterling's sides with her thighs, wondering how long she'd have to hold on before this was over.

She didn't have to wonder long.

Sterling and Alec each bent their legs, pushed off the side of the building, and released a massive length of rope through the attachment points on their harnesses.

Then all three of them were in freefall.

Blair's stomach leapt into her throat as the mirrored windows of their skyscraper swept upward. Her wild eyes caught the reflection before her: Sterling's and Alec's silhouettes in black, rappelling in tandem high above the streets of Century City. She caught a glimpse of her black hair trailing over Sterling's shoulder, arms and legs desperately wrapped around him, with Alec beside them.

Suddenly the reflections swelled in size. They were soaring back toward the glass on the opposite end of their pendulum swing, and as Blair braced for impact, Sterling's and Alec's boots struck the outside window and pushed off again.

All three of them swung out over the street a final time, releasing a length of rope in a horrifying descent. There can't be much rope left, Blair thought. But this time, as they swung back toward the building, Blair saw something she hadn't noticed before.

Below them, along the trajectory they were rappelling toward, one of the building's mirrored glass panels shifted. A section of window was suddenly disappearing, the resulting hole filled with a single tall, masked figure.

It was the third man in their heist crew.

Sterling and Alec slowed their fall, their boots slamming to a stop on either side of the newly opened gap. Blair was in a full panic now, resisting the instinct to clamber over Sterling in a feverish bid to get back in the building.

And in that moment, she locked eyes with the tall robber. He wore his bag of cash on his back, and his face looked even more bewildered than she felt.

"What is *she* doing here?" he asked in a Russian accent.

"Blair," Sterling grunted. "Go!"

He rolled sideways on one boot, swinging her toward the gap. The tall man reached under her armpits and shouted, "I've got you. Come on."

Blair was frozen.

"Let go!" Sterling shouted.

Against all instincts, Blair's hands released their grip.

The second they did, the man inside the building hoisted Blair through the hole. He spun her around and set her down on a carpeted floor—Blair wanted to kiss it; the ground had never felt so good—and then he turned to assist Sterling and Alec.

As Alec entered the building, he bellowed an explanation.

"Princess Blair was rescued from the castle tower," he said in a regal voice, "by Sir Sterling, fair of skin, fit of frame, with glorious locks of gold."

Blair struggled to stand, hyperventilating in dizzying relief that she was still alive. The removed section of glass was face-down on the carpet, with two handled suction cups affixed to it. When had he cut the glass, she wondered—and what was this escape? FBI SWAT was near the roof and LAPD SWAT was near the ground. The crew was still inside the same building, now between two SWAT elements instead of above both. The situation was, arguably, even worse.

Alec detached the rope from his metal clip and released it. Then the tall man helped Sterling back inside, and he detached from the rope as well.

"Hurry up!" the Russian robber directed, leading them at a run through the office and down the hallway to the right.

Blair moved as quickly as her boots allowed, hearing the distant thunder of SWAT helicopters touching down on the rooftop. Then she heard a far more terrifying noise than the helicopters landing above her head.

It was the deafening blast of a shotgun, not on some separate floor but *right here*, just around the corner.

A second shotgun blast followed within two seconds—someone was blowing the hinges off a door—and then the great metal clanging of that door slamming onto the tile floor erupted, sending its echo washing over them.

"Federal agents! Don't move!" someone shouted, almost as loud as the shotgun blasts that preceded it.

But it wasn't the volume that made Blair freeze in her tracks, nor the fact that she was about to be taken into custody.

The voice belonged to *Jim*.

Suddenly a hand was on her wrist, jerking her forward with such force that her shoulder was almost thrown out.

It was Sterling, of course, pulling her out of her stupor. Together they ran forward down the hall, and Blair saw that the other two robbers were far ahead, having never broken stride. Sterling must have come back for her, and before she could reflect on what that meant, the other two robbers stopped at their destination.

It was an elevator shaft, the exterior doors frozen open to reveal a gaping hole with a group of vertical cables. Affixed to the thickest cable were three sets of equipment, each a clamped footrest below a hydraulic descender with two handgrips.

She heard Jim swiftly closing in on them, could tell by the cadence of footfalls that he was moving tactically, hurriedly.

Before she could contemplate this, Alec put a headlight over his forehead and stepped over the mount holding the elevator doors apart. Grasping the grips of the lowest hydraulic descender, he stepped onto the footrest with one foot and then the other.

Then Blair heard a tremendous group of men rolling toward her, a full SWAT team moving in a mad dash, followed by shouts of "FBI! Don't move!"

Alec looked to Blair. Below the blaze of his headlamp, she could see a mischievous expression playing across his eyes as he shot her a wink.

Then he thumbed a button on his hydraulic descender and rocketed downward out of sight.

Blair's breath caught in her throat just as she heard, right around the corner, "ASAC Jacobson here! On me! On me!" He was announcing that the SWAT team should move to the sound of his voice, indicating that he'd partially cleared the floor and needed backup.

More footsteps raced toward them as the tall robber mounted the lower remaining hydraulic descender.

Then he disappeared from view in a split second, the sound of his descender now a vanishing echo as he zipped down the cable.

Sterling put a hand on Blair's shoulder and whispered urgently, "Arms around me, exactly as before."

He turned away from her and toward the elevator.

She quickly routed her arms around Sterling and clasped her hands together over his sternum. They weren't going to make it. The men clearing the floor were sweeping toward them too quickly, but she couldn't do anything about it now.

Now, it was up to Sterling.

He grasped the handholds of the last remaining hydraulic descender, and then grunted and strained to reach the footholds while maneuvering Blair's body into the cold, hollow shaft. Blair looked down, seeing the cable disappear into darkness.

Sterling pushed the descent button, and they dropped three feet before their fall was halted. Blair gasped in fear, but Sterling merely reached for a rubber doorstop wedge stuck in the side of the elevator door. He pulled it free, and the door's sensor latch clicked back into place before the doors slid shut, encapsulating them in darkness.

A barrage of automatic gunfire erupted outside the elevator shaft.

Blair involuntarily clutched Sterling tighter, fearful that bullets would puncture the elevator door beside her.

Then Sterling pressed the button on his descender, and he and Blair launched into a freefall.

29

JIM

Jim's pace increased with repetition: hurdle down a flight of stairs, shotgun in hand; check the door on the landing, find it unlocked; and continue moving.

By now, the entire law enforcement response was synced with what Jim had intuitively known when the suspects were reported kneeling over their hiking packs.

"*Suspects are rappelling down building...*"

"*Copy,*" Vance replied, sounding frustrated. "*Blue Team is at 32nd floor on our way back down.*"

Jim reached the landing of the 23rd floor, the distant sound of men rushing down the stairs echoing high above him. He hastily pulled on the door handle, already half-turned to continue moving down to the next level.

But the door caught.

He pulled on it again.

Locked.

"*...three suspects are re-entering the building on 23rd floor—fourth suspect is helping them inside. I say again, all four suspects confirmed 23rd floor.*"

Jim was now facing a personal crisis of sorts.

When Vance's men arrived, they'd take the lead and he'd be relegated to last shooter in the stack.

The smart tactical play—other than not separating himself from the SWAT team in the first place—would be to maintain eyes on the stairwell door. Once SWAT reached him, he could confirm that Blair's crew hadn't taken the stairs and so definitively remained on that level. Then SWAT would take the lead and conduct a deliberate clearance.

If Blair's team was still *on* the 23ʳᵈ floor when SWAT arrived. Because however the bandits planned on leaving, he now guessed they had something less obvious in store than simply taking the stairs.

Entering the 23ʳᵈ floor alone was tactical suicide, one man against four. But to do so would give him the chance he desperately needed—a direct line of sight to Blair. Then he could take his shot, and drop her once and for all. Of course, he'd be pinned down immediately, if not running for his life; but he had the best tactical shooters in LA racing to back him up.

These considerations flipped through Jim's mind in the span of seconds, and he lifted the barrel of his shotgun to the top door hinge.

"Helos are touching down on roof..."

Jim pulled the trigger, and the 12-gauge bucked in his grasp with a deafening roar.

"...Red Team moving to stairwell..."

Racking the slide, Jim dropped the barrel to the lower door hinge.

"...to link up with Blue Team..."

Jim fired again, and the second slug blasted the lower door hinge clear. He racked the shotgun a second time, kicking the metal door as hard as he could.

The door fell free of the frame, and Jim quickly sidestepped in case someone began firing at the sound of the breach. When a second passed with no response, he plunged through the doorway, shotgun raised.

"Federal agents!" he shouted. "Don't move!"

The hallway spread in both directions, and on a whim, Jim cut right. He moved quickly—having lost the element of surprise, he could only rely on speed. The hallway wound through a row of office doors, and Jim stopped at the corner to angle his shotgun. All he needed now was a noise. His twin radio earpieces had a decibel cutoff for hearing protection, so he yanked the left one out. Now only the slightest whisper, or the shuffle of a person repositioning himself, would be sufficient to orient his movement.

He got far more than he needed: the sound of hurried footsteps, the clatter of Blair's footfalls. He picked up the pace, then slowed as he reached the next corner.

And as he stopped to listen, his senses on full alert, all other sounds were lost in the storm of boots as Vance's men rushed off the stairwell.

"FBI! Don't move!"

He mentally cursed them, and then cursed Vance for not bringing his men here in the first place.

"ASAC Jacobson here! On me! On me!"

The SWAT shooters began sprinting to back him up, and for a moment Jim thought he heard a muffled hissing sound around the corner. He wanted desperately to advance but hesitated, thinking that if he was killed turning the corner solo, his tombstone would read: *JAMES JACOBSON. SHOT IN FACE BECAUSE HE DIDN'T WAIT 3.5 SECONDS FOR SWAT TO BACK HIM UP.*

He knelt at the corner as officers rushed in behind him, and thought he heard it again: a faint hissing sound, followed by a scrape of metal and a soft thumping noise.

Then a SWAT officer stopped behind him, giving Jim's shoulder a squeeze.

Jim pivoted around the corner, aiming his shotgun from the kneeling position as the SWAT officer behind him did the same while standing—a maneuver known as a "high-low," putting two barrels around the corner while maintaining cover behind the wall.

Jim's eyes were wide, his focus wired as he searched for Blair amid the black silhouettes of her crew.

But the short hallway before him was empty, save the brushed stainless steel elevator doors and a set of potted plants. Where was she?

Then chaos erupted.

The rapid-fire staccato blast of gunshots rang out, and for one terrified second Jim thought it was the last sound he'd ever hear. The burst of fire was deafening, forcing him to cower behind his corner until he determined he wasn't being shot at—yet.

"*Shots fired, shots fired, 23rd floor—*"

These gunshots were coming from somewhere past the elevator hallway. Rapid, undisciplined bursts of automatic fire. The space was too confined for him to identify the exact weapon, but it was definitely an assault rifle. Some element of Vance's SWAT team must have begun clearance on a separate part of the floor when they took fire from Blair's crew.

Everything happened very quickly after that.

SWAT shooters flooded past Jim, maneuvering into position around the gunfire. He stood as they cleared the short elevator hallway, hearing the shots continue.

Jim followed the SWAT officers around the next corner, the direction of sound narrowing the source of gunfire to a closed office door.

Was the crew firing through an open window at police on the ground? It would be a pointlessly audacious move, wild and chaotic. Then again, nothing about Blair's methods during this heist had been particularly rational. Maybe she'd wanted to die in a blaze of glory this whole time—and Jim would certainly oblige.

Vance's men were already blasting the locked door with a shotgun breach and then hurling a flash bang inside. The concussion grenade exploded in a blast of noise and light, and the team began flowing inside to clear.

It must have been a massive office, because the SWAT shooters kept disappearing inside the doorway. Jim brought up the end of the stack, racing inside and raising his shotgun.

A great mahogany desk faced him, the window beyond it overlooking an adjacent building. Filing cabinets lined one wall, and the other bore a long sofa. SWAT shooters were flowing along the walls to shift their sectors of fire in a coordinated clearance behind every possible blind spot.

But nobody else was there.

The gunshots had ended.

Jim stood, his nostrils filled with a peculiar cordite stench that stung his eyes. It wasn't just the flash bang, he realized. This smell was unfamiliar to him, and he couldn't figure out what it was.

He moved around the side of the desk, steadying his shotgun, refusing to believe this was over.

Sitting on the ground was a device he'd never seen before—a long gray box with a timer blinking 0:00, connected to a coil of yellow wire that dovetailed into multiple rows of thin cylinders. There were dozens of them, all but one smoking and burst open in the middle like some kind of firecracker party favor. He examined the lone intact cylinder seated at the end of the final row. It was rust-colored, its exterior bearing small lettering that he leaned in to examine.

SQUIB, AK-47. MADE IN CHINA.

The cylinder exploded with a loud pop. Jim jumped in fear, his adrenaline waning to embarrassment. His left ear was ringing badly as radio chatter erupted through his remaining earpiece.

"*—confirm no casualties?*"

"*Who is taking fire—*"

Jim transmitted, "Break, break, break. Negative shots fired. They're squibs."

"*Say again?*"

"Squibs. Miniature explosives."

"*EOD standing by. Send location of explosive device.*"

"Negative! It was firecrackers. Hollywood firecrackers. Break." He took a breath as the SWAT officers flooded out of the room to continue clearing the rest of the floor. Why wouldn't they? After all, the bandits were all sighted re-entering this level of the building after rappelling from the roof. And once that happened, law enforcement response went from positively identifying all four suspects on the 23rd floor to losing all of them in the space of thirty seconds.

Jim knew that Blair and her team were gone—he just didn't know how. LAPD SWAT controlled the ground level and had cleared the first few stories of the building; FBI SWAT now controlled the roof down to the 23rd floor, where Jim now stood, feeling foolish. He'd gone from triumphant in anticipating that the crew would flee the roof for a lower level to almost stupidly audacious in conducting a one-man breach and clearance to press the initiative.

Now he stood, shotgun lighter by two slugs used for a door breach, wearing a throw-down piece hidden on his ankle and no closer to catching Blair—who, he reminded himself, held more than a few secrets about his past that he couldn't have circulating.

His mind raced through Blair's possible locations. Everything indicated she should still be on the 23rd floor—so how did he instinctively know that she *wasn't*? Something had informed his subconscious, he knew, because his instincts were rarely misleading and never completely wrong.

Mentally inventorying every piece of information he had to go on, he found one area unexplored: the noise he'd heard before the false gunfire. First was a zinging hiss, then a scrape of metal, and finally a soft thumping. He'd been close to the noise, so close that when he pivoted around the corner with a SWAT shooter, he was certain he'd see the suspects.

But instead, all he'd seen were the elevators...

And then he understood.

Jim keyed his radio and transmitted, "Suspects descended through the elevator shaft. I say again, suspects descended through the elevator shaft. Mission Control, confirm every elevator outlet is barricaded—especially parking lot sublevels."

"Confirm; they're all locked down."

"I need every elevator shaft opened and spotlighted, now. And tell the elevator barricade crews that one of them is about to get attacked."

30

BLAIR

Blair held tight to Sterling's back, their dizzying slide down the elevator cable feeling like it would never end.

Sterling held an iron grip on the descender, confidently looking down in a move that Blair hadn't yet summoned up the nerve to do herself.

Instead she clenched Sterling's chest, telling herself the freefall couldn't last much longer. Slits of light from elevator doors formed a blinking strobe that raced upward as they fell.

She could only manage a series of stunted half-breaths. The air was stale and humid, and smelled of oil, metal, and concrete. And though she was still scared, Blair now felt a peculiar sense of confidence in Sterling and his team. Their plan was equal parts daring and ludicrous, a combination that had resulted in them successfully outpacing the police at every turn —so far.

She'd played out the sordid memory of Jim's betrayal a thousand times before—she'd certainly had time to do so in the aftermath. And now, knowing full well that he was trying to have her killed, she should have felt utterly defeated.

Instead, Blair felt something different altogether.

Alive.

It wasn't an alien feeling, though it had certainly been some time since she had experienced it. As a paroled ex-agent reduced to bouncing between waitressing jobs, she hadn't expected any source of exhilaration in the coming years, if ever again.

But now, she'd reclaimed it. She felt more alive than she ever had—total freedom, a current of adrenaline underscored by the thrill of doing something for herself. For once. She didn't know what she wanted, but she knew she had nothing to go back to on the outside. Things had been bad before. Now that Jim had declared her a criminal mastermind on national television, they were far worse.

And Blair was done putting up with it.

When these men had captured her, she'd wanted nothing more than to reclaim her old life. Now that she'd briefly been party to the ease with which they usurped every institutional safeguard designed to catch them, she felt a begrudging sense of admiration. Envy, even. In this moment, so many things in her past seemed ludicrous: subjecting herself to such a vast system, with all its policies and bureaucracy; compromising her integrity, first with an affair and later by lying. That huge machine had chewed her up and spit her out, it had controlled her entire world, and yet these three men were dancing around it, outwitting the jaws with ease.

Then she felt her descent begin to slow; Sterling must have been able to control their speed through the hydraulic descender. He was still looking down, and after taking the deepest breath she could summon, Blair did the same.

A glowing orb of light was stationary beneath them—Alec's headlight. The tall robber slowed as he approached it, and Sterling adjusted his rate of descent like a bird flying in formation.

Alec was reaching for some outlet on the side of the elevator shaft that Blair couldn't quite make out. Then he vanished into the side of the wall, his headlight illuminating the square opening into which he'd climbed. The tall, Russian-accented robber followed suit, his height making the movement an awkward clamber off his descender and footrest.

Sterling eased himself downward until he and Blair were level with the square hatch.

"Go ahead," he whispered.

Blair reached out and accepted the tall robber's hand, and he helped her off Sterling's back and into the shaft. It was lined with a fitted exterior frame and extended through a slab of concrete that appeared to be roughly sawed apart—professional equipment had been used in constructing this access point, Blair thought, but not by professionals.

The amateur job had been effective enough, however, as Blair found herself in a tunnel big enough for her to stand with a slight hunch. And while the tall robber couldn't fit without awkwardly contorting his lanky frame, Alec was shuffling forward to parts unknown with relative ease, his headlamp blazing a trail for the others.

She turned to take guidance from Sterling, and saw that he was hurriedly stripping all three sets of hydraulic descenders off the elevator cable and dumping them onto the ground with a series of echoing clanks.

"What were those gunshots?" she asked. "FBI doesn't 'spray and pray' on full auto."

"Squibs," Sterling said, tossing down the last hydraulic descender. "Hand me that drill."

"What...drill?"

He donned a headlight and turned it toward her legs, and she saw a power drill leaning against the tunnel wall at her feet. She picked it up, noting its heft and a thick hexagonal bit.

Sterling took it from her, using his gloves to wipe off the grip where her hand had touched it. He performed the action fluidly, naturally, as though he were opening a can of beer at a party.

Then he performed what Blair considered a master stroke for the getaway.

Beside him, leaned flush against the wall, was a filthy square metal panel. In the center was an ominous yellow triangle with a lightning bolt symbol, and the large print beneath it read, *DANGER: High Voltage. Back of this panel is live.* An assortment of other official-looking labels were on the panel—Blair particularly liked one demanding that anyone seeking to remove the panel comply with, quote, *NFPA 70E for electrical safe work practices, including all protective equipment.*

But the rest of the warning labels vanished from view as Sterling rotated the panel into place to cover the gap behind them. He used the drill to bolt the panel against a frame fitted around the tunnel entrance, then turned to Blair.

"Shall we?" He extended his hand forward to indicate that Blair should proceed down the tunnel.

She turned to see that it stretched only twenty feet or so, and the other two robbers were already gone. In their wake was a square exit that Blair approached, the space beyond dimly lit by the shifting glow of a headlamp.

When she reached the end of the tunnel, she stepped through an identical square frame delineating its boundary, and had to sit on the edge and lower herself into the room beyond.

Her first breath was full of hot air and choking dust. "What is this place?"

"Utility tunnel," Alec said simply, as if that should have been obvious.

As Blair stepped away from the passage to make room for Sterling to exit, she took in her surroundings with a sense of awe. All around her were pipes of varying diameters, extending in all directions and sparsely lit by periodic dim light bulbs high above them. Amid the snaking pipes were industrial crank handles, access panels, long stretches of network cables, and electrical wiring crisscrossing through the shadowy depths.

Blair had never seen anything like it. An entire labyrinthine universe existed just beneath the surface, and in a way it was more beautiful than the building's public architecture.

Sterling handed the power drill to the tall robber, who remained at the tunnel exit.

Alec was weaving his way through the pipes, calling over his shoulder to Sterling, "She can walk now. Start pulling your weight again, scumbag."

Blair saw that Alec had abandoned one of his bags of cash on the ground, and Sterling begrudgingly hoisted it onto his back, waving at Blair to follow.

She complied, casting a glance backward to see the tall robber sliding another mock-electrical panel into place over the tunnel outlet, bolting it on from the outside. The panel bore all the same precautions as the one connecting to the opposite end of the short tunnel—a conglomeration of yellow doomsday stickers proclaiming impassably high voltage beyond.

"Where are we?" she asked Sterling, now following Alec in a twisting path between the pipes.

"Between ground floor and the first parking sublevel. Try not to touch anything."

No sooner had he said this than her bare arm brushed a pipe, and she hissed with pain from scalding heat. A second later she banged her head on another pipe, ducking beneath it with a curse.

"I told you not to touch anything," Sterling reprimanded.

She heard a noise behind her, and looked back to see that the tall robber was following their trail far more gracefully than she was, despite his height, and with the drill in hand.

They passed over an enormous pipe rising to waist-height, straddling it one at a time to cross. Sterling lent Blair a gloved hand to assist, indicating that he didn't want her leaving fingerprints. Occasionally he stopped to shine his light at a puddle that Blair needed to step around, ensuring she didn't leave wet footprints either.

Alec stopped suddenly, reaching between the pipes to recover a large orange duffel bag. He threw it down beside a nondescript padlocked rectangular panel in the floor stamped *SEWER ACCESS*.

Then Alec opened the lock with a key as Sterling unzipped the duffel bag.

Blair winced as Alec slid the sewer cover off. As expected, she smelled the contents at once.

But the putrid stench that reached her eyes and nostrils didn't smell like sewage; instead, it reeked of sulfur.

Whatever the original purpose of the compartment, it had been repatriated into a giant tub filled halfway with clear liquid. The tall robber tossed his power drill into the tub as the men began stripping their masks and outer jackets, depositing them into the liquid. Every splash intensified the sulfurous odor in the unventilated space.

She could tell the tall robber was hesitant to remove his mask in front of her, doing so at great reluctance.

He had long hair worn in a bun, and distinctive cheekbones and a cleft chin. He'd be hard to miss in a lineup, she thought.

Alec, by contrast, didn't seem to care. He removed his mask at once, revealing Asian features on a round face, spiky black hair in a high fade.

Blair asked, "Is that sulfuric acid?"

"If you know a quicker method to denature DNA, we're all ears." Sterling handed her his black jacket and added, "Here. It's better than nothing."

She pulled on the jacket, watching the men strip a few objects off their belts—namely the holsters, guns, and handcuffs. The tasers stayed.

As Sterling removed his detachable holster, Blair held open her hand. "May I?"

He slapped the gun into her palm, and she removed the holster and tossed it into the acid. Holding the pistol with one hand, she dropped the magazine into the other and checked the load—as she suspected, it was filled with blank rounds.

Blair dropped the pistol into the tub.

The tall robber asked, "Anyone going to explain what Blair is doing here?"

Sterling cleared his throat. "Surely you've heard that she's a former federal agent."

"Yeah, I caught that part on the news. Hence my question."

"Well, she needed to get out of the situation I put her in. And yeah, I know—RTB."

"No," the Russian replied. "You're way beyond RTB at this point. A future generation of thieves is going to be telling themselves, 'Remember Sterling.'"

Blair could feel the tension rising between them. The tall robber was none too happy about her presence—why would he be? Still, she sensed that a far more uncensored conversation would transpire when they were alone.

She asked, "What's RTB?"

"Remember the Baron," Sterling said without elaborating.

Beneath their outer jackets, Sterling and Alec wore nondescript black uniform shirts with Department of Water & Power patches. The tall robber had EMT patches that he quickly switched with Velcro ones to match his teammates.

Then Sterling began handing the men items out of the cached duffel bag—an orange safety vest with reflective tape and a white hardhat with a circular logo between the words WATER and POWER.

Blair was surprised at how quickly their appearance reversed completely: with the loss of pistol and handcuffs, the tactical belts became tool belts. Notably, the men didn't remove their tasers, though with the addition of the orange vest and hardhat, the tasers were barely noticeable. To all appearances, they were now Los Angeles Department of Water & Power workers.

The last three items that Sterling removed from the bag caught Blair's attention. One was a blue crowbar-like device. The other two were large cylindrical grenades, their metal casing labeled *RIOT CONTROL: CS*. Blair recognized the letters CS at once: it was tear gas, an agent she'd had to endure once in her FBI training. To her, entering the CS chamber felt like entering a fog of mace, lighting her eyes, nose, and throat on fire. Seeing, smelling, or tasting anything but the choking gas became impossible, and recovering to full sensory power had taken her half an hour after leaving the chamber.

Sterling kept one CS grenade, tossing the other to Alec as the tall robber slid the metal cover over the tub and locked it. He retrieved the blue crowbar-like tool and stood.

And just like that, their metamorphosis was complete.

"Ah," Alec gasped with satisfaction as they donned their bags of cash, "that's better. Perfectly natural now—just your everyday group of three city maintenance workers with a centerfold model in a red dress."

They proceeded through the utility tunnel. There were doors and hatches everywhere, labeled as numbered mechanical rooms or simply by a cryptic alphanumeric code. Blair wondered which door the team would eventually exit through.

The answer, as she found out a minute later, was none of them.

Instead, they stopped at a manhole cover in the floor labeled STORMWATER. The tall robber slid the curved end of the blue tool underneath the lid, popping it up as Sterling and Alec helped shift it out of the way.

Then the tall robber lowered himself through the hole, taking the tool with him.

"Blair," Sterling said, "go on down." He and Alec both held their gas grenades, apparently planning to toss them before descending into the hole.

She sat at the edge of the manhole. "The SWAT team will have respirators, you know."

Sterling looked troubled, as if he hadn't thought of that. "What about their tracking dogs?"

"Oh." Blair nodded. "Never mind."

But Alec wouldn't let it go. "Because if the canines have respirators, then they'll find our path pretty quickly. So real quick, Blair, which is it? The dogs have respirators, or they don't?"

"You've made your point. Let's move on."

Sterling and Alec pulled the pins on their gas grenades, rolling them in opposite directions. The canisters gave a small *pop* and began hissing gas, and Blair lowered herself through the hole as the tall robber reached up from below to help her.

31

JIM

Jim walked out the front door of Geering Plaza, making way for two men and a woman from LAPD forensics.

He stepped into the street, running a hand over his drenched scalp. An FBI support agent ran up to him, taking the shotgun from Jim as he stripped off his jacket and vest. Then he handed the vest to the support agent, who wisely left Jim alone.

His shirt was soaked with sweat. Having worn a favorite tie for his press conference, he saw the silk was now distorted from being crushed under the armored plate.

Jim shrugged back into the navy FBI jacket, looking around the street, or, rather, what little street was visible at the moment—evacuees from the building were still being processed, and every first responder element from the county, city, and state level had packed the streets around the bank, eager to do their duty in the wake of this robbery-turned-hostage-situation.

Except, Jim thought, there wasn't a hostage situation. Not really. He'd seen his share of those during his time on SWAT. Armed robbers got caught, got desperate, and threatened civilian lives to try and get away. They were never successful—Blair should have known that.

And apparently, he corrected himself, she did.

Meanwhile, the hostage debriefs hadn't helped his cause. According to the agent he'd just spoken to on the ground floor, half the employees released from the bank emphasized the wise-cracking robber who released them with a speech akin to an airline stewardess's landing brief. Blair? She was a fellow hostage, by all accounts as courteous as could be. Jim's stomach churned at the thought of giving his next press conference.

Because here were the facts: a bank was robbed, sure. Hostages were taken, and most would be humorously relating their account on every primetime talk show within forty-eight hours—probably in exchange for a greater sum than they earned in any given month of their day job. Police response? FBI SWAT had assaulted from the street up *and* roof down, using ground and helicopter-infiltrated teams—and the robbers had let the two elements close in before rappelling between them. The thieves re-entered the building and vanished, while the FBI had run to the sound of the "guns"—in this case, Chinese knockoffs of gunfight squibs straight off a low-budget movie set.

Meanwhile, the building had turned into a complete disaster. FBI SWAT was bracing open the elevator doors with assistance from the fire department. LAPD officers had swarmed into the building, conducting deliberate floor-by-floor clearing operations that would take until nightfall. The wake of their clearance was quickly filled by forensic crews looking for any possible clue that would lead to the robbers' arrest.

He could see it now, and knew what was transpiring without even checking the news feed on his phone. Images of a daring daylight rappel by masked men—and Blair, of all people, looking like some kind of action hero starlet in her red dress—outwitting the forces of justice.

And the money? Gone. All of it, except the dye packs.

What had they needed to pull off the heist? He did a quick mental tally, and couldn't attribute more than a few grand worth of climbing gear, glass-cutting equipment, and weapons. They'd rappelled using existing rooftop anchor points intended as lanyard tie-downs for maintenance workers operating close to the edge. Anyone *could* have done the job—but the sheer brilliance of their plan, and the audacity with which they'd executed it, was unlike anything Jim had ever seen. Had he underestimated Blair?

Perhaps he had, and that would make it his second mistake of the day. Mission Command had been right—every elevator outlet had been barricaded by police at the outset of the heist, including the parking sub garages.

He'd been certain that a set of doors, probably in a sublevel, would be pried open and Blair's team would shoot it out with a police element.

But nothing had happened.

And after a few minutes, Jim knew in his core that the team was gone.

Vance's voice crackled in his earpiece. "*Elevator doors are open on all shafts. No sign of where they went. Blue Team is preparing to rappel to investigate further.*"

Jim gave a frustrated groan and transmitted, "You're looking for a tunnel. If they're good, they've built some kind of barricade to block your pursuit. If they're really good, that barricade will be something innocuous. But start looking below the ground floor, and do it quick."

"*Copy all.*"

Then he turned and looked toward the gaps of sky between Century City buildings. The helicopters were gone now, apparently in anticipation of the weather.

A drop of rain stung Jim's eye. He wiped it away, and then felt a half dozen more hit his face and hair.

He steadied himself with a long, exasperated breath.

"Sir." A woman jogged toward him, extending an umbrella. "Take this. It's about to open up."

Jim turned to see the buxom redhead from his task force.

He reached out and took the umbrella, his hand grazing hers. "Thank you, Peggy."

She smiled. "No problem, sir."

Then she swept past him, and Jim glanced sideways to watch her enter the bank building. Her figure looked particularly curvaceous today, and Jim wondered why he hadn't taken more notice before. Peggy was a real woman —all breasts and hips. Blair was too skinny. He could do better.

As the patter of rain danced across his umbrella, Jim trotted down the steps and onto the sidewalk. Then he strode toward the hostage containment area, where the mob of people was now up in arms over being held in the rain by the LAPD.

But that wasn't Jim's problem. There was only one person from that mob that he wanted to talk to, and Jim was going to find him.

32

BLAIR

Blair's boots splashed softly in shallow water as the tall robber led her down a circular drainage pipe. The air was thick with wet concrete, and the sound of their footsteps echoed around her. She could faintly hear the CS grenades spewing tear gas overhead, though the sound disappeared altogether as Sterling and Alec dropped into the pipe and replaced the manhole cover.

The standing water they were splashing through suddenly came alive, a barely detectable current causing it to flow forward.

"There's the rain," the tall robber said in his slight Russian accent.

"Yep," Alec agreed. "There it is."

They sounded solemn, almost forlorn at the prospect.

"What's wrong?" Blair asked.

Alec looked genuinely confused. "With what?"

"The rain."

"Ah, there's nothing wrong with the rain. Nothing at all."

"Then why do you sound worried?"

The tall robber answered impatiently, "There's a flash flood warning."

"So?"

"So if we get hit with more rainfall than the infrastructure can handle, we won't have to explain anything else. You'll see for yourself."

Blair didn't respond; instead, she continued shuffling forward. This couldn't be how they planned on outdistancing the police cordon.

It wasn't that they couldn't make forward progress; to the contrary, they ambled along at a decent rate. But the drainage pipe was so narrow that the tall robber had to hunch over, his waterproof bag of cash scraping the roof and sides of the tunnel, and she could hear Sterling's bag brushing the walls behind her.

But she followed without comment as the tall robber led the way, his headlight illuminating a bright streak of reflection against the inch or so of water running along the centerline.

This was all fun and games, for perhaps a block or two of walking. After that, the narrow space would become unbearable for all but the shortest members of their party—her and Alec.

She didn't have to wait that long.

After a few minutes, their path intersected a far wider drainage tunnel, so massive that even the tall robber could comfortably stand. But instead of continuing to chart their course, he stopped abruptly, his headlight illuminating two amorphous shapes before them.

Blair sidestepped to take in the pair of great stationary mounds covered in chest-high plastic tarp. Sterling and Alec stopped behind her, gasping simultaneously in relief.

"So," Blair asked, "what now?"

Alec walked to the second mound and grasped the plastic cover, looking back at Blair for dramatic effect. "Now," he proclaimed, whipping off the cover with a flourish, "we *ride!*"

Beneath the tarp was an all-terrain vehicle.

Blair looked at the ATV, tilting her head, and tried to sound impressed. "Oh. So, kind of like '86. The Hole in the Ground Gang."

Alec stammered, "Not like the—they couldn't—we *rappelled*, man."

"And let's talk about that," Sterling said, uncovering the lead ATV. "Why does the FBI have such stupid names for criminals? 'The Hole in the Ground Gang.' 'The High Incident Bandits.' Why is the FBI still calling people bandits at all? Or gangs?"

"It's disrespectful," the tall robber agreed, pushing Alec aside to mount the second ATV.

Alec straddled the seat behind him, grasping the tall robber's midsection and briefly laying his head against the man's bag of cash with a dreamy sigh. The tall robber threw a halfhearted elbow jab backward to knock him away, then fired the engine.

Sterling mounted the lead ATV and started it, headlight blazing to reveal an endless stretch of drainage pipe. He turned his gaze back to Blair.

"Well," he called over the engine noise, "you coming, or what?"

Blair gave a disapproving grunt, then approached and swung her legs onto the ATV seat behind him.

Leaning forward, she called to Sterling, "How much of this soiree am I supposed to spend hanging onto you while—"

Her last word was cut off as Sterling accelerated the ATV forward, launching from zero to near-highway speed in the time it took Blair to clench the bag of cash on his back.

The headlight from the trail ATV cast a halo of light on the tunnel around her as it followed suit, and they were off.

33

JIM

The rain was striking harder against Jim's umbrella now, his footsteps cresting pavement greased with a slick of water.

He reached a young patrol officer guarding the entrance to the hostage containment area, now an impromptu set of traffic barricades corralling hundreds of building employees wailing in collective agony at being forced to stand outside in the rain. Officers guarding the periphery were shouting threats, the primary one being a charge of accessory to armed robbery for anyone who dared step outside the line.

"How can I help you, sir?" the patrol officer in regulation raingear asked courteously.

As Jim opened his mouth to reply, his radio earpiece crackled to life.

"All stations, all stations..."

Vance's Alabama accent was unmistakable.

"Excuse me." Jim dismissed the officer with a raised index finger, half turning to listen to the remainder of the transmission.

"Blue Team found a possible tunnel entrance between ground floor and the first parking sublevel."

"Then what's the problem?" Jim transmitted. He pressed a finger into his earpiece, trying to listen above the pelting rain.

"It's labeled as an electrical access point. Risk of electrocution, all that jazz."

"So?"

"*So one of our guys used to work in his dad's industrial electric service. He says the safety placards are correct, but there's no reason for that panel to exist where...well, where it does.*"

"Are we honestly having this conversation?"

"*He's giving his dad a call now, asking if—*"

"Here's what he can ask," Jim seethed. "Ask if the risk is greater if he opens that panel, which is a guaranteed tunnel access point, or if"—he heaved a breath, trying to stop himself and deciding to proceed anyway—"I come down there and smash that panel open with his face." Jim ended his transmission, and then re-keyed to add, "That's what he's allowed to ask, Vance. What are your questions?"

"*No questions,*" Vance answered. "*Copy all.*"

Jim turned to face the young officer and opened his mouth to speak, then

whirled away again to transmit, "Whatever you find down there, it's going to be a labyrinth. That's why Blair chose it, and you can bet the bank on that." He cleared his throat. "No pun intended. Put in the call for canine support, or you'll be searching for days."

"*Copy, calling for dogs.*"

Jim paused for a moment, considering whether to transmit again. He decided not to, but his thoughts were clear enough.

Vance, you dumb ox, if you'd had the wherewithal to go back down the stairs when I told you to, we'd have had them dead to rights. Now we're chasing ghosts, hoping they surface into a trap that now has to cover half the city, whether you realize it yet or not.

But deep inside, Jim knew the truth.

His ultimate frustration lay with himself. Jim was pissed that he hadn't *cleared that corner* in front of the elevators, despite the movement he'd heard. Instead he'd chosen to wait for SWAT backup, mitigating his entire advantage while the crew escaped. He was more than capable, his individual reflexes rock-solid despite the longstanding lack of practice in a team environment.

How much had he missed his chance by? Five seconds?

Even less?

He should have cleared that corner alone. If any cause was worth his life, it was silencing Blair forever.

Now she'd made it out, and the chances of her being captured alive were rising with every second that Vance didn't kill her first. And if she was arrested this time, nothing in the world would stop her from spilling everything she knew about Jim.

Except for one thing.

Jim pulled a cheap throwaway cell phone from his pocket. He hadn't even bothered pulling the laminate off the screen. What was the point? He replaced this thing on a weekly basis.

He entered a four-digit pin to unlock the phone, then keyed in a phone number from memory—there were no contacts—and typed a three-word text message.

need the Jester

His thumb hovered over the button to send the text. Did he really want to do this? There would be consequences, potentially grave ones. To himself, to his career, and potentially, in the worst-case scenario, to the person on the other end of the message.

But Jim had to do this. If Blair got arrested and started talking before he could get to her, he was done for. She simply knew too much; he'd been too reckless during their affair.

He pressed the button to send the text, and the words *need the Jester* disappeared.

Then Jim dialed a six-button sequence into the phone, the action reflexive from repetition. After all, he'd done this after every text or call from his rotation of burner phones. At this point he could do it without looking, though he watched closely to make sure he didn't make a mistake. The person he carried the phone to contact wouldn't tolerate any of them.

Finally, the screen displayed a message. *You are about to clear all memory. Are you sure?*

Jim pressed a button, and the phone's usage history vanished.

Pocketing the phone, Jim spun to face the officer standing at the entrance to the evacuee processing area. Then he spoke from the coverage of his umbrella, briefly feeling bad for the patrol cop in regulation raingear that looked like it wasn't doing much to keep the rain out.

"Ground zero," Jim said, flipping his identification open. There was something reassuringly familiar in the weight of his FBI badge being exposed to view. "Every infection has one. And in this case"—he pocketed the identification, sufficiently satisfied with the officer's look of recognition—"it's the bank manager, Gordon Schmidt. I want to talk to him. Now."

"Let me call my captain," the cop said, taking a step back and keying his radio.

Jim heard a few hushed words after that—the LAPD officer murmuring the phrases, "that FBI agent from the press conference," "requesting access," and "sounds urgent."

He waited, trying to appear patient but feeling anything but under the circumstances. These people were burning time.

"Right this way," the patrol officer finally said. "An escort will be here shortly to take you to Mr. Schmidt."

And with that, he moved the barricade across wet pavement for Jim to enter.

34

STERLING

Sterling throttled the ATV as fast as he could, but it progressively felt like driving across quicksand.

What had started as a roaring jaunt at 40mph down the main storm sewer had slowed incrementally with the rising water level that seemed to engulf more of Sterling's ATV wheels by the second. He'd installed snorkel kits on both ATVs, which would buy them some time before the engines flooded. How much time, he wasn't certain. They had already covered almost three miles toward their destination, with only one more to go. But now, progress was becoming impossible. With an extremely limited number of exit points before then, their situation was growing direr by the second.

Clinging to the moneybag slung to his back, Blair asked, "What's going on up there, a tsunami?"

Sterling shouted back, "We're in the main pipe—it's fed from more side pipes than I care to consider at present. Whatever rain lands up there"—he nodded skyward—"it's going to be funneled into us at maximum force."

"So what happens if there's a flash flood?"

"If there's a flash flood, then we panic."

For once, he hoped for a smart quip from Blair. But none came. She realized the gravity of their situation, he knew. How could she not? It didn't take a meteorologist to see they were in trouble. The tunnel was wide enough to drive in—but that convenience would come at a cost if they couldn't outrun the storm. They could drown in this tunnel, their bodies washed downstream along with bags of cash from the heist.

The trail ATV fell back, the glare from its headlight now barely distinguishable in his periphery. Marco and Alec were tired of getting sprayed with water.

He knew what they were thinking—that he should've canceled the op when the weather report came in. Alec had flat-out told him he would have, while Marco's admonition the previous night had cut far deeper. Sterling's track record certainly wasn't flawless, but no one could point out that nuance quite like Marco.

Of course you're not a loose cannon, Sterling. You're something worse: a lion. You get hungrier the closer you get to a steak, and every minute you don't abort this thing reduces the chances that you will, regardless of how the situation develops. Coupled to that is the fact that you feed off risk like a leech off blood, and one of these days, it's going to burn you.

At this moment, they were surely recalling their words of warning, just as Sterling was. Committing heists was a rare vocation where participating in the first place was a freedom-or-jail, life-or-death risk. And like most vocations falling under that category, a level of grim respect was reserved for cold, analytical risk analysis. No one judged the guy who decisively made his call based on the data and stuck to it.

For Sterling, though, it wasn't just about data—or emotion, for that matter. His persistence wasn't greed; it was grit. Anyone could find a hundred reasons to back down off an op. Sterling's strength was in finding the one way to succeed. Marco was far smarter than him, and Alec far stronger. But Sterling had a chip on his shoulder, one that wouldn't let him quit.

Or fail.

Leading a crew into the arena was a big deal. It didn't help that this one was so difficult. Sure, most of their jobs were technically more complex than this. But the involvement of two outside parties—Gordon and Blair—introduced an infinite number of variables. Blair had very nearly single-handedly derailed the entire operation. Now Mother Nature was casting her vote on the outcome of the op. They'd scarcely had a problem yet with law enforcement, who had more or less performed according to expectations. Police succeeded by having protocol. Thieves succeeded by having none—at least, none that the outside world could decipher until after the job was done.

Sterling felt an uncharacteristic attack of doubt. He reminded himself that the risk had been worth it, that this operation would be a strategic success provided they got away—and that no one suspected their true intentions, at least for a few days. It would happen eventually, but the idea was to delay it long enough to be wildly profitable for everyone involved.

Sterling watched the foggy periphery of his headlamp: more and more water flowed out of the side pipes as they careened forward. The collective rivulets swept into the water at the center of the pipe, causing the trail of water they moved along to expand up the tunnel sides.

He looked down with irritation—the water level in the main pipe was now up to his ankles, the ATV wheels churning a frothy, splashing wake around them.

Then he felt an abrupt and tectonic increase in the subterranean air pressure.

The barometric shift caused the hair on the back of his neck to stand up in some primal instinct, and he suddenly felt an almost crippling sense of claustrophobia.

Then he heard it. The ATV engines were loud, but they couldn't completely shield a perceptible noise coming from the pipe ahead. It was a low, growling whistle that rose at a steady rate.

A moment later, Sterling saw the source of the noise and called out to Blair, "Here it comes."

Ahead of him, a frothy current spewed from the black abyss of the main pipe—the combined rainfall from countless city blocks funneled into a single wave that snowballed in size and momentum as it proceeded downstream.

He braced against the wave as it struck, splashing instantly to knee-height in a gushing flow that he struggled to drive upstream against. Something cracked against his shin—he looked to see a thin metal pipe spinning downstream.

Sterling swung his view forward, fighting against the water level that continued to rapidly rise. It wasn't freezing, and that was something—but the prolonged saturation would soon take its toll. Especially on Blair, who was riding in a dress and suede ankle boots that would become water-logged and double in weight if they hadn't already. The jacket Sterling gave her would do little to combat the chill.

"You okay?" he asked.

"Don't worry about me. I've been through worse."

An army of debris raced along the water's surface, everything that would fit through the city's drainage grates and a few things that wouldn't: empty cigarette packs, fast food wrappers, the lid to a trash can. A beer bottle bounced off the front of his ATV. The water level wouldn't stop rising, and he glanced back to see that the other ATV was trailing far behind as progress became more difficult.

The water was now up to his thighs, cresting the ATV's hood as he drove it to destruction. Without the snorkel kits, the ATV engines would have flooded by now. They were moving at a crawl, slower than they'd be able to walk on the surface. Almost slower, he thought, than they'd be able to walk down here in the water.

Facing front, his light reflected off the matte surface of something ominous whipping over the water.

"Rock!"

He tried to block the object, which turned out to be a dinner-plate-sized slab of concrete. But it struck his right knee as it passed, causing him to gasp with a sharp, stabbing spike of pain.

The slab narrowly missed Blair's leg. Sterling could feel her clutching the waterproof bag of cash on his back, and knew that if she wasn't visibly shivering yet, she would be soon. Better that he couldn't see her, he thought.

What had he done to this woman?

Sterling could see his next checkpoint on the right. On their planning maps it was labeled "Vault No. 341," though that term sounded more prestigious than the space appearing before him.

It was little more than the small cutout of a utility room set into the pipe above the current water line. Above it, a circular tube with rusty ladder handholds stretched upward to a distant manhole cover. The assemblage was designed for maintenance workers to climb down to the main storm sewer as needed.

But Sterling needed it for the opposite purpose: to ascend to street level, because they couldn't feasibly proceed on subterranean ATVs. By now they'd long outdistanced the police cordon but hadn't yet reached the next leg of their getaway route.

He was going to have to improvise.

Bringing the ATV to a halt beside the utility room cutout, he called to Blair behind him.

"Go on up!"

He felt her release the bag on his back and then climb the handholds into the side of the pipe as the trail ATV came to a stop behind him. The next access point upward wasn't for another half mile, and they weren't going to make it that far.

Sterling killed his engine. As Marco did the same, the tunnel went dark save the glow of their personal headlights.

The three men clambered up the handholds, out of the water, and into the small utility room where Blair already stood. Then they unslung their bags of cash and aligned them neatly on the ground, straps facing up.

Sterling couldn't handle the sight of Blair—hair drenched, soaked from head to toe in his black jacket.

But her face wasn't desperate; if anything, her expression was one of fortitude.

"Well," she called to them, starting to shiver, "this is going pretty well so far."

Sterling felt Alec's and Marco's eyes turn to him, and he gave his command.

"We can't proceed and we can't wait out the storm. You three stay here. I'm going up."

"I wouldn't do that," Blair said. "You can bet that Jim has figured out this little tunnel trick and has units canvassing every manhole cover from here to Koreatown."

"I don't have a choice."

Marco asked, "Sure you don't want one of us to go with you?"

"They're looking for three men. I'll draw less suspicion alone."

Marco opened a pouch on his belt and handed him the Pegasus.

"Range is a thousand feet. Should be sufficient for most of Station D, and the entire Yard. Remember, if it doesn't work, they're using an RFID case or a Faraday of some kind—"

"Yeah, yeah. I got it. If I'm not back in half an hour, it means I'm in a squad car. You and Blair can flip a coin to see who's in charge, so long as it's not Alec."

"I should at least be picked before Blair," Alec protested. "She's been here for like five minutes." Then he looked to her and mumbled, "No offense."

"None taken." She looked confused, wondering about the small black box that Marco had just handed over.

Sterling reached for the ladder handholds set in the wall, then ascended a circular tube ending in a manhole cover.

Once he reached the top, he braced his feet against a ladder rung and pressed his back against the manhole cover. He waited a beat to see if any traffic vibrated against his back and, feeling none, took the chance and heaved upward.

This was always a variable prospect—sometimes he could unseat a manhole cover from below using his hands, sometimes with his back, and sometimes they were so insanely heavy that several people had to move them. In this case he used his back from the start, hedging his bets and finding it paid off as the cover began to move. It shifted up and away from its seating, and he used his arms to assist it to the side as a torrent of rain fell onto his hardhat.

Sterling knew that a street was directly above Vault No. 341, and after sliding the cover off he ducked back down, half-expecting a car tire to wheel into the gap. But he was met with only the downpour from the storm, and squinted upward to see rain falling from a dark rolling mass of storm clouds between buildings.

Hazarding a glance above the manhole cover, he saw a road stretching either direction. Cars were halted at a stoplight ten yards distant—no police vehicles in sight. Sterling clambered out of the hole and stood in the street.

Then he stood officially, pointing at the cars like a traffic cop and directing them around the manhole cover.

There were precious few times to feel a sense of gratitude for The Average LA Driver, Sterling knew, and this was one of them. When the light turned green, the cars whipped around him in an inconvenienced rush, making no effort to avoid spraying him with groundwater. So much the better, he thought. No rubbernecking, and very few sideways glances at the maintenance worker in vest and hardhat. Once the wave of cars had passed, he knelt and slid the manhole cover back into place.

Then Sterling rose, darted onto the sidewalk, and began moving to his destination.

35

JIM

The LAPD escort led Jim through sheets of rain and into the building adjacent to Geering Plaza. Jim lowered his umbrella, shaking it off and following the escort. The hallway was filled with cops guarding the bank employees, who'd been brought into hastily cleared office spaces for questioning and to provide details about the bank layout to aid the SWAT assault.

Normally, anyone employed by a robbed bank was scrutinized for complicity in an inside job. That type of thing was more common than most people thought, though the police would frame their questioning to indicate no suspicion whatsoever. Putting a subject at ease was usually the first step in getting them to slip up.

But in this case, they had something very different altogether. The bank manager, Gordon Schmidt, had spontaneously confessed to inside involvement, though he claimed it was under duress. All the other witnesses had independently corroborated his story, and what's more, Jim had been assured that Gordon's immense family wealth gave him no motive whatsoever to rob his own bank.

It was that last fact that Jim seized on, mentally filing it for presentation if Gordon should choose to resist his questioning. Blair and her crew's escape indicated a high degree of advance planning, and Jim sensed that she'd chosen the Mayfield National Bank largely because of Gordon himself.

The escort led Jim to a closed office door, and Jim thanked him. He set down his umbrella outside the door, and then reached for the knob before Vance's voice crackled over his earpiece.

"*Update follows, how copy?*"

Jim turned away from the door and transmitted, "Send it."

"*Blue Team has breached the electrical panel in the elevator shaft—it's connected to a twenty-foot tunnel. Looks like it was dug in the last week or so. And the suspects used hydraulic descenders to come down the elevator cables—we recovered three sets.*"

"Where does the tunnel lead?"

"*Utility corridor.*"

Jim began nodding. He knew it, and now they just had to press the advantage while they could.

"*We got a guy from Public Works here, he says these utility tunnels go all over the city. There are access points to sewer, wastewater, regular water, electrical—and this isn't the only place where they share a walled boundary with an underground parking garage. Or a machine room. In some places, the utility access expands to three or four sublevels—so if these people did any more creative tunneling ahead of time, they could be anywhere right now.*"

"Fine," Jim replied. "The dogs will be able to sort the trail."

"*No dice on the dogs. The suspects popped tear gas, and a lot of it. It hit our guys as soon as we breached the far end of the tunnel. There's no ventilation down there, so it's gonna be about twenty years before a dog will be able to pick up a trail in that tunnel. We're having some respirators brought down, but it's going to be a physical search to find out where they went.*"

Jim grimaced, but he spoke in a measured tone. "Here's what I want you to do. Get a map of storm water outlets from Public Works, and request LAPD to canvass them for movement. Tell them to pull in any Sheriff support they can get from County, and be on the lookout for people trying to emerge. With this rain, our suspects are either in a tunnel and drowning like rats, or they're waiting out the storm in some hole before they move topside. If they go up, I want the first thing they see to be a police cruiser. If they stay down, I want the last thing they see to be your team. Got it?"

"*Copy all. Will comply.*"

Jim turned back to the door, collecting his thoughts before entering.

The map of this heist continued to unfold, and every turn brought with it an increasing layer of complexity. Their rappel and building re-entry was one thing; now hydraulic descenders were in play, along with a tunnel dug in advance. Blair must have linked up with an established crew and provided her knowledge of law enforcement. The CS gas was just another step in foiling the SWAT pursuit, and a good one at that.

All of these factors reinforced Jim's assumption that Gordon hadn't been selected at random. If anything, the heist was designed around him as a central weak point to exploit. Jim thought he knew why, but he wouldn't play that card unless he had to.

Taking a breath, Jim turned the door handle and entered the office.

Gordon was seated at the table, head nestled in his arms as if he were asleep. Jim observed him as he eased the door shut. Innocent people tended to remain active when alone in interrogation rooms, usually pacing or examining their surroundings with a fleeting sense of interest.

The guilty ones, by contrast, almost universally put their heads down.

Jim flashed his credentials to Gordon. "Jim Jacobson, FBI. Assistant Special Agent in Charge. I'd like to have a word with you."

Gordon took a moment to sit up, and Jim caught his first impression of the heavyset man. He was freshly shaven, but that was about the extent of his concessions to external composure. His suit looked so disheveled—tie askew, collar undone, one lapel flipped under the jacket without him noticing—that Jim wondered how professional his appearance could have been under the best of circumstances.

Perhaps most peculiarly, Gordon's deep-set eyes didn't focus on Jim.

Instead, he looked to the window with a haunted expression.

"You ever seen rain like that in LA?"

Jim looked out the window where sheets of rain were battering the masses of people standing outside. The crowd, still corralled for police processing, looked like they were on the brink of a riot. Police officers had donned ponchos and were beginning to shuttle people into an adjacent building lobby to get them out of the weather.

"It's been a while," Jim agreed, putting his identification away. He briefly wondered if this man was in shock or socially awkward...or both.

"Mind if I sit down?"

"I've already answered every question under the sun. There's nothing else for me to explain about our alarms or security protocol. Everything I did, I did to protect my employees. None of my actions violated my bank's protocol for a robbery."

"No one's questioning that, Mr. Schmidt. You're the victim of a tragic situation, and I don't need to know the specifics of your bank. I'm here to ask about Blair Morgan."

He recoiled at the mention of her name, looking at Jim for the first time since he'd entered. "Blair? Why?"

Jim pulled out a chair and sat across from Gordon.

"I have reason to believe she's the mastermind behind this heist."

Gordon scoffed. "I don't think so. She was a hostage, same as me."

"I assure you, Mr. Schmidt, that she was no more a victim than the three other monsters that broke into your home last night. Let's take it from the top. How did you meet her?"

"I went to a bar. She was there when I came in."

"Who initiated contact?"

"I did."

"And then?"

Gordon shrugged. "Just small talk. She seemed...interested. We went to my place from there."

Jim had to suppress a smile. This poor man thought himself appealing to a woman like Blair. "Mr. Schmidt, how was the security at your house disabled?"

"I turned off the system from my phone."

"From the driveway?"

"Before we pulled in. I didn't want the...the camera on. When we pulled in."

"And then were you ambushed by the three men?"

"Not at first. We went to my living room with drinks."

"And then they took you hostage."

"Me and Blair, yes."

Jim gave a soft laugh. "And aside from Blair's acting skills, what makes you think she was a hostage?"

Gordon looked perplexed. "What do you mean? She was terrified. She tried to escape."

"How?"

"They put her in a bedroom, and she got out somehow. Two of the men ran her down—I don't know how far she got. I was afraid to ask. But I could hear her yelling at them outside. Then they were gone for a long time, and when they came back they were all exhausted. They'd been running down-hill through the trees behind my house."

Jim sat back in his chair, considering Gordon's account of last night. Blair must have had some motivation behind the act. How much convincing did she think Gordon needed to believe her a genuine hostage?

"Mr. Schmidt, I think you're hiding something from me. You don't have to protect Blair. She can't hurt you anymore."

"Hurt me? What about those three dickheads in ski masks—why are you worried about the girl?"

"I know you have information about her complicity. And it's in your best interests to tell me before anyone gets hurt. These people are still on the run."

Gordon waved a dismissive hand. "Get out of here. You don't know what you're talking about. Go ask my lawyer if you need any more—"

Jim slammed a fist on the table. "You don't want to hold out on me. Because if these people leveraged you without violence, I'll bet there's something else they could hang over your head. And with a little selective investigation, I could uncover it."

Gordon's face turned ashen. Jim had hit the pressure point, and he'd continue pressing just as long as he needed.

"Now I don't care about your sideline ventures. Given your position and your family, I can hazard an educated guess on where to look. So don't give me a reason to."

Gordon jammed his hands into his armpits. "What do you want?"

"The truth."

"I'm telling you the truth. You want me to lie and say the girl hand-cuffed me instead of the robbers? Type up the sworn statement, and I'll sign it. Provided, of course, that my attorney approves. I'll repeat whatever version of events you want, as long as you stay out of my life. You want me to lie, and I'll lie. But man to man, the truth is that girl was just as surprised as I was when those robbers came through the door."

Jim tried to speak with empathy and patience, though he felt neither.

"Mr. Schmidt, I don't doubt that Blair Morgan conducted an elaborate act to allay your suspicions. But do you honestly believe that her intentions were to go home with you for the purposes of sex?"

"Well, what was I supposed to think? She offered to come back to my place. Can you blame me? I mean, have you seen the body on that little piece of—"

Jim leapt up and grabbed Gordon by the suit jacket, partially hoisting him up over the tabletop.

"What's that supposed to mean?" Jim shouted.

Gordon's face twisted into a reddening knot of fear as he stammered, "I mean... please don't... oh, God." He began to sob uncontrollably.

And with Gordon's fearful submission, Jim began to accept the reality of his situation. He was so emotionally tied to Blair that the sideways mention of her name caused him to lash out on a traumatized hostage, a man already in shock and now more so.

Jim released Gordon, who sank back into his chair. He was crying harder now, a pitiful display of cowardice. Even if Jim dared to stick around, he wasn't going to get any further information from this man.

"I apologize," Jim said flatly, straightening his tie. "I wasn't myself."

He turned to leave, making a move for the door.

"Wait," Gordon called after him.

Jim turned to see the man composing himself remarkably fast. He was staring at Jim, sniffling back tears.

Gordon said in a shaky voice, "What do you want my story to be? I mean, do you want me to say Blair was one of the robbers or not?"

Jim watched Gordon for a moment, searching for signs of deception and finding none. He spun and opened the door, stepping outside and closing it quietly behind him.

The nearest LAPD officers were watching him curiously—they must have heard Jim's outburst.

He took three steps away, then reversed course to snatch his umbrella from its resting place beside the door. Walking to the front door to distance himself from the attending officers, he pulled out his phone and paused. The first vestiges of doubt were entering his psyche. He still couldn't believe that Blair hadn't been a party to this entire robbery—though he could no longer decide whether that was due to the facts he knew to be true, or denial since he'd already hosted a press conference where he adamantly declared the contrary.

He pulled the burner phone from his pocket, seeing that he had yet to receive a response to his request for the Jester. Readying his umbrella, Jim pushed open the door and stepped into the torrential rainfall. When he reached his SUV, he quickly collapsed his umbrella and ducked out of the rain. Once inside, Jim checked his burner phone again. Still nothing.

He started driving anyway—when the response came, he'd have to move fast. If Blair was captured before then, it'd be too late. Jim's secrets would be out. His only choice was to reason with Blair first, and that required his mentor's help.

As he left Century City and drove south toward Manhattan Beach, he thought about the Blair Morgan he'd met when she got assigned to his task force—the bright-eyed woman with such professional bearing that he expected to find military service in her jacket. Where was she now?

He'd been so physically taken with Blair that he had to have her. A man with many loyal years of marriage, he'd nonetheless initiated his first affair. But it wasn't the affair that was burning inside him now. It was everything he'd told Blair in the course of their time together. He'd needed her to lie on her surveillance report, and couldn't convince her to do so without explaining the way of the world—the cases he'd closed using similar methods, the sacrifices and risks required in the world of criminal justice investigations. Jim had built a solid career out of employing methods that transcended conventional morality, and Blair could have, too.

Or at least, she should have. There had never been cause to suspect Jim of falsifying a report. Why should it have been any different for her? There had never been a hidden surveillance camera covering a blind spot in official coverage, no legal team swooping in with cutting-edge LIDAR data to contest a federal official's version of events.

None of that mattered now. Because Blair had refused to turn herself in, and she surely knew by now that Jim had done everything in his power to kill her. Now that she was likely to be captured alive, he had no choice but to set things in motion to incentivize her voluntary silence.

Suddenly his burner phone chimed with an incoming text. Jim fumbled for it, checking the screen as he drove.

. . .

Will call soon. Be ready.

Smiling, Jim accelerated and swerved around a car to his front, heading south through the rain on his way toward the Jester.

36

BLAIR

Blair huddled in the small utility room with the two robbers, waiting for Sterling to return from parts unknown.

She looked down after he left, seeing the water level in the huge pipe beside them continue to rise as it churned past. If it got much higher, the water would begin seeping into their maintenance cutout.

The two men removed their hardhats. For the second time, Blair got to clearly observe their faces, which couldn't have been more different. Alec was—well, Alec. Short, strong, with a round Asian face full of childlike enthusiasm and mischievous eyes. But the tall robber was solemn, lean with long hair. His gray eyes watched Blair coldly.

She asked him, "What did you hand Sterling before he left?"

"What do you think?"

"Based on your comments about RFID, Faraday, and range, I'm guessing that it was a device for a relay hack. Probably custom, because if it truly has a range of a thousand feet, it's something that you can't buy off a shelf. Or pay a tech firm to build, because it's illegal as can be. You'd have to design and build it, which is no small feat."

The man suppressed a small grin of tacit approval, and Blair seized on the opportunity.

"So," she said casually, "I've already met Sterling and Alec. What's your name?"

Alec tousled his hair. "You're not very good with icebreakers, Blair."

The tall robber nodded. "He's right."

"Be that as it may—"

"It may."

"—there's no reason we shouldn't meet."

"There are a hundred reasons. Maybe more. And whatever discussion went into your convincing Sterling to bring you along, I wasn't privy to it. But whatever the logic, I can assure you that Sterling means well but is not acting in the best interests of this operation."

"You don't trust me?"

"I didn't say that." The tall robber's lanky posture suddenly grew rigid. "But while we're on the subject, no, I don't."

"I've practically incriminated myself with you every step of the way. What exactly are you afraid of?"

"Everything you've done could potentially be leveraged to get you in your former colleagues' good graces. Whether that has been your intent all along is beside the point."

Blair's mouth went dry. "If you think the FBI would speak to me before this heist, much less after, or much *less* welcome me back with open arms, then you're deluding yourself."

He lowered his head in response, as if to study her. "There's surely a way you could play this to your advantage if we are captured. And while I imagine the thought of how to do so has crossed your mind already, I selfishly hope you don't have the chance to find out how you'd react in that event."

"There's no way that—" She caught herself. There *was* a way, she thought, and Jim was probably scrambling right now to make it feasible. "I will never go back."

Alec cut in, addressing his partner. "We had to bring her. Blair was betrayed by a scoundrel. Convicted for following her boss's orders, and he would've killed her if we left her behind. Plus, she was swept off her feet by my debonair persona and overpowering pheromones."

The tall robber asked her, "I've got to question your sanity if you immediately trusted three bank robbers who kidnapped you the night before."

"I don't trust three bank robbers. But I *do* believe in the abilities of the

186

crew that I believe has pulled off a majority of the successful California heists in the past few years."

"Then go find them."

"I believe I have. There was one image of a thief captured in the Shea Jewelry Emporium heist, and he was wearing Sterling's vintage watch."

The tall robber's response was immediate. "Sterling got that watch last week, at a pawn shop at the corner of Pico and La Cienega Boulevard. I was there."

Blair rolled her eyes. "That's the location of the *second* bank that the Hole in the Ground Gang robbed in the '80s. After their first heist at Spaulding Avenue, namesake of the alias where they bought their ATVs."

"Well," he murmured, "there's a pawn shop there now."

"Sure there is. You're forgetting I spent a year on the task force."

"That doesn't mean you understand anything about heist crews."

"No? You already know what I did for the FBI. I've been on dozens of covert entries, defeated all kinds of security to install surveillance devices. You can't tell me there's no overlap with what you people do."

"You people?" Alec said. "Is that, like, a racial dig because I'm Asian, or—"

The tall robber interjected, "Your TacOps experience is impressive. But let me ask you a question. When you did a break-in to install a surveillance device, how many people were involved?"

"Depended on the job. Could be a few dozen, could be a hundred. Scouts, lookouts, agents tailing the keyholder, agents providing diversion, local PD support—"

"Exactly." He cocked his head at her, then shook it. "There may be some overlap in technical skills, sure. But don't think for one second that you've been on a heist before today. What you did with TacOps was legally sanctioned by court orders. There are no consequences if you get caught."

Blair felt her eyes prickling with tears as she shot back, "Oh, so I don't understand consequences? Not to take away from your many successes, all of which I'm sure were hard-earned, but I've *been* to prison. I know what awaits when you get caught committing a crime, and I know what it means to be in solitary confinement. What it's like to lose your humanity, to go insane in a cell. Can you say that?" She looked to Alec. "Or you?"

Neither man spoke.

"That's what I thought. Now you can lecture me on a lot of things, but not understanding the risk and not being prepared to face consequences aren't on that list."

Blair stopped speaking, suddenly cognizant that she'd overstepped her bounds. She was trying to earn their respect, and instead she'd come off as a self-entitled brat. Worse still, she began shivering even harder from the dampness.

The tall robber took a step toward her.

Then he extended his hand.

"Marco."

"Blair." She took his hand and gave it a shake.

But his eyes still held a calculated resentment—whether toward her or the situation, she couldn't tell.

She said, "You're still pissed that I'm here."

Marco shrugged. "It's not your fault."

"Then whose is it?"

"Sterling's."

"I asked him to bring me along."

Alec cut in, "Circus chimps ask for machetes all the time. Doesn't mean you should give one to them."

Blair raised a quizzical eyebrow, and Marco spoke.

"What my friend here is trying to say is that your heart is in the right place. So is Sterling's. But his decision to take you out of Geering Plaza is going to get one or more of us pinched."

"Pinched?"

"Arrested."

"When?"

Alec set his hand on her shoulder and gave her a light shake. "In a few minutes, Blair. Probably three."

Marco shook his head, trying to explain. "A heist is a fickle thing, Blair. It's like an engine, or maybe the inside of a—"

Alec said, "A watch."

"Yeah." He nodded. "Exactly. Nothing about a heist exists in a vacuum. Every aspect from your equipment to the environment is an intercon-nected, three-dimensional system, and a complicated one at that. A lot of factors, a lot of risk and research and planning. Now you take that already volatile system and toss in a wrench—"

"Or an exotic, lithe woman with smoky, smoky eyes."

"—you're going to have problems. And we didn't think through bringing you along."

Blair felt her stomach fluttering. "So?"

"So now we're playing against the law of averages. When one thing goes wrong, or isn't taken into account, it doesn't exist in isolation. It ignites a chain reaction, and often a disastrous one."

"RTB," Alec agreed.

Blair asked, "What does that mean?"

Alec said, "We already told you. 'Remember the Baron.'"

"I recall. So who is the Baron?"

Marco answered. "Herman Lamm, also known as the Baron. Ever heard of him?"

"No."

He grinned. "All this expertise of heists and you've never heard of the Baron?"

"I said no already."

"In the '20s and '30s he was the king of bank robbery. He pioneered casing a bank, planning getaway routes, rehearsing the job, you name it. The Baron did more meticulous planning than anyone ever had before— more than 99.9% of criminals have done ever since."

"Okay," Blair allowed. "So you say RTB as a reminder to stick to your plan?"

Alec said, "We don't need any reminders about that."

"Then...what?"

Marco replied, "We don't say RTB as a reminder to stick to the plan; we say it as a reminder of what can go wrong even when you do. To be careful and not overstep your bounds, because no matter how well you plan, the universe will fight you every step of the way."

"What does that have to do with the Baron?"

"His last bank robbery was in 1930. He and his crew had just made it to the getaway car when a shotgun-toting vigilante appeared. Their getaway driver panicked and flipped a U-turn, popping a tire on the curb. Car door flies open, and their spare gas can falls out. With me so far?"

"Sure."

"They gain enough distance to do a tire change, and the rolling gunfight begins. Then their spare goes flat. So they steal a car—turns out it has a speed governor, so it can't go over thirty-five. They steal a truck—but there's not enough water in the radiator, so they steal a fourth vehicle. That one is almost out of gas. They pull over at a farmhouse to get a fifth vehicle, but someone had just left for an errand with the family car."

Alec said, "Then they're cornered by a lynch mob of cops and vigilantes. The Baron fled into a cornfield, there was a big shootout, and he died."

"Who shot him?" Blair asked.

"You tell me. Could have been one of his crew, could have been a cop or vigilante, or it could have been suicide. Forensic procedures were somewhat lacking in 1930."

Marco continued, "The point is, the best planning and rehearsal can fail under a cascade of absurd chance. So RTB means pulling off a heist in the first place is pushing your luck. So don't make it any worse with stupid decisions. But pushing our luck—with the storm, much less bringing you along—is all we've been doing today."

Then Marco lowered his head, considering his words before adding a final thought on the matter.

"And one way or another, we're about to pay dearly for that."

37

STERLING

Sterling continued walking through sheets of rain, orienting himself at the nearest intersection with Cadillac Avenue. He was now less than a mile from their intended point of departure from the drain, a distance that would have been a few minutes of ATV driving under their intended conditions. Given the flooding below, his current course of action was the only one left.

He had his destination; now he just had to get there, and perform well once on-site. Everyone else was literally depending on him—their measures to discourage pursuit would slow the cops, not stop them completely. Now, Sterling was counting on his contingency planning, skills, and no small amount of desperation to ensure success.

It was all up to him now.

And to be honest, he was almost grateful for the distraction.

Anything was better than facing the watchful eyes of Blair, a woman he'd dragged into this mess and was now attempting to drag out. Or the skeptical gazes of two teammates who had told him to abort mission when the flash flood warning hadn't lifted that morning.

If the flooding had held off just a few more minutes, they would've been long gone already.

And if the flooding had arrived a few minutes earlier, he reminded himself, they could have been trapped without their ATVs, left to navigate a subterranean labyrinth directly below the police perimeter.

No reason to think over what *hadn't* happened, he thought. Look too far into the chaotic maelstrom of possibilities when you disrupted the universal order with a heist, and you could go crazy. Besides, plenty enough *had* occurred for him to remain gainfully employed for the time being.

The rain meant almost no foot traffic. Lots of cars were parked on the street if he dared a brazen theft, but none were suited to his needs. That was perfectly okay with him: he'd planned ahead for this.

The beauty of the Los Angeles Department of Water & Power as a cover, of course, was that the DWP had facilities scattered across the entire city. Throw a dart on a map of LA, and if you didn't hit one of them, you'd be able to locate two almost equidistant from your impact. The city was covered with DWP converter stations, control facilities, and receiving stations, each of which had dedicated and frequently unsupervised maintenance vehicles and a shifting cast of inspectors, supervisors, and workers totaling nearly ten thousand people.

And with an organization that large came a correlating mess of regulatory minutiae, an ocean of bureaucracy that Sterling could talk his way into and out of at will.

For someone who needed to run, hide, and/or steal a vehicle at any point in LA proper, a DWP uniform and a bit of working knowledge could be the difference between a skillful near-miss with the law or spending the rest of your life in prison.

Sterling took the crosswalk through Cadillac Avenue and followed the sidewalk past the DWP's Receiving Station D on his right. But he didn't plan on entering the actual electric receiving station unless he had to. Security measures tended to be higher around elements of public infrastructure that, if disabled, could shut down power to a quarter of the city. Anything that a terrorist would find appetizing was the last place you wanted to have to explain yourself to security.

Instead Sterling was headed to the adjacent Western Water Yard. The Yard had multiple buildings, so new faces came and went frequently enough that no single person could possibly know everyone else. Most importantly, however, was the presence of a motor pool housing a veritable armada of maintenance vehicles.

As he approached the Yard, he pulled an identification badge out of his pocket and slid the lanyard around his neck, tucking the badge under his vest for now. It was totally illegitimate, of course, identifying him as a DWP headquarters employee granted general access to any facility. And while the badge was sufficient for him to get through the security checkpoints and onto DWP properties, he wouldn't subject himself to that unless absolutely necessary to avoid being filmed at face-level by one of the facility's security cameras.

The Yard's triangular compound was fully fenced, he knew from previous reconnaissance, but two of the three sides were little more than a last resort—both exposed to the constant supervision of nearby residences.

That left him with one primary route into the compound. With a public sidewalk running the length, and just enough attractive vegetation to conceal a man cheetah-flipping over the fence, it would be an easy "in." Granted, six lanes of traffic ran along this stretch—but half of the drivers would be texting, the other half not looking or caring what went on in the world outside of their traffic lane. And for the few people who did have the situational awareness to observe their surroundings, it took merely the slightest indication of credibility—hardhat, badge, or tool belt—to assure them that someone had a right to be doing what they were doing.

The perimeter in front of the main building at the corner was a green cast-iron fence with an outward-curving top. For Sterling it would have been pitifully easy to negotiate, but the exposure at the intersection was far too high.

So Sterling continued walking through the rain.

He counted six trees planted directly beside the perimeter wall and extending far above the barbed wire. It never ceased to amaze him how often people employed perfectly effective security measures—cameras, lights, fences—only to plant shrubs or trees that either impeded visibility or provided easy access, or both. The absence of vegetation could be a huge impediment to a thief; its presence, a gift from the heist gods. There was even a second row of trees between the sidewalk and traffic, providing a further layer of cover. The heavy rainfall was the icing on the cake, reducing visibility to a fraction of what it would be in sunlight. No need to get creative or fancy here; just wait for the traffic flow to subside and make your move.

The first few trees were too close to the guard shack and camera. He wanted to shoot for one of the last two, and quickened his pace to exploit an upcoming gap in traffic toward him.

Sterling began drifting off the sidewalk, now crossing the mulch toward the wall.

As the last cars passed him, Sterling slid between the narrow tree trunks with his back to the brick wall. Reaching up, he hoisted himself up along the thickest trunk and scanned through the twin rows of overhanging barbed wire to confirm there were no fence-mounted cameras.

He planted one boot on the brick wall, the other in a fork of the tree, and rotated himself around until he was facing the wall. Then, pulling himself up the final few feet, he placed one foot on the upper edge of the wall and the other in the center of the barbed wire.

On the other side of the wall were rows of dumpsters and parked vehicles. He could've jumped into the back of a pickup if he wanted; instead, he chose the space between two trucks.

Shifting his weight onto the foot between rows of barbed wire, Sterling leapt.

His feet struck hard on the pavement between vehicles, and he came to an instant kneeling position as he let his legs absorb the shock. Then he stood, adjusting his now-tilted hardhat.

And that was it; he was in.

He heard the rain continuing to fall in sheets, splattering on the ground —no sounds of yelling or running footsteps, though he wasn't going to remain at his entry point to test his luck.

Sterling walked away from the main building, his path taking him past a series of overflowing dumpsters, and he peeked inside to look for anything that would aid his DWP disguise. He hoped to score an empty pack of cigarettes tossed at the top of the trash—particularly useful when diffusing suspicion by asking for a smoke. But instead, he saw something far better. The ultimate symbol of being a very busy person with a lot of authority.

An aluminum storage clipboard.

Sterling snatched it up at once. Sure, the metal clip at the top was broken and the bent lid no longer closed all the way, but who cared?

Holding the clipboard in one hand, he continued strolling confidently through the compound.

There were vehicles everywhere: vans, trucks, and immense utility rigs. Sterling passed between stacks of pipes and building supplies, heading away from the main building until he'd gotten some distance from his entry point.

Cutting right, he began to circle toward the vehicles parked against the back wall. He could make out a group of four pickups, all quad-cabs, all looking brand-new. Sterling set off toward them—his quickest way out of here was to use the Pegasus, and that lent itself to the most modern vehicles he could find in the DWP fleet.

"Hey!" a voice shouted behind him. "Stop right there!"

38

JIM

Jim was parked now, but he left his engine idling. He watched the surroundings beyond his windshield turn to an unfocused blur before the wipers streaked the glass clean, revealing the office building overlooking Manhattan Beach. He counted upward nine floors, knowing the Jester would be at the top. He vaguely wondered if the Jester was looking out the window toward him now. Who was he kidding? The Jester's office would be on the opposite side of the building, facing the ocean. Probably on a corner suite.

The view blurred once more with rain.

He caught himself twisting his wedding ring. Forcing himself to stop, he instead picked up his burner phone and flipped it end over end against his thigh, waiting for a response to his text.

Jim's mind was tearing itself apart. He was a few hours removed from planning on shooting Blair himself, and now, faced with the likelihood of her capture, he couldn't bear the thought of her exposing him. He could, of course, keep her from testifying against him—but only if his proceedings with the Jester went as he hoped.

He continued toying with the burner phone as he rehearsed what he'd say when the call came; that much was necessary, after all. He cared about keeping his career intact. But the person he carried that burner for, the one he switched it out for on a weekly basis, dealt with only one currency.

Power.

Jim was waiting for the phone to ring; he'd been expecting it, if not on his drive over, then shortly after he arrived here at his destination.

Even though Jim was waiting for the phone to ring, when it did, he jumped regardless.

He quickly answered, "I'm here."

No response.

He added, "I wouldn't call if this wasn't critical."

The voice that responded was synthesized to an almost unrecognizable baritone.

"I would know if you were being investigated. OPR hasn't called me. Why are you?"

"It's not for me."

A longer pause this time. "Then I suppose this is related to the news."

"She can burn me."

"You've already gone public to accuse her. So instead of wasting my time, you should be making sure she can't contradict your version of events." A pause, and the synthesized voice continued. "You should have taken care of it already."

"I tried. But now she's out there, and she's going to be arrested soon. It's time for Plan B. I can consolidate power from this." He quickly corrected himself. "*We* can consolidate power from this."

"I don't think so, James."

Jim grimaced. Only his mentor still called him James. To his mentor, he was still a kid.

"I can restate my public condemnation of Blair as a misunderstanding. My logic was sound, and voiced out of a concern for public safety. And my willful support of Blair in the aftermath of this will show me to be a secure man. A man able to withstand fire from the press and public, capable of pivoting when required to preserve his reputation. In short"—he took a breath—"everything required of a politician."

His mentor paused. "The media attention around this thing is turning into a juggernaut. That means it can break down the walls standing in your way, or it can destroy you. If you're going to do anything but get out of the way, you need to be certain."

"I am certain. I can ride this wave forward, leverage the media spotlight to advance my position."

"This is thin. And it's a big risk to take for your side piece."

A muscle ticked in Jim's jaw. But the first time he talked back would be the last.

Instead he used his mentor's own words to get what he wanted. "When we made our arrangement, you said that I'd get enough rope to either hang myself or climb to the summit of power. That's what I agreed to. Now I need you to trust me in how to use the rope."

He waited for a response, holding his breath.

"You want the Jester? You've got one free pass. But if you expect me to make a call on your behalf, it better be quick."

"I'm in the parking lot of the modeling agency right now."

"Good. My flight leaves in eighteen minutes. You have until then if you need a Hail Mary."

"It might take a little longer for me to—"

"My jet doesn't stay grounded for anyone but me. And you, James, are still far from being me. Mess this up, and you may never arrive. You have eighteen minutes. You'll figure it out before then—or you won't."

The call ended.

Jim killed his engine, leapt out of his truck, and slammed the door, leaving his umbrella behind. Then he ran through the rain toward the office building.

The granite slab in front of the entrance was innocuous, reading only *YATARI BUILDING*.

But the business directory that Jim passed on his way to the elevator held a more specific designation for the occupant of the 9th floor:

Law Offices of Damian Horne Wycroft, P.S.

39

STERLING

Sterling stopped in place, frozen in the middle of the DWP's Western Water Yard.

Then he turned around, raising a hand to one ear as if he hadn't heard the man running toward him in the rain and now jogging to a stop. The man was large and physically imposing, though Sterling didn't care about that. It would make resorting to his taser more difficult, but not impossible.

Instead, Sterling's mind registered what did matter.

The man's boots were well broken in but clean: somewhere between labor and management.

His identification badge was properly displayed, a rarity within DWP facilities: cared about regulations.

He had challenged Sterling alone: confident in his ability to make split-second judgment calls without someone else guiding his decisions.

"What did you say?" Sterling asked.

"I said stop," the man answered.

"Well." Sterling shrugged. "I'm stopped." Did this man see him jump the fence, or was he just challenging an unknown individual in his sphere of influence?

The man hesitated at Sterling's response. He appraised Sterling's hardhat and vest—both DWP-issued—and seemed somewhat more satisfied. "No one's supposed to be back here. Can I help you?"

Sterling gave a slow nod. "I'm hoping you can help me."

He said nothing else, and the man's eyes ticked to the aluminum storage clipboard and back up.

"You an inspector?"

Sterling watched the man expectantly, saying nothing.

"Because Debbie Baker isn't here at the moment."

"Well," Sterling said, "that explains a lot. And I see why you don't want anyone walking around back here: there's no drip pan under half these vehicles."

"None of these trucks have oil leaks. They're all cleared by—"

"What's the 130-53 say? And not the old version. I'm talking last week's update, because I know the memo has circulated by now."

The man went silent.

Sterling pressed, "What's your name?"

"Hank Paddock, Senior Chief. May I see your identification?"

Sterling looked confused, then glanced down and saw his lanyard was tucked into his vest. He pulled the lanyard free, exposing his ID card and holding it up for Hank, but only very briefly, dismissing the query altogether. "I meant your first name. Listen, Hank, you're lucky I'm not from environmental compliance, because they cleaned house at RS-K Olympic about an hour ago. I know word has gotten around by now"—he waved toward the trucks—"so why hasn't Baker fixed this up already?"

"She's been on a job since ten."

Sterling gave a good-natured shrug, remarking almost to himself, "You know what? It doesn't have to go that far." Then he checked his watch and looked up, stern once more. "Hank, I've got about fifteen minutes left on my rounds. Please do me a favor and get these vehicles compliant before I go. If everything's tip-top by the time I head to RS-H, I'll mark it all as satisfactory. As long as everything else looks good, I won't mention this to Debbie. Capeesh?"

"Yeah, okay," he said. "Thanks."

"Don't worry about it. But Hank"—Sterling took a half step closer—"if you guys haven't heard of the regulatory update, then for the sake of your management, I don't want to know. Just make sure it gets posted."

Hank nodded, saying nothing.

"Have a great day," Sterling said cheerfully, turning and walking in his original direction. He didn't look back, instead glancing in the reflection of rain-streaked vehicle windows to see Hank watching him leave, standing still for a few seconds before walking toward the main building.

Sterling cut between parked vehicles, approaching the row of four white quad-cab pickups that he'd identified as his best prospects. They all looked new, and their front bumpers were fitted with two baskets storing twin stacks of inverted traffic cones for easy access.

It wouldn't get any better than this.

Sterling walked around one to its driver door, which sported a DWP logo. Grabbing the handle with one hand, he used the other to withdraw a black plastic box from his pocket: Marco's self-proclaimed Pegasus.

Turning it on, he began rhythmically testing the door handle.

Pull.

Pull.

Pull.

The truck remained locked, and Sterling kept testing it. In theory, it should open any minute now. At least, if Marco was correct. His so-called Pegasus had worked in their training and rehearsals but hadn't yet been utilized in an actual situation.

But Marco's assurance was this: keyless vehicle entry and ignition systems were at the mercy of their key fobs, which worked by transmitting a low-frequency signal verified by the vehicle's computer.

As long as the fob's signal was paired to that individual vehicle and detectable within a few feet of the car, it provided access to open doors. Even starting the engine had no additional protections in place beyond requiring the vehicle to be in park with the brake depressed.

And for the technologically enterprising, there were a half dozen ways to leverage this system to steal a car.

The simplest was a relay hack, and that's what Sterling was doing now —or, more correctly, attempting to do.

Average car thieves performed this procedure by working in pairs, with each man holding a relay box. One thief stood as close as possible to the key fob—which could be in a house, café, or shopping mall several hundred feet from the car—allowing his relay box to capture the fob signal. This would be transmitted to the other relay box held by a second thief, standing at the vehicle and testing the door handle. And presto, the relayed signal would allow the doors to unlock and the vehicle to start.

That much wasn't impressive. If you knew what you were doing, you could build two such relay boxes out of parts totaling the price of a decent steak. More advanced car thieves would amplify the signal to triple the workable transmit distance, allowing them to steal cars from a colorful variety of locations.

Not to be outdone, Marco had constructed the device in Sterling's hand, which he'd dubbed the Pegasus.

The Pegasus combined both relay boxes into a single unit. When activated, the Pegasus passively collected fob signals within a thousand-foot diameter of the user—in this case, encompassing the centrally managed DWP lockbox in the adjacent building that Sterling dared not enter—and then actively broadcast those signals one at a time in half-second intervals.

So the user only needed to turn the box on, then stand there like an idiot testing the door handle until—

It clicked open.

Sterling opened the driver door and slid into the pickup, tossing his clipboard onto the opposite seat and closing the door behind him. With a foot on the brake, he began pressing the vehicle's push button start.

Nothing happened.

So he pressed again, and again, and then finally resigned himself to tapping the button over and over in a way that resembled no secret agent or gentleman thief in any movie, ever. The process instead required him to act like an impatient child at the elevator switch. He'd have to talk to Marco about this, he decided. It was undignified.

Finally, after thirty to forty button pushes, the engine turned over and the truck growled to life.

Sterling turned on the wipers, and the water-covered windshield streaked clear until the next barrage of rain hit it.

Back in business, Sterling thought. And with a satisfied nod, he put the truck in drive and pulled out of the spot to recover his team and Blair, and save his heist.

40

BLAIR

Marco consulted his watch with a frown. "Sterling's been gone for thirty minutes without radio contact." He lowered his hand. "My turn to boost a ride."

Alec nodded solemnly. "If Sterling got clipped in a DWP outfit, they'll be looking for others. Lose the costume once you're clear of the manhole cover."

"I will."

Then Blair added, "Wherever Sterling went for a car, you should go the opposite way. His point of arrest will become ground zero for the new search radius."

"Thanks." Marco turned to the ladder. Looking over his shoulder at Alec, he said, "Put another thirty minutes on the clock. If Sterling shows before I'm back, get out of here as planned. Mark the manhole cover with a load signal so I can assess at a glance. I'll displace to Area J and lie low until I get the call for a sterilized pickup."

Then he grasped a ladder rung with one hand and reached up with the other, but before he could pull himself upward, a ray of light shone on him. The light expanded in size as Marco stepped out of the way to dodge a torrent of water from above.

They looked up to see the manhole cover being removed. It was replaced by Sterling looking down at them, complete with hardhat.

"DWP, assemble," he called down. "Time to make our way to the ranch."

Blair felt a surge of relief that was quickly replaced by embarrassment as she looked to the ladder rungs embedded in the wall and then her dress. When she'd selected it for an evening with Gordon, she hadn't planned on climbing ladders ahead of men.

"You two go ahead."

Both men donned their bags of cash, and Marco reached for the third.

"I'll get Sterling's bag," Blair said. "You guys have carried enough dead-weight today."

Marco withdrew his hand, darting up the ladder behind Alec.

Blair tried to lift the bag of cash, and it barely moved. Redoubling her efforts, she hoisted the enormous bag over her back, the strap pulling tension between her breasts. These were waterproof bags, so it wasn't like the contents were waterlogged—the cash was just *heavy*.

She considered the irony of the situation as she climbed from one rusty ladder rung to the next. Using her legs to push herself, she struggled against gravity to ascend with the loot from a bank robbery. There was something bizarrely Shakespearian about it—the tragic story of a former FBI agent facilitating a crime in order to get away from her own people— but Blair didn't feel like a criminal, despite being soaked, chilled to the bone, and weighed down with cash as she followed two bank robbers up a ladder. Going to Gordon's house had felt far more unnatural. Being in prison—*that* felt unnatural.

But her current situation, against all odds and for reasons she couldn't explain, seemed like just another day at the office. Even her fear of heights didn't strike as she ascended skyward, though that very well could have been because she was underground.

Couldn't it?

As she reached the top of the now-empty ladder, Sterling reached through the manhole.

"Hand me that bag," he called.

"I'm going to feel really foolish," she grunted, struggling to lift the strap from around her shoulders, "if you take the cash and then leave me down here."

"Not my style, Blair. Have a little faith."

The weight was removed as Sterling took control of the bag, pulling it up and out of sight.

Blair tried to climb the final rung, but Sterling said, "Wait right there."

He reappeared a moment later, handing her a hardhat and vest.

"It's not much," he said, shrugging, "but better than nothing."

She put on the hardhat and worked her arms through the vest one at a time while clinging to the rung.

Finally, she climbed through the hole and pulled herself to ground level.

Rain was exploding off the street all around her, and Sterling had blocked off the area around them with orange traffic cones.

A white utility truck was parked in front of the hole, its emergency flashers on. Alec was holding open a rear door and beckoning for her to get in the backseat.

As she approached him, Alec announced, "Blair Morgan, Master of Disguise."

He was right to mock her—she felt ridiculous in her haphazard assortment of clothing. Blair slid onto a rear canvas seat, and was immediately blasted by hot air pouring out of the vents. She felt a sense of comfort bordering on ecstasy as her core temperature soared to what felt like normal levels. Marco jumped in the passenger seat, and Alec got in the back with Blair as they slammed the doors shut. Sterling collected the traffic cones, returned them to their mount on the front bumper, and let himself into the driver seat before pulling the truck forward into traffic.

Blair dropped her hardhat on the floor, then stripped off her soaking wet safety vest and Sterling's black jacket while sighing with almost delirious pleasure. The truck's interior felt like the inside of an oven, and Sterling must have had the heat running full blast since...

"Wait a minute," she cried. "Where did this truck come from? Did you use a relay hack?"

Sterling didn't have time to respond before Marco added, "Yeah, did the Pegasus work?"

"No. I had to hotwire this thing like a barbarian."

"What? Were you within—"

"I'm kidding, relax. The Pony worked great."

"Pegasus," Alec corrected him.

Marco shouted triumphantly, "The first real-world application!"

Blair asked, "But did you just find this truck parked on the street, or what?"

Sterling made an ambiguous clucking noise with his tongue.

Alec replied, "I may have overstated the value of improvisation in our creative process. Planning is still a key ingredient."

"So you memorized the location of facilities correlating with your cover along potential exits of your getaway route? Or planned your cover based on the accessible facilities? That's so...so..."

"Impressive?" Alec leaned toward her. "Physically attractive, even?"

Blair leaned away from him. "I was going to say premeditated. The Baron would be proud."

"You told her about our mono-acronym?" Sterling asked.

Alec shrugged. "Well, there was a lot of free time while you were off gallivanting in search of this rust heap."

"I got you freeloading expletives a quad-cab! A brand-new one, at that. I thought you'd be slightly..." He trailed off, eyes darting from the windshield to the rearview mirror and then back again. "Well, this is awkward."

Blair asked, "What is?"

"Look behind us."

Blair glanced over her shoulder, and felt her jaw drop.

Directly behind them was a Los Angeles County Sheriff's Department cruiser.

Blair whipped back around, facing forward with a rush of light-headedness.

Behind the wheel, Sterling said, "He just turned in from a side street. Missed seeing our pickup by about thirty seconds."

"No way," Blair gasped, then added, "RTB."

Alec shot back, "What! Totally inappropriate usage, Blair."

"Seriously," Sterling agreed. "Who even taught you what that means?"

"Well what are you supposed to say under these conditions?"

"Nothing," Marco said. "You act steely cool under pressure. Comment on the weather, if you must."

"Okay, then it's very *rainy* with a ninety percent chance of *life without parole*. And weren't you the one saying this is all going to go terribly wrong, Marco?"

He nodded solemnly. "I still am. The day is young, and we'd better hope Lady Luck is on our side in what's to come."

Blair asked the others, "How often is Marco right?"

Sterling gave a conciliatory shrug. "Pretty much always. But look at the bright side: this truck hasn't been reported stolen yet. Otherwise, that deputy would let us know. What's the Sheriff's Department doing here, anyway? Thought this was LAPD jurisdiction."

Blair looked at him incredulously. "Oh, I don't know, Sterling. Probably because Jim has called in every peace officer in the western United States to assist with our capture. And if we don't get out of here quick, we're all going to end up behind bars."

41

JIM

Jim was out of the elevator before the doors had finished opening, turning the corner and pushing his way through a pair of glass doors. He forced himself to a measured pace as he strode across the marble floor tiles toward the receptionist.

Whoa, he thought, unable to remain focused even in the urgency of the current moment. The woman behind the desk—perhaps the correct term would have been *girl*, as she didn't look a day over twenty-five—was gorgeous.

She looked up at Jim, her pouty lips spreading in a dazzling smile.

"Welcome to the Law Offices of Damian Horne Wycroft. How may I help you?"

Jim stopped before her, squaring his shoulders before removing his identification and opening it to reveal his badge.

"ASAC Jim Jacobson. Federal Bureau of Investigation."

The woman gasped.

Jim continued, "I need to speak to Damian immediately." He felt ridiculous. For holding his badge, for being here in the first place acting authoritative after groveling in his car and kissing his mentor's proverbial ring. For using Wycroft's first name. To everyone in the world, he was simply Wycroft or the Jester. The use of three names—Damian Horne Wycroft—was an act of stroking his own ego, and little else.

The receptionist thrust an index finger toward a glass door to her side. "Right through that door. End of the hall, to the right. I'll let Shelly know you're coming."

Jim let the badge linger for a moment longer, and then replaced it in his pocket.

"Thank you," he said in a deep voice, a throaty voice, the voice he was reduced to in the presence of beauty.

The voice he'd used around Blair.

Spinning on his heels, he strode toward the door. Behind him, he heard the receptionist pick up the phone and whisper, "Shelly? The *F...B...I* is here to see the boss..."

Pushing open the door, Jim strode confidently toward the desk of a woman who must have been Shelly, Wycroft's personal secretary.

And, God help him, she was beautiful too—a tan brunette with cleavage tightly contained within a blouse open a full two buttons below where it needed to be.

He shouldn't have been surprised. The running joke was that Wycroft didn't have a legal office; instead, he ran a modeling agency. If you saw a man or ugly woman in his building, the rumor went, then you were looking at a client and not an employee.

Shelly had the phone to her ear, surely talking to the awestruck receptionist, but hung up when she saw Jim.

He procured his identification and announced, "ASAC Jim Jacobson. Federal Bureau of Investigation."

Shelly gave a bored nod toward his badge. "And are you here in that capacity right now?"

Jim hesitated a second. "Yes. Obviously."

"Okay. Have a seat." She gestured behind him, where an Italian leather sofa resided before a glass coffee table with an untouched spread of *The Economist* magazines. As if any of Wycroft's clients were in danger of reading *The Economist*.

He turned to face Shelly, pocketing his credentials. "Maybe you didn't hear me. I'm here on official business, and the federal government waits for no man—"

"I'm a woman," she said in a voice a little too stern. "Clearly you've noticed by now."

Jim cursed himself—had she caught him checking out her cleavage?

Shelly continued, "And unless there's a search warrant stapled to that badge, you can wait."

Jim checked his Rolex, a final measure of posturing for an important man who couldn't be kept waiting. Shelly didn't break her stare—of course she didn't. Her boss probably wore a watch worth twenty times what Jim's Rolex had cost him, produced by some Swiss company or another that was unknown to ninety-nine percent of the world's population and unaffordable to a majority of the remaining one percent.

"Very well," he announced in his throaty voice. He cursed himself for having no formal authority here, for being at the behest of this civilian tumult of egos and agendas that didn't conform to the rules of rank and order, morality and discipline.

Jim turned and negotiated the coffee table, falling into the soft leather surface of the sofa and smoothing his pants. Crossing a leg, he watched Shelly expectantly.

But she only stared at her computer screen, re-inserting the single bud of a headphone. She picked up the phone with her free hand, tucking it between ear and shoulder, and pressed a single button.

"Sir, you've got an FBI agent here to see you. Jacobson." A pause. "Yes, sir, same guy."

She paused another beat, then hung up the phone. Her eyes were riveted to the screen, her hand guiding a computer mouse through multiple clicks. Probably checking social media, Jim thought. His eyes ticked to Wycroft's office door, imagining the corner suite view beyond and waiting for the door to open.

And then—nothing happened.

Jim lowered his eyes, pretending to be unconcerned and eternally patient. This was a power play, he knew. He discreetly slid the shirt cuff up his left arm, checking his Rolex again. In doing so, he verified that every second felt like four times that span of time.

The office door opened abruptly, and Wycroft—or more properly, Jim corrected himself, *Damian Horne Wycroft*—stood in the gap.

"Jim," Wycroft announced, "sorry to keep you waiting. Please"—he waved an arm inside—"come on in. Can I get you anything? Coffee? Bourbon?"

Jim rose, casting Shelly a resentful sidelong glance as he approached Wycroft. But she didn't notice—her eyes were still fixed on her computer screen.

"No thank you," he said, accepting Wycroft's outstretched hand in a firm shake before entering the office.

He stepped inside, closing the door behind him as Wycroft rounded his desk. It was exactly as he suspected: a corner suite, one wall of glass facing the Pacific coast. The other faced north, to Jim's own task force headquarters in El Segundo, and LAX beyond.

"Please, have a seat," Wycroft insisted. Jim obliged, sitting down in the chair opposite the desk, drinking in the view of coastal sky.

Then, he observed Wycroft himself.

His hair hadn't gone gray, it had gone white as snow, and Wycroft had done nothing to stop that. Nor, Jim thought, had he done anything to assuage the unrelenting onset of age, other than festoon himself in absurd horn-rimmed eyeglasses, gold cufflinks, and bespoke clothes subtly matching windowpane patterns of lavender amid charcoal. The man was wearing a pocket square, of all things. And what was worse, it paired well with the shirt and jacket, just as intended.

It was such a defense lawyer thing to do, Jim decided. Flaunt his excessive wealth and surround himself in a palatial tower with a beach view and a bevy of supermodels doing his every bidding. The only thing Wycroft was missing to complete the picture was a gaudy diamond pinkie ring.

And then, Jim witnessed firsthand why they called this man the Jester. He flashed a wide, perpetual, and almost insulting Cheshire cat smile as he said, "Mind if I imbibe? I'm a sucker for Greaney's Espresso Roast." Then he took a seat and poured a fresh cup of coffee from a silver carafe on his desk. Jim caught a glimpse of his watch, didn't recognize it, and looked away before Wycroft said, "So to what do I owe the honor? The last time I saw you, you were over there."

Confused, Jim turned in his seat to see what Wycroft was indicating.

Then his face reddened. Behind him was a massive flat-screen TV.

He faced Wycroft.

"That's what I'm here to talk to you about. Blair may not have masterminded this heist. She may have entered it as a hostage."

"But in your press conference you said—"

"Forget my press conference. New information has come to light."

"I'm honored that you would think of me, but if you're seeking to rectify the truth, you might want to get back in front of those cameras and tell it to the reporters."

"I will," Jim said through gritted teeth. "But I suspect that the robbers will soon release Blair since they haven't killed her already. She's emotional; I can't guarantee she won't say something to a public defender or even the police. She needs to be under your protection immediately."

"There is no question that her rights must be protected by a competent and licensed defender. Of which there is no shortage in the City of Angels. What brings you here, to my office?"

Jim checked his Rolex—he only had minutes remaining before his mentor was closed for business. If there was anything in Jim's power he could do to avoid making that cry for help, well then, by all means, he'd avoid it.

"Surely you've noticed the national media attention surrounding this event. Well, I'm here to tell you there's going to be a lot more. And you can be leading the charge."

Wycroft took a sip of coffee, then waved the mug dismissively. "Now, Jim, I've been the beneficiary of all the media attention I care to handle. I own more homes than I have time to visit. Where *do* I find the time to create balance? And unless I'm mistaken, federal salaries are insufficient to cover the costs of my representation."

"You've done pro bono representation for lesser incidents, and bene-fited from it in the long term. You've got the legal chops and connections with judges and testimony experts to pull off a peerless defense, and a high-profile-enough law practice to reap the collective rewards."

Wycroft chuckled merrily. "The only case I'll be taking on a pro bono basis that has anything to do with you would be when you capture the heist network operating in our fine state. That's the kind of national attention I require, Jim, but as of yet you haven't been able to deliver any of them. When you do, tell them to call me. Until then I've got more than enough serial killers vying for my attention. If Blair Morgan went on a nine-state killing spree tomorrow, she'd still be competing for my client list."

Jim gave a tight smile. "This could be a redemption story under your belt. Think along the lines of 'wrongful imprisonment.' A previous conviction that can be overturned—given the right legal representation—and a former agent cleared of wrongdoing, her dignity reclaimed in the public eye. This would be a great final chapter in the autobiography you're working on." Jim nodded behind him toward the television. "You saw the news. They'll be replaying that rooftop footage on every major network for weeks."

"My autobiography is coming along quite well, thank you," Wycroft began. "And while I agree that the rooftop footage of these bank robbers with Blair is quite compelling, and even the stuff of legendary book and movie deals, I tend to favor the indefensible. If there's a scrap of merit to Blair Morgan's participation today, then I dare say that it can be sufficiently represented by any number of excellent attorneys. I'd be happy to refer you to some more economical options with availability in their case load."

Jim snapped, "You're a glory hound seeking recognition with any major national case that comes to light. Why wouldn't you want to take this?"

Wycroft smiled warmly, steepling his fingers. "Why Jim Jacobson, the sheer paradox of being accused of craving the media spotlight by a man like yourself is simply staggering." Then he leaned forward, pressing a button on his conference phone.

"Yes, sir?" Shelly asked.

"Shelly, I can't possibly continue to work today. I'm paralyzed by shock. Please call an EMT to take me home by stretcher."

Before she could reply, he tapped another button to end the call, then said, "Shelly couldn't respond because she's just been killed by irony. I'm quite sorry, Jim, but I have other clients to attend to. If you'd like to take me up on that fresh cup of Greaney's coffee, you'll have to take it to go."

Frowning, Jim yanked the phone out of his pocket and entered a text.

Wycroft squinted at it; he hadn't seen a phone that old in some time, and they only served one purpose. No GPS, easily replaceable...he knew he was looking at a burner phone, could sense it in the core of his being, but he wouldn't give any concessions until his suspicions were confirmed.

Jim pocketed the phone and looked back to Wycroft, letting a few seconds pass before he spoke.

"I'm sorry, you were saying?"

Wycroft's desk phone began to ring.

He gave a small grin, unable to help himself or suppress his curiosity. He pressed a button, and his secretary's voice erupted on speaker.

"Sir, you've got an urgent call on line one—"

"Don't you dare say another word, Shelly," he cut her off. "You know how much I do love surprises."

Reaching for the receiver, his perpetual smile grew wider as he said to Jim, "Trying to strong-arm me? It's unbecoming. And not to slight your profession, but an FBI agent doesn't have the firepower necessary to force the legal hand around here."

Jim said nothing. He watched Wycroft pick up the receiver.

"Law Offices of Damian Horne Wycroft." He paused for effect. "This is Damian. Horne. Wycroft."

And then, Jim watched the metamorphosis.

It wasn't the first time he'd seen it—and, if he could pull this off successfully, it wouldn't be the last.

Wycroft's countenance paled, the grin fading to an expression of solemnity as he listened to the phone receiver.

No words were spoken; they never were.

Wycroft leaned forward to hang up the phone, letting the receiver fall into its cradle from a one-inch drop.

Then he looked to Jim with renewed curiosity.

"Why Jim, why didn't you simply say that this poor defenseless woman had her reputation as a federal agent falsely besmirched? Given her tragic involvement in the horrifying events today—my God, man, have you seen the television footage—it's the least I can do to be of service. Besides, she must be extremely emotional and at a high risk of saying something most regrettable to the police or even, heaven forbid, a public defender. I'd say overturning her conviction is well within my means on any number of grounds. With time served, I could even make a case for reinstating her to some form of federal service."

He tapped a button on his phone, and Shelly replied, "Yes, sir?"

"Shelly, I will personally be representing Blair Morgan. Pro bono. Please notify the LAPD that I am to be considered her attorney and that I will rain fire and brimstone for any, I say again *any*, violation of my client's constitutional rights."

"Sir—"

"And furthermore, I want you to begin monitoring the police transponder for any traffic related to Blair Morgan's whereabouts. And notify me the second her location is known. I need to be present at her apprehension."

"Yes, sir, and—"

"This very second, Shelly. No time to waste."

Wycroft leaned back in his chair, folding his hands over his suit vest and giving Jim his trademark Cheshire cat smile for a second time.

Jim nodded, satisfied.

Then Shelly continued speaking.

"Sir, it's already happening."

"What is?" Wycroft asked.

"Police just spotted Blair Morgan fleeing in a vehicle. They're starting pursuit now."

42

BLAIR

Sterling maneuvered the utility truck through the residential neighborhoods southeast of Century City. They were only a few miles distant from Geering Plaza, but the areas were worlds apart—the scenery outside the truck was row after endless row of suburban houses. The rain was still falling continuously, though not at the same pelting rate.

"So close," Alec lamented. "If it weren't for the flash flood, this weather would've been perfect."

Blair looked at him, incredulous. "Traffic and riots are LA's weather. You're telling me you guys *meant* to do this in the rain?"

"Daylight robbery in public?" Marco asked rhetorically. "You bet. It's our highest chance of getting compromised on escape. You want us to try that in clear weather?"

"What difference does it make?"

Alec answered, "There's nothing like a getaway 'in the wet.' Police helicopters get grounded, and CCTV footage at intersections will be lousy and make it harder to identify license plates and who's in our cars."

"Cars—plural? You guys have multiple getaway cars?"

"Thanks for reminding me. Cars are another thing. Regular cops aren't going to have the experience to drive in wet conditions, and for the most part they're using rear-wheel-drive cars with all-season tires. But professional drivers in all-wheel-drive cars, with the best wet weather tires available, well, that's a different story. I'm telling you, there's nothing like a getaway 'in the wet.'"

"Can you please stop saying that?" Blair asked.

"Particularly when we've prepped by driving the routes and know every surface condition and corner. Stop saying what?"

"'In the wet.'"

"Your words, not mine. Now as for why we have two cars, that's just Getaway 101. If both cars get away clean, it's no harm. If one gets burned, the other is on call to pick up the occupants after they ditch the car. And if both get burned, then it's a race in opposite directions to divide the police pursuit down the middle."

"Okay," Blair conceded, "but why would you stash the cars in suburbia?"

Sterling answered. "We wouldn't. For something like that you want a multi-level parking garage with exit points to two separate streets. And, you know, storm drain access nearby, which is regrettably going unused."

She saw what he was referring to: ahead of them appeared a shopping center with a three-story parking garage.

Sterling drove under a sign marked *Mall Parking* and killed the wipers.

Blair watched with heady anticipation as they drove to a distant corner of the garage. Given the resources and planning of this team, she expected a pair of exotic racecars in disguise, capable of turning the LA freeways into the Indy 500.

But Sterling pulled the truck into an open spot beside two vehicles that looked like they belonged to a pair of soccer moms.

One was a small, unremarkable black BMW sedan.

The other was even worse: a white Volvo station wagon.

Blair managed, "Please tell me I don't have to flee a bank robbery in a station wagon."

"Turbo wagon," Alec corrected her, "and no. Clearly you're not worthy of this magnificent chariot. You know what BMW stands for, right?"

"No."

Marco said, "Bring Mechanic's Wrench."

"Yeah," Alec agreed. "Good luck, you two. Come on, Marco, let's take the *reliable* transportation."

Their vehicle transition was remarkably efficient. Marco and Alec threw two bags of cash into the back of the turbo wagon and then disappeared inside without a further word. The engine turned over as Sterling told her, "Lose the outfit."

He'd already deposited his bag of cash, hardhat, and orange vest into the BMW's trunk. Then he removed a spray bottle of what Blair could only assume was more sulfuric acid, and began hosing down the interior of the maintenance truck before they ditched it for good. Blair threw her own DWP accessories into the BMW trunk, seeing that a majority of it was filled by extra fuel cells. Closing the trunk, she opened the passenger door and slid inside as Sterling took the wheel.

He pressed the push button ignition and the BMW roared to life with a throaty growl. Blair thought it sounded abnormally loud, but her attention was drawn to an odd configuration of narrow tubes and valves installed throughout the cabin. Then the navigation screen glowed with a customized display—a three-block radius was visible around the car's beacon, with multiple routes marked by different colored lines stretching in various directions. As the screen activated, the BMW's speakers played the radio transmissions of a police transponder in full high-definition stereo.

Sterling ordered, "Put your seatbelt on."

He clicked his belt in place as Blair obeyed, still watching the navigation screen and wondering what custom programming it contained.

Before she could consider it further, Sterling piloted the BMW out of the parking spot. The turbo wagon was already vanishing out one street exit, and Sterling drove in the opposite direction to pull out on a separate road.

The police transponder went temporarily silent as Alec transmitted, "*Bullet Two is away.*"

The view outside became blurred with rain as they left the parking garage, and Sterling activated his windshield wipers. Turning left onto the street, he pushed a button on the steering wheel and the speakers went silent. "Bullet One is away."

Blair oriented herself—they were heading east on Sawyer, and she expected that any second now, he'd take her south to the I-10.

Then she noticed a patrol car parked on the curb to their left, just in front of a McDonald's. A second glance showed the vehicle to be a Los

Angeles Sheriff's Department cruiser. A deputy in a poncho and hat was striding briskly back to it with a cup of coffee in hand.

"Just relax," Sterling said, "and get your head down after we pass this cruiser. You'd be surprised what people don't notice if they're not expecting—"

Blair didn't hear him. She was busy rubbing her forehead and glancing through her fingers to see the deputy's eyes widening.

Sterling drove past, and Blair turned in her seat to see the deputy racing to his cruiser.

"Uh-oh," she said. "That was Pearson."

"What—you *know* him?"

"He was one of the first responders for the Shea Emporium heist," she offered hesitantly, seeing Sterling's jaw clench. "He asked me to dinner. I declined. Nice guy, though."

Sterling pressed a button on his steering wheel and the police transponder muted.

"Bullet One is compromised and evading."

Alec transmitted back, *"Bullet Two on support."*

The police transponder noise flooded back into the BMW, punctuated by a single urgent transmission.

"10-33, give me the patch."

"That's Pearson," Blair said. "'Give me the patch' means—"

"No kidding," Sterling shot back, accelerating toward the intersection to their front. "I know what it means."

A female dispatcher replied to Pearson in a clinical tone, *"10-33, you're on the patch, go."*

Pearson continued, *"283 in pursuit of two-eleven suspects heading east-bound on Sawyer and La Cienega. Black BMW sedan, plate's gonna be two George David uniform, zero two three. Occupied times two."*

"Traffic?"

Sterling whipped a left turn at the intersection.

"He just blew the light and went northbound on Fairfax, traffic is light, one unit in pursuit."

Blair looked to Sterling, trying to gauge the severity of their circumstances by his expression.

But at that moment, his features solidified into a deadpan intensity. His eyes gave one mechanical flick toward the navigation display, then back to the road, before he floored the gas pedal.

Blair was thrown backward, her spine and shoulder suctioned into the seat as the BMW accelerated so fast that she braced in anticipation of rear-ending the car to their front. Sterling effortlessly whipped the BMW into oncoming traffic, passing the car and cranking back into the lane a split second before a head-on collision with an SUV.

Then he accelerated even faster, the BMW's turbos activating to launch them to highway speeds at an impossibly fast rate, and their chase began.

43

STERLING

Sterling drove the BMW hard toward the curb as houses whipped past in a rain-streaked blur. He was approaching five lanes of Pico Boulevard, and prepared to cross all five on a yellow light.

Sterling braked to 50mph as he approached Pico, seeing his traffic light flick from yellow to red as he ripped the steering wheel left. The BMW carved a line through the momentarily empty intersection of five divided lanes just as vehicles began moving from all sides.

Angry horns blared to his left and right, but Sterling's focus was distilled down to tracking possible crashes and impulsively reacting with control inputs to the steering wheel and pedals. He drifted wide off his ideal line to avoid hitting a coupe that had stopped halfway into the inter-section, then corrected his direction back to the two lanes stretching west ahead of him.

Sterling reduced his steering angle as he exited the turn, allowing him to accelerate without his tires locking. As he straightened his trajectory and floored the gas, he actually felt himself smiling as the flow of traffic closed the gap behind him.

But a flick of his eyes to his left side-view mirror revealed the Sheriff's cruiser threading its way through the crossfire of civilian traffic, sirens flashing between cars that struggled to brake to a halt.

Sterling's mind clicked over to the contingency for this. He surveyed the wall of retail storefronts visible through a veil of falling rain, then saw traffic parting in his rearview to make way for the cruiser speeding toward him, siren on.

Sterling made a split-second decision to exit Pico Boulevard with a pro maneuver. He could pull it off near-effortlessly to cost his pursuer more time, sure; but deep down, he thought it would be fun.

Sterling braked the BMW as the cruiser sped toward him from the rear.

"What are you doing?" Blair cried.

He didn't answer, instead watching his speed plummet on his instrument panel.

When his car had slowed to 25mph, Sterling pulled his emergency brake.

The rear tires locked instantly, and he cranked the steering wheel a quarter turn to the right.

The BMW's back end swung 180 degrees, completing a stomach-churning rotation in less than two seconds. Sterling's vehicle was near-stationary as the patrol car skidded helplessly past him, and he dropped the emergency brake to hit the accelerator. The spin of tires on slick pavement subsided to the BMW's engine noise as he sped forward in the wrong direction, cutting left into a residential street.

He checked his rearview, noting with pleasure that the deputy was nowhere to be seen. The Sheriff's cruiser was probably still sliding down Pico after its tires locked without traction.

Sterling allowed himself a smug grin as he sped north, beginning a zigzag course through the neighborhood for the next phase of his escape.

Blair said, "It's only neighborhoods north of here. There's nowhere to—"

"I know," Sterling cut her off. "I just need to draw this guy into residential, then lose him. The police helicopter can't fly in this rain. Once we lose our tail, we move back to a high-speed road before responding units can box us in."

"But they've got our license plate."

"We just need enough distance to ditch the BMW and get picked up by Alec's turbo wagon. Come on." He shot her a sideways glance, seeing her tense expression and hoping to reassure her. "You trust me, remember?"

He looked up to see the Sheriff's cruiser skidding to a halt at the intersection to his front.

Sterling threw on the brakes, and the BMW crested to a stop in the spinning red glow of the cruiser's light bar. Deputy Pearson was staring at Blair through the flickering windshield wipers, his expression, in that moment, matching Sterling's—a look of mutual astonishment, as if neither could believe they'd entered a maze of suburbia and managed to meet at the same point in time.

Blair raised a hand and waved.

"Hi, Pearson," she said quietly.

Sterling flung the transmission into reverse and floored the gas, throttling backward between dual rows of cars parallel-parked in front of houses. He watched the backup camera to adjust his steering, glancing up to see the cruiser finishing a short Y-turn before speeding down the road toward him.

When Sterling returned his gaze to his backup camera, it showed the flashing lights of a second police cruiser gunning toward him from behind.

Blair was looking over her shoulder. "There's another cop behind us."

"I noticed," he replied curtly, barreling backward down the road. Two blocks now separated all three cars: both cruisers speeding toward each other, with the BMW reversing between them.

"You're going to hit him!"

Sterling didn't answer, his vision fixed on the backup camera. He reversed toward the last remaining side street between him and the cruiser to his rear, braking sharply to 20mph.

Both cruisers sped toward him, the drivers eager to box him in.

They were seconds from impact when Sterling ripped the steering wheel to the right as far as it would go.

The BMW's rear bumper careened ninety degrees, reversing the car out of the final four-way intersection as Sterling straightened out his wheels to keep the car on the street.

Both cruisers were left to find their quarry backing out of the way, leaving them to face one another head-on. They braked simultaneously, swerving right to avoid colliding.

But their cars couldn't cope with the control inputs against the wet streets, and the BMW's front bumper backed out of the intersection a moment before the cruisers hit each other.

A blasting twist of metal erupted as the cruisers collided at a slight angle. They jolted to a halt, hoods and front fenders crumbling against one another as a front bumper fell in the din. Sterling saw both cabins fill with the white dust of airbag deployments before he cut the wheel to reverse into a driveway.

Sterling bragged, "Guess he's not getting dinner with you now!"

Blair gasped. "We've got to help them."

Sterling tried to hide his amusement—Blair's kindness was endearing, if misplaced.

"They're fine, they've got airbags." He accelerated out of the driveway, taking the street away from the crash. "We don't, by the way."

"Why in God's name don't we have airbags?"

"Hopefully you don't have to find out. You know," he went on, making a right turn to break visual contact with the cruisers, "there really is nothing like a getaway 'in the wet.'"

44

BLAIR

Blair's concern for the officers in the two crashed cruisers was quickly subverted by a wave of near-gleeful euphoria. She thought she'd gotten Sterling busted, thought she'd be going back to prison for sure and dragging him along for the ride; now he was taking them in a circuitous route through the neighborhoods, headed south—opposite the direction of travel he'd led the officers.

Her presence had almost put him behind bars, she thought, and still he didn't complain.

He couldn't, really—he was busy driving.

If you could call it that.

To Blair, the BMW seemed a marionette at Sterling's fingertips. Judging by the intensity of his eyes, he was steering by thoughts alone. But his arms maneuvered the steering wheel with practiced repetition, as if he'd been doing this his whole life. Maybe he had.

"You're not bad at this," she said.

"I've been to more driving schools than any of these cops. But there are hundreds of cops"—he spun the wheel to corner a turn—"and only one of me."

"You're doing all right so far."

"We're not racing the patrol cars, we're racing the weather. We need to make it to the I-10 before the sky clears any further."

Blair implicitly understood what he meant. Once a police helicopter arrived overhead, this chase was over. She'd watched plenty of high-speed chases unfolding on live TV—everyone in Los Angeles had. It was practically the city's official pastime, uniting spectators around live news feeds whose grim appeal transcended that of any organized team sport. The getaway drivers never had a chance.

But the helicopters couldn't fly in rain like this. She wanted to ask where he planned to go after they made it to the I-10, which stretched from the Pacific coast all the way to Florida.

Before she could raise the question, Sterling took a right turn to see three patrol cars skidding to a halt to their front, blocking the path.

Blair's body was flung forward against her seatbelt by the force of Sterling's braking. No sooner had the BMW jolted to a stop less than ten feet from the cruisers than Sterling threw the transmission into reverse and floored the gas.

Blair saw the cruisers recede in the windshield as the BMW rocketed backward. She felt nauseous with the sudden change of trajectory, gasping with relief when Sterling let off the accelerator.

But then he spun the wheel wildly to the left, and the BMW whipped a sliding turn that sent the world beyond the windshield spinning in a blur of motion. Suddenly the cruisers were gone from her view, and the BMW pointed back down the way they had come. Blair never sensed Sterling putting the car from reverse into drive, but he must have at some point because her shoulders were once again suctioned to the seat. The BMW was now screaming forward once more, away from the cruisers.

But a fourth cruiser skidded to a halt to his front. Now they were pinned between police, with no way out. She looked to Sterling, fearful, but he calmly addressed her with a question.

"You wanted to know why we don't have airbags?"

"I guess..."

"This is why."

Sterling slowed the car as if he was going to comply with the barricade, but when the BMW was a car length from the cruiser, he floored the gas.

Blair braced for a mighty impact—but it never happened.

Instead, the BMW's driver side bumper impacted the rear wheel of the cruiser, and the squad car flipped neatly out of the way in a tight quarter spin. The BMW proceeded forward with little more than a slight shudder, as if Sterling had momentarily tapped the brakes.

Then they were off again—accelerating forward at the maximum possible speed, Sterling speaking above the sound of the engine and police transponder.

"Everything that helps a civilian driver is bad for a trained getaway driver. Airbags, fuel pump shut-offs, traction control."

"Where did you learn all this?"

"I'm a student of the world, Blair. Interstate 10, here we come."

"After that, where to?"

Sterling smiled. "How about 11000 Wilshire Boulevard?"

"Very funny." She was surprised he knew the address by memory—it was the Los Angeles FBI headquarters office.

"Sure you don't want me to drop you off there? Thought you might be getting homesick."

"Wilshire is the main headquarters. I worked out of the task force office in El Segundo."

"El Segundo? That part of town isn't on the agenda."

"Good," she breathed. "I've had enough of the FBI to last me a lifetime."

And just like that, they were at the ramp for I-10 westbound.

Sterling approached it like a normal Sunday drive, activating his turn signal and negotiating the long entry road at normal merging speed. The road drifted along a lazy curve, lifting them high above the tight streets and swarming police response of West Los Angeles.

His effort to get there had been nothing short of miraculous, she thought. Blair half-grinned at the traffic over the police transponder. The dispatcher was speaking in a patient, clinical tone, like a waiting room attendant. Meanwhile the police officer transmissions were rapid-fire bursts spoken against a backdrop of wailing sirens and growling engines. They were still combing the residential and retail districts, failing to mask the frustration in their voices as they tried to regain visual contact with the black BMW now merging into five lanes of traffic heading west.

"Seriously," Blair said, looking to Sterling. "Where are we headed?"

Sterling didn't answer. His eyes seemed unfocused, and he leaned forward slightly as if in disbelief.

A third type of transmission sounded over the police transponder. The speaker's voice fell somewhere between the dispatcher and the officers: not completely sterile and detached, and not particularly adrenaline-filled either.

This voice spoke with a new background noise: a warbling, high-pitched whine more distant and steadier than any of the sirens.

"Air 21, we are now overhead with the suspect vehicle."

Blair whirled in her seat, scanning upward out the passenger side window.

Roaring above, offset from the interstate and visible against a benign shale sky, was the green and yellow silhouette of a Sheriff's Department helicopter.

Sterling accelerated and maneuvered around a car to their front.

The transmission continued, *"SCC, we are westbound on the 10 from La Cienega. Vehicle is accelerating through 90mph in the number two lane, traffic is moderate. Vehicle is occupied times two. Can you ask responding units to parallel on majors to the south, to the north, and can I get units on the ramps at Overland. And can you ask CHP to stage a traffic break for the 10 and the 405 interchange, and patch me in with Marina Del Ray station, South LA, Carson, and Century?"*

The dispatcher replied, *"Air 21, responding units are en route. CHP is 914N, and you're on the patch."*

Sterling was flooring the gas now, weaving the BMW forward through a dense web of civilian traffic. Blair didn't know what to do or say. She checked the sky for some dark bank of storm clouds to save them.

But the sky only continued to brighten, paradoxically dooming their escape. Sterling could outdrive any cop in LA, it seemed, but with a helicopter overhead they were faced with one thing that no expert driver could compete with: a radio.

"Sterling?" She looked at him, waiting for some humorous comment, some momentary assurance, however false.

"Sterling?" Blair repeated. But he was focused on the road, as if he didn't hear her at all. Maybe he didn't.

Pressing a button on his steering wheel to transmit to the other car, Sterling spoke quickly.

"Bullet One has a helo overhead, bumping to Route Black to lose them in LAX airspace."

Alec replied, *"Bullet Two on support."*

Blair didn't know how she could help now.

"Can I help you navigate or...something?"

"No. We're taking Overland, West Jefferson into Sepulveda, then Slauson east to La Cienega. West Florence to Aviation. Zero dead ends, four lane majors for evasion, six freeways to access."

His response was quick and confident, but Blair could hear his looming sense of dread. Of course she could, she thought. How else was he supposed to react? The best driver in the world would be at the mercy of uncontrolled conditions trying to run from police anywhere in the world, much less Los Angeles. Heading toward LAX was a common tactic for high-speed chases trying to lose their aerial surveillance. The helicopter would now be requesting LAX airspace clearance to continue pursuit, Blair knew. It was extremely rare for this clearance to be granted, but if it was...there'd be nothing Sterling could do.

Blair looked forward, seeing they were now approaching terrific speeds in the gaps between commuter cars. And with a great sinking feeling of horror, Blair thought they were going to get arrested. Or killed.

She considered the latter, and thought that it may have been the more preferable of the two options. Because the alternative would be a return to prison—and could she really do that?

She thought of her previous incarceration, and how she'd reacted. To her credit, Blair had started strong. It was a strength, she later considered, forged out of ignorance and self-deception. But now she knew what became of that type of strength in the crumbling hillside of time that was her solitary confinement.

Something out the window caught her eye, and Blair glanced up to see a new helicopter flying above them. This was no police or sheriff chopper; instead it was bright blue, with gauche yellow lettering boasting a local news station. Beneath the helicopter's nose was a mounted sphere that orbited to keep its black pit of a lens trained on the BMW.

And with that, Blair realized, she and Sterling were on TV yet again.

45

JIM

The news commentator said excitedly, "*It appears the suspects are making a run for LAX, a common move for criminals trying to lose their overhead surveillance...*"

"We're in luck!" Wycroft exclaimed, greedily pouring another cup of coffee as he nodded toward the window of his corner suite. "We'll be able to see the choppers soon. Man oh man, how I love my office."

Jim said nothing, turning back to watch the huge television behind him. What an Angelino thing for Wycroft to say, he decided, studying the footage unfolding on the screen.

There were two types of car chases in the US, Jim thought to himself: those that took place in LA, and those that occurred anywhere else in the country.

Visually, the average viewer couldn't tell the difference. Just like any other car chase, a blue bar crossed the bottom of the screen announcing the pursuit and current location, leaving room, of course, for the network logo. In the corner of the screen was a tag reading LIVE, the best ratings-booster for any news footage.

"*The pursuit began just minutes before our chopper arrived, and police believe this car contains suspects from this morning's daring bank robbery in Century City, including a woman the FBI has identified as Blair Morgan...*"

The screen divided, the right half designated EARLIER and showing aerial footage of two men in black rappelling down the side of the skyscraper, with Blair in tow. She clung to the taller of the two men, falling free over the streets of LA in her red dress and boots, black hair whipping in the wind.

The rest of the screen was filled with a panning view of the chase in progress. But that, Jim knew, was where the similarities ended. Beyond those staples, no city in America did car chases like LA.

"If I didn't know better, Tom, I'd think this was part of a Hollywood action movie. But police say the dramatic scene unfolding now is anything but a carefully scripted film shoot..."

For LA, high-speed car chases were the equivalent of tornados for the Midwest: a break in all programming, cause for streaming coverage to be watched in rapt fascination by anyone not in the path of destruction. Wycroft was, at present, a living personification of this effect. Tens of thousands of Angelinos would tune in just to watch a fifteen-minute escape attempt by some thug who'd just held up a gas station. Viewership would increase for every second the chase continued, more so if the getaway attempt was unique, such as an RV crashing through the streets or a stolen Lamborghini ripping down the interstate at a buck eighty. Both had unfolded on live television in LA in the past few years.

But for the spectacle unfolding now, he knew, the entire city would be watching.

"I couldn't agree with you more, Amanda—this morning's footage is straight off the set of a James Bond movie. And this chase doesn't disappoint either. I've followed a lot of car chases, but never seen one like this..."

The soundtrack of such chases was inevitably Tom Stillman, the local station's aerial newsman. He had inadvertently gained a cult following in Los Angeles, and the entire city reveled in listening to him calling the shots of each chase with the enthusiasm of an Argentine soccer announcer.

"...the black BMW has been eluding police like I've never seen and—OH! OH! Amanda, we've got another cruiser down trying to pursue, that's got to be the fourth or fifth that has wrecked attempting to follow the suspect who, I've gotta tell you, could make a decent living as a race car driver if he wasn't going to spend the rest of his life in prison..."

Jim was disgusted—these newscasters, who'd never been any closer to the action than their filming set, were virtually cheering on the BMW driver. And why wouldn't they? All these people cared about was their ratings. Beyond their sterile teleprompter they had no idea what animals prowled the streets of this city, kept in check by law enforcement under the best of circumstances and endangering the populace under the worst.

Keep cheering, he thought. Wait until that BMW loses traction and takes out a minivan with a family of five inside. Then we'll see who was on the right side of this pursuit.

The public, it appeared, wasn't nearly so concerned with their own safety. The footage revealed drivers holding phones out their windows to film the chase as it passed, waving excitedly to the BMW.

Tom Stillman went on, *"He's been weaving in and out of traffic, in the emergency lane, on the shoulder, moving at extremely high speeds. Every time I think he's driving erratically he pulls off some crazy driving maneuver and changes direction. At this point I can't tell if he's desperate or a genius...this guy simply cannot be running on luck anymore."*

Jim gritted his teeth. On this point, Tom wasn't wrong. Apparently Mario Andretti himself was piloting the BMW sedan barreling down the slick road, minimizing wheel spin and sliding while police cars were literally and figuratively spinning their wheels, skidding and crashing at the end of great oversteering slides.

"The driver is described as a Caucasian male, and he's got one female passenger who police believe is Blair Morgan. So far it appears the only injuries have been officers involved in the pursuit...and at this rate of speed, the suspect should be arriving in LAX airspace any minute now. It'll be up to police to negotiate helicopter clearance past that..."

Wycroft leapt out of his seat, striding to the northern-facing window of his corner office that overlooked El Segundo and north of it, LAX.

"Jim," he said, taking a sip of coffee, "come over here before this ends. Get a load of my new client outrunning every cop in LA."

232

46

STERLING

Sterling swerved right, taking the exit for Overland Avenue and hearing the police helicopter report his departure from the I-10. He accelerated along the lane as it curved right and over the interstate he'd just exited, noting with almost comical resignation that a California Highway Patrol truck was approaching from the top of the ramp, lights blazing.

"Get in line, pal," Sterling muttered, flinging the BMW over a short curb and into the opposite lanes to bypass a cluster of cars waiting at the red light. Cutting left onto Overland, he saw a long stretch of straight road shooting southeast. It was a getaway driver's playground—for now, at least—and he punched the gas and throttled south toward the airport.

Easily swinging the car through gaps in traffic, he observed cops beginning to pour onto Overland behind him. One cruiser burst out of an intersection to his front, nearly sideswiping him before accelerating toward his rear bumper.

Blair said, "They're going to try a PIT maneuver, Sterling."

"I know, I know," he answered, somewhat impatiently. The PIT stood for Pursuit Intervention Technique—a police favorite for ending a high-speed chase. It was remarkably simple to execute: the police cruiser simply pulled its front bumper even with the suspect vehicle's rear quarter panel, then conducted a lane change toward the target car.

Properly executed, the fleeing car would spin out of control. Follow-on police cars would then speed in, block it front and rear, and presto: the reckless driver or armed robbery suspect was suddenly in the sights of a half dozen cops with guns pointed, screaming for him to show his hands.

And in a perfect universe, Sterling would have been near-immune from such a maneuver. The combination of his vehicle and driving skills would make it nearly impossible for a cop to catch up to him, much less attempt a PIT maneuver.

But here, in the real world of LA traffic, no matter how carefully selected the route, there were civilian vehicles to contend with. And Sterling would avoid striking one of them at all costs. It was one thing if cops got injured while trying to pursue; but he would let himself get arrested before he risked hurting a bystander.

That thought weighed heavily on Sterling's mind as he braked to enter a cluster of vehicles, weaving through their ranks before the sound of police sirens cleared a swath of open lanes on the road. The effect was doubly bad—civilian vehicles parted like the Red Sea in his rearview, too late to help him but soon enough to allow the police unrestricted passage. Sterling cursed his failure to consider this, and vowed to install an audible siren on his getaway vehicle the next time.

If there was a next time.

He made a hard right onto Jefferson Boulevard, which tightened down to a divided road. The trees on the side of the street would give him some momentary respite from aerial surveillance, but not enough to save him— and as he whipped through the angled intersection where Sepulveda Boulevard merged with Jefferson, disaster struck.

A white Toyota minivan suddenly swerved toward him from the right lane; Sterling juked the BMW left, catching a fleeting glimpse of a middle-aged woman texting, oblivious to the chase in progress. His sudden avoidance prevented a collision, but put him in the wake of an eighteen-wheeler in the adjacent lane that Sterling had to brake sharply to avoid contact with as it swerved out of the way.

The BMW's all-wheel drive chirped to a clean deceleration on the wet pavement, but the maneuver cost Sterling whatever distance advantage he maintained from the ground pursuit. A police cruiser shot the gap to Sterling's BMW, a flashing red light bar brightening in his driver side mirror. It was the last thing Sterling saw before impact.

He felt his rear tires lose traction in a split second, the BMW whipping counterclockwise in a flat spin. Sterling steered in the direction of the turn, straightening his wheels when the windshield faced backward on the road.

A train of police cruisers was racing toward him as Sterling threw the transmission in reverse and punched the accelerator, quickly backing away from the lead cruiser's attempt to ram him from the front.

Sterling checked his mirrors, a second's glance confirming enough open lane space to his four o'clock to reverse his fortunes. He took his foot off the gas and cranked his steering wheel to the right.

The BMW whipped a tight rotation. Sterling reversed his steering input as he cleared the first ninety degrees of the turn, straightening the wheels as he shifted from reverse to drive.

He floored the gas pedal as the storefront of a dry cleaner whipped past his windshield. The BMW completed an additional ninety-degree spin to face forward on the road, which was as long as it took for the transmission and gas inputs to take effect.

All four wet weather tires grabbed traction at the same time, launching the BMW forward ahead of the main pursuit.

"Whoa!" Blair shouted. "Yeah!"

"Are you—cheering?"

"Did you see that? Of course I'm cheering."

"There's no cheering until the chase is over. You're jinxing our getaway."

As if on cue, the sound of the police transponder muted, and Alec transmitted from the other getaway car.

"*Bullet One, they must really want to nail you—police just got airspace clearance for LAX. You'll lose the media, but the police chopper will be in it for the long haul.*"

Sterling felt a painful tightness in his chest, his mouth going dry in one instant.

That airspace clearance was the death blow to their escape, plain and simple; he now had three police cars immediately behind him and an additional unit—the one that had spun him out with a PIT maneuver—to his front. But those were just the immediate pursuers. Law enforcement would be realigning their disposition of resources along the chase corridor as the pursuit progressed. He could break visual with a helicopter by driving into an area of dense buildings and tight streets, but this put him at much greater risk of a police barricade or spike strip, and it wouldn't take the helicopter long to reorient its flight to locate him. He had driving maneuvers for days to outpace ground units, and the right car to do it in, but that meant nothing with a helicopter announcing his actions at every turn.

Sterling forced himself to key the radio and replied, "Copy. I'll think of something."

As he whipped a left turn onto Slauson Avenue eastbound, the police transponder dutifully reported his change in direction. Sterling was now proceeding along his course for little more than lack of better options—ditching the car was useless without overhead cover blocking the helicopter's view, and even then he wouldn't let Marco and Alec come near him unless he was certain he'd shaken all surveillance.

Sterling had spent weeks driving potential routes, and had the training and experience from braking and acceleration to cornering and line theory to make a high-speed getaway "in the wet." The BMW was dancing at his fingertips now, ready to do everything he asked of it.

The sad truth was that none of this preparation had mattered.

And it was completely and utterly his fault.

His ambition had gotten the best of him, and not for the first time. He was aware of the consequences and willing the pay the price if necessary, with one exception: now, he'd gone too far. Risking the flash flood warning and even proceeding with the heist after the woman revealed herself to be a minor escape artist were simple matters of risk versus reward. He'd gambled and lost; that much, he could live with.

But what plagued him was involving *this* woman. A woman who, if Sterling had known her past, he never would have involved. A woman who'd desperately asked to be removed from Geering Plaza, a request that he'd agreed to despite the risks involved.

Blair couldn't have understood what their escape entailed, regardless of what she knew—or thought she knew—from working in law enforcement. And Sterling should have taken that into account before allowing her to come along. So why hadn't he? Why had he capitulated to her will?

He couldn't conceive of an answer. Instead he spoke numbly, saying, "This is embarrassing. I think we're going to get arrested."

Sterling watched Blair's jaw go slack, saw her place trembling fingertips over her open mouth without saying a word.

"You'll be okay," he insisted. "Tell them you were my hostage. I made you come after you saw my face. You resisted at every turn."

"They're not going to believe that, Sterling."

"I can't be responsible for you ending up in prison. I've already screwed your life up enough, and I've got to live with that for the rest of mine. I'm sorry about this. About all of it. It wasn't supposed to go this way."

"I know," she replied in a quavering voice. "Why did you guys do this in the first place?"

Sterling whipped a turn, accelerating to merge with La Cienega Boulevard southbound.

"It's all a game, Blair. A game to make them think we're someone we're not."

"Why? Why the fake bank robbery, the hostages, all of it?"

He looked at her hesitantly. "I regret to say that you'll know soon enough."

47

BLAIR

Blair turned over Sterling's last words in her mind. *I regret to say that you'll know soon enough.* She began hyperventilating, feeling like she was having a heart attack, panic attack, or both. She couldn't go back to prison, she decided—couldn't possibly go through that again. And yet she was about to, and this imminent return meant that her next prison cell would be the one she died in.

Blair leaned her head back and pinched her eyes shut, her body jolting as Sterling maneuvered the BMW—toward what or why, she didn't know anymore. And lurking beneath the physical sensation was a single gut-wrenching reminder: this was all her fault.

She demanded that Sterling take her along on the getaway, remove her from the circumstances of a life that was barely recognizable anymore. Weighing heavily on that impulsive decision was the assurance that they were the wildly talented heist crew she'd envisioned, much to the amusement of everyone else on the task force who insisted that a vast network of robbery teams was collaborating across Southern California. Now she was beginning to doubt herself. And if they weren't the crew she thought, then...who *were* they?

Regardless, Sterling had drastically altered his plan to concede to her request, placing himself and his team at great risk.

And what had Blair done in return?

Gotten him caught.

Now she was about to go to prison. *Back* to prison, she corrected herself.

Blair thought back to her incarceration. She had gone straight into solitary confinement, though not for any egregious violation of inmate rules. Instead, an entire prison wing was dedicated to people considered too at-risk to serve their time in the general population.

Chief among them? Former officers of the law.

So Blair had gone to her cell, isolated from the human race save meal delivery and an hour in the yard each day. At first she'd passed the time with rigorous physical training, burning with the determination that she'd be released ahead of schedule. She told herself that Jim would be swooping in with Wycroft at his side, ready to save her with some litigation that had been kept secret until the time was right. She'd kept herself going with that thought, until all hope was lost when she finally realized that no one was coming to save her.

Then the despair had set in, the unceasing hopelessness. Once the prospect of ever reclaiming her career became a pipe dream, her spirit broke. Her sense of identity had been so intertwined with her job, she realized, that once the job was gone, her identity seemed to evaporate just as quickly.

Now, the FBI was like a black hole that she couldn't escape. She'd so willfully tried to get in, painstakingly filled out every application and regarded her acceptance letter as a defining moment of her life. Taking the Oath of Office upon graduating the Academy, yet another milestone. Now, wanting nothing more than to start over, she was reminded of the FBI's immense power, its inescapable gravitational pull. The FBI SWAT teams had attacked the bank building top and bottom, and she'd narrowly escaped only to flee with a police helicopter overhead, marshaling patrol cars ready to take her and Sterling into custody.

Then Blair thought of the day's events—her panic at the top of Geering Plaza, the unbridled freedom of descending through the elevator shaft. How natural it had felt to ascend the ladder to the street, a bag of cash from a bank heist slung across her back.

At first she thought today represented the first freedom she'd felt since her incarceration. But now she realized that she hadn't felt free since the start of her affair with Jim, since she began slinking to various locations around LA for their sexual encounters. By the time she agreed to fabricate her report, she hadn't felt free; not for some time.

With that thought, it felt like a weight was lifted off her. In that moment she felt—bizarrely, yes, and in contradiction to the events around them— totally *free*. And that feeling would sustain her no matter her surroundings, would nourish her in a way she'd never felt before.

She had her dignity again. She'd earned that much on the rooftop in Century City, and she was never going to let it go again. Her heart rate began to subside, and she took a deep, centering breath before opening her eyes.

The sky beyond the windshield was beautiful after the storm—still gray, but lifting and letting in more light on the city below. The BMW continued to whip through traffic on Aviation Boulevard, as if Sterling was operating on instinct until escape became fully impossible.

She looked to her right and saw LAX whipping by, passenger jets halted on the runway until the chase had passed.

And in the improbable chaos of that moment, sitting as a passenger in a high-speed police pursuit, Blair Morgan found peace.

She looked to Sterling and announced, "It's okay."

"What do you mean, it's okay?"

Blair shrugged. "All of this. Getting arrested, going back to prison."

"That couldn't be further from 'okay.' Blair, I'm...I'm so sorry I dragged you into this."

She waved an indifferent hand at him. "Don't be. Freedom isn't living outside of prison bars. There are people who've never been imprisoned that aren't free. Looking back now, I realize that I was in solitary confinement before I ever broke the law. Jim controlled me because I couldn't control myself. After today—well, I can. You can be truly free in prison, or imprisoned in a penthouse. By risking every- thing today, I think I've found true freedom for the first time in my life. You've shown me what that is." She gave him an icy glare. "In a real messed-up, roundabout way." Watching the road, she continued, "No one's ever breaking me again. Whether I go back to my one- bedroom apartment or my one-person cell after this is beside the point."

"That doesn't mean you belong back in prison, Blair."

"Well this time, I'll go in with my head held high." She looked over to him. "What about you?"

"The only words they'll hear me say are asking for a lawyer. I recommend you do the same."

"I'm no rat," Blair said. Then she considered how she'd preserved Jim's secret and added, "Even when I should be. So count on this—no matter what happens, I won't say a word that helps them find Marco or Alec. I offered to go along so you wouldn't take other hostages, period. Though you may want to ditch your Omega before getting caught."

Sterling looked quickly to her before changing lanes to pass another car. "Decision time. Where do you want to get arrested? Manhattan Beach? Torrance? We could head back to Wilshire and get caught at the FBI headquarters."

"I told you, that's just the main headquarters. The task force is based out of an office in..."

Her voice trailed off, and then she shouted, "Head to El Segundo!"

"Why?"

"Because I know a way out of this—a place we can hide long enough to get picked up by Marco and Alec."

"What place? Woman, five seconds ago you were ready to get arrested."

"Arrested?" she yelled at him. "Are you crazy? I can't go back to prison! Just take us toward El Segundo!"

He glanced at the nav screen, then back at the road. "We just passed it. Couldn't you have had this revelation a few minutes ago?"

"Well you're the world's greatest getaway driver, Sterling. Figure it out."

Sterling didn't have time to evaluate his options—instead, he made a visual sweep of his mirrors and prepared to act on instinct.

Three police cars were close behind him and one remained to his front, ready to box him in when the opportunity presented itself.

And Sterling needed to go the opposite direction.

He punched the gas, easing past the police cruiser to his front.

The cop driving the cruiser saw the opportunity for another PIT maneuver, and drifted toward the BMW. Sterling let him get close and, before the cop could initiate contact, tapped the brakes.

The wheels chirped on wet asphalt, a momentary deceleration that caused the police cruiser to begin overshooting Sterling's car.

Then Sterling swung the BMW's bumper into the cruiser's rear wheel, holding the turn to pivot the cop car sideways.

The cruiser's rear tires lost traction, and the black-and-white spun sideways in a great wheeling arc.

Sterling saw the cruisers behind him swing wide to avoid the car now spinning out of control—and that, he thought, was exactly the gap he needed.

Before the police could re-form their pursuit, Sterling checked his speedometer and saw he was now at 80mph.

He activated his emergency brake and turned the steering wheel a quarter turn to the left. The BMW rotated sideways in a long, drifting slide, coming to a stop facing back the way he'd come. Sterling pushed the emergency brake downward and then punched the gas to accelerate toward the police cruisers. They were trying to form a unified front to block him, but with three cruisers and five lanes, Sterling was able to whip around them before they could constitute a barrier across the road.

He kept the BMW roaring north on Aviation Boulevard. To stay out of civilian traffic, he drove in the median over shards of blown-out tires and fast food litter. His rearview mirror revealed the pursuit cruisers scrambling to reorient themselves, and Sterling looked forward to see the intersection for Rosecrans Avenue.

It wasn't his green light, but that hadn't stopped him yet. Sterling chose a path in between cars in the oncoming lane, successfully diverting around the rows of traffic dutifully awaiting their legal turn.

A bright red Ferrari was crossing the intersection and the driver braked to a panicked stop upon seeing a black BMW coming at it nearly head-on.

Sterling slowed to 20mph before cranking his emergency brake and spinning the BMW ninety degrees, orienting his front bumper with the westbound traffic lanes before dropping the brake and accelerating forward to El Segundo.

48

JIM

"Jim," Wycroft probed, "it sounds like she's in the passenger seat of that BMW."

"I know," Jim said impatiently, leaning in to watch the television.

Tom Stillman was saying, *"They've attempted to PIT this guy without success, and even had one of their black-and-whites pitted by the suspect on Aviation Boulevard southbound before the BMW turned back to the north..."*

Jim shook his head. In most parts of America, coverage of a car chase resulted in reporters trying to explain the PIT maneuver to their audience. In LA, reporters critiqued the police's PIT maneuvers on the air, turning it into a verb: "pitted."

The news anchor continued, *"There must be close to ten police vehicles out of commission in the pursuit of this BMW..."*

Wycroft sounded hesitant. "Jim, are you entirely certain that Blair is a hostage?"

Jim snapped his head toward Wycroft. "Of course I am."

Then he spun back to the television.

The getaway driver was locating and moving to the dull, porous sections of wet pavement, which would provide more grip than the shiny stretches.

But the cops could only react to the BMW's changing route and attempt to follow in vehicles unsuited for the conditions. The view behind the suspect vehicle looked like a drifting contest, with cop cars spinning their wheels and sliding past corners and into the curb.

Jim shook his head. What sense did that make—why was the driver going off the main roads? Taking a chase to side streets was begging the cops to anticipate your route and box you in with spike strips.

Wycroft probed again, "What if—and obviously I'm speaking in hypotheticals here—what if Blair doesn't want to come back?"

Jim waved a dismissive hand. "Don't be ridiculous. No one's walking away from clearing their name and securing a government pension."

He continued squinting at the screen, trying to make sense of what he was seeing. The driver had clearly outfitted his car for wet-weather operation—and had the driving chops to back it up. Based on that, Jim could reasonably assume the vehicle was equipped with additional fuel cells for extended range. But where could he go with helicopters in pursuit?

The news footage was more distant now, the media helicopters trying to zoom in from outside LAX airspace while the police helicopter alone remained directly overhead.

"Now he's maneuvering in tighter streets, where this gets very, very dangerous...police can't tell where to throw spike strips because this guy's changing direction constantly. But his general movement seems to be toward El Segundo..."

Jim froze, feeling the tingle of goose bumps rising from his lower back up to his shoulder blades.

"El Segundo," Wycroft noted, completely oblivious, "that's a few blocks from here! We'll get some extra viewing pleasure yet."

"The Assignments Desk has just told me that... hang on a sec... yes, police report that this is the area of the FBI task force where bank robbery suspect Blair Morgan used to work...if revenge is a motive, they speculate she may be planning a desperate last stand. Units are barricading that building in anticipation of..."

Jim bolted to his feet.

"I have to go," he blurted.

Wycroft looked startled. "You sure? I mean, I can see the police chopper right here."

But Jim was already moving out of the office and past Shelly, who watched the footage on her computer screen, entranced.

By the time he passed the receptionist he was at a run, headed for the elevator.

The door chimed open and Jim strode inside, tapping the button for the ground floor in a furious cadence.

49

STERLING

Sterling had many problems at that moment, but driving wasn't one of them.

He careened right through an intersection, swerving around bewildered drivers screeching to a halt around him. Sterling could drive circles around them all day; and given the additional fuel cells installed in his BMW, he meant that quite literally.

But regardless of how confident Blair was in her plan, the Eye in the Sky continued tracking them from above. Were it not for the flash flood dooming their ATVs in the tunnel, he lamented, his entire crew would have been ghosts by now.

The transponder blared, "...*additional units needed at the task force head-quarters in El Segundo. Suspects appear to be increasingly desperate, may be looking to attempt a suicide attack of some kind...*"

Sterling asked Blair, "How good is this spot of yours?"

"Couldn't be better. I can tell you how to get there—and the media heli-copters are already gone because they don't have airspace clearance. You just need to lose the police chopper long enough for us to get in."

"Oh, 'just' lose the police chopper. Great, that'll be a cinch."

Sterling wheeled the BMW left, accelerating as he wound his way toward El Segundo.

Evading a police helicopter in the daytime was very different from evading at night, and at this point he wasn't sure which he'd have preferred more. Neither, actually. And now that he was stuck with a daytime evasion, most workable tactics were out of the question.

In certain circumstances, it was possible to escape a helo. It had certainly been done in the past, although rarely and more often by luck than any discernable skill. Most successes involved the fleeing suspect ditching their car in the covered parking garage of a mall, and then blending with the mass of people inside. Or exiting amid the urban tangle of their own neighborhood, and breaking the helicopter's line of sight by running through houses on foot. In either case, the procedure was to lose the helicopter and restrict the police arsenal to ground units only.

But Sterling had to do the opposite: lose the ground units first, and then lose the aerial surveillance. That was a far trickier proposition.

"Well," Blair objected, "if you have a better idea, I'm all ears."

"Just let me think."

It didn't take long. He knew more about police helicopter procedures than many patrol officers; right or wrong, this was his life's work.

First off, the pilots would avoid hovering. They were flying at several hundred feet; in the event of engine trouble, their only hope was to "auto-rotate" to the ground by using the helicopter's forward momentum to spin to ground at a survivable angle. If their engine lost power in a hover at that altitude, the helicopter would plummet to the earth.

This meant the aircraft would stay moving, which forced the pilots to either circle over an area or, in the event of a high-speed chase, anticipate the car's direction of movement and set up their flight path to maintain visual.

Sterling could give them every indication of his direction of travel, and then subvert this expectation with a sudden change of direction. If he did so when their line of sight to him was obstructed, he'd buy time before they could reacquire visual—it would be tight, but doable. But even if he was successful, he'd win himself seconds, not minutes.

And he'd have to reach Blair's hiding spot before the helicopter found him again.

"Okay," Sterling said. "Here's what we have to—"

"You're done thinking already? That was, like, two seconds."

"Thanks. I need you to navigate while I drive. We won't have any margin for error."

"El Segundo is my backyard. I know the streets—what do you need?"

"Before we head to your spot, we've got to break line of sight. Narrow road, lined with trees or tall buildings. Preferably both."

"Continental Boulevard, between Grand and Mariposa. Next?"

"Are there outlets where I can change direction quickly?"

"Multiple. Unlimited, if you're willing to jump a curb. And there are huge outdoor parking lots all around it, filled with cars—if they lose sight of you, they'll have to start searching for a needle in a haystack. Plus access to covered parking they can't see from the air."

"Good. Next: we have to get the helicopter confident in our direction of travel, so when we hit Continental and they lose us in the trees, they try to pick up visual on the other side."

"That's the easy part."

"It is?"

"They think we're headed for the task force headquarters. Let's not disappoint them."

"So approach the tree-lined part of Continental like we're headed to your old job, then pull the switch before the helo realizes their mistake... that might work."

"It better. Prison sucks."

"All right. I'm in your hands now, Blair."

"Relax, Sterling," she said. "Now it's your turn to trust me. Take this next right."

50

JIM

Jim accelerated his SUV, roaring through the intersection as the light turned green.

He listened to the police transponder, where dispatch still speculated that Blair was headed toward the task force office.

But Jim suspected something else entirely. He'd been wondering where she could go, and the thought had first struck him as he saw the news in Wycroft's office. As soon as he heard El Segundo, he started asking himself... What if? What if Blair went to their old rendezvous spot?

It would certainly make sense. She was a brutalized hostage, under duress, terrified of dying in a fireball during a high-speed chase. Blair had made it through nine months in prison, all of it in solitary. She was a survivor. She'd do whatever it took to stay alive, to keep hope until law enforcement could rescue her.

It wasn't a sure thing, by any means.

But there was a chance—and only a chance—that she'd advise the driver to go to the hidden garage. The spot was perfect: only one way in or out by vehicle, and one by foot. Both entrances appeared to be under surveillance to anyone who didn't know better, so the odds of anyone venturing inside were slim to none.

After all, that's why Jim picked it for their workday affair, and later, to stash his throw-down piece.

He considered the odds, repeatedly assuring himself there was at least a chance. Was it worth checking out? Of course it was.

But only by him.

He couldn't call backup—every possible police asset was tied up in the ongoing chase. And *if* Jim was right, how could he explain that he knew that extremely obscure spot? Admitting his suspicion would be as good as admitting he'd screwed Blair in the backseat.

Besides, he thought with a wry smile, why would he want backup?

He knew that location better than anyone, definitively knew how he could enter undetected. If he was wrong, no harm no foul. If he was right, he could get the drop on the one captor sighted in the car and save Blair himself.

That solved everything. He'd heroically rescue Blair, and even if she still hated him for what he'd done to her, he could now explain that Wycroft was standing by to overturn her conviction. Whether she loved him or not, he would have righted his wrongs against her. Imagine the press conference, he thought. Jim and Blair, side by side, explaining the events of her rescue from violent criminals.

So too could they explain the misunderstanding that had led to Jim's faulty conclusion that Blair was involved in the heist—a misunderstanding that was about to be corrected via Blair's pro bono legal representation. Justice would shine like a diamond, and the resulting media frenzy would secure Jim's Bureau legacy and pave the way for his next move up the ranks —ultimately, to a position as Special Agent in Charge.

His mentor would be most pleased, and Jim would be a hero among heroes.

Don't get ahead of yourself, he thought as he braked for a red light. You'll probably get there and find it empty.

But in a few minutes, he'd know for sure.

51

BLAIR

"Chopper is at one o'clock," Blair said.

"Good." Sterling slowed to 45mph on westbound El Segundo Boulevard, causing the trailing police cruisers to bunch up on his tail. It took them only a few seconds to begin maneuvering into position for a PIT.

And then Sterling dropped the hammer.

As he floored the accelerator and the BMW blasted forward, Blair was thrown against the seat. The cruisers faded from her side view mirror, struggling to give chase. But the distance kept expanding, and by the time they'd reoriented themselves, Sterling was yanking the parking brake for a near-instantaneous ninety-degree turn onto Continental northbound.

Dropping the parking brake, he throttled forward at maximum speed. Blair caught glimpses of the helicopter between the trees and multi-story buildings to her right. It began to outpace them to the north, repositioning to maintain a line of sight with Continental Boulevard.

"You're clear!" Blair said.

And with that, Sterling made another gut-wrenching turn with his emergency brake. This one swung them right into an access street that passed between multi-level parking garages and office buildings, and he accelerated through the L-shaped turn to emerge on Grand Avenue eastbound.

In a four-second blast of full throttle they were passing under the elevated track of the Metro Green Line. As Sterling made his next turn, Blair heard what sounded like a sweet, sweet symphony over the vehicle speakers.

"*Air 21 has lost visual, do any ground units have eyes-on?*"

"Take a left here."

"*...don't see him on Continental...*"

They were two turns removed from the last speed and direction seen by the police, about to be three.

"Another left."

"*Be advised, suspects may have gone stationary in an adjacent parking lot. Advise ground units to sweep both sides of Continental, there's a lot of black cars down there...*"

Now Sterling did what felt to Blair like a bizarrely alien act: he started driving the speed limit.

"Take this right, we're almost there."

"*And we need barricades on the covered parking garages on El Segundo and Nash, El Segundo and Pacific, and Continental and Grand...*"

"This is it—right turn into this parking lot."

"*...no sign of suspects on foot, they could be waiting us out...*"

"That's us." Blair pointed at the vehicle entrance into the brick building before them.

Sterling piloted the BMW toward it as Blair caught a glimpse of the twin signs on either side.

VIDEO SURVEILLANCE IN EFFECT. ALL TRESPASSERS WILL BE PROSECUTED TO THE FULLEST EXTENT OF THE LAW.

Then the building exterior was swept from view, the BMW's headlights activating to illuminate the tunnel leading to the small garage.

"What about that camera?" Sterling asked.

"Inoperative. Trust me."

They reached the garage interior with six executive parking spaces and he stopped the car, facing the lone pedestrian exit. Blair saw him scanning the space around them as if looking for answers. Finally he shut off the engine and asked, "How do you know about this place?"

"Don't ask."

Sterling didn't. Instead he keyed the button on his steering wheel and said, "Bullet Two, this is Bullet One."

No response.

Sterling repeated, "Bullet Two, this is Bullet One."

"You think they're okay?" Blair asked.

"Yeah. Just radio problems. It's fine—they've been trailing the chase, waiting for our call. And they're about to get it."

He pulled out his cell phone.

Blair began, "There's—"

"No reception in here," he finished her sentence.

Blair pointed at the pedestrian footpath in front of them. "This walkway leads to an outdoor lot and side street on the other side of the building. We can go outside and call from there."

He nodded, leaning over to press a button on the console and holding it down. The nav display flashed a message that read, *Zeroing all software and radio programming. Hold to continue.*

Three seconds later, the screen went black.

Sterling and Blair exited the car, the sound of their doors closing echoing like gunshots in the enclosed space. He looked to her.

"We'll need to figure out what to do with you from here."

"I've been thinking about that."

"And?"

She felt lightheaded as she responded, "I want to join you guys."

"Join...us?"

She nodded slowly. "In the FBI, I sent people to prison. They were people that needed to go, yes—but after going myself, I don't have it in me to do that kind of work anymore. Not that the FBI's offering, mind you, but...still. You guys have been hitting doubles and triples, not hurting anyone—"

"Tell that to the bank guard."

"—other than bank guards," Blair corrected herself. "Not only do you guys not send anyone to prison, but you avoid it yourselves. That's kind of the epitome of freedom, on both counts. I loved working covert entries. That feels like what I was born to do. But," she continued, "I'd rather be doing it in a way that doesn't put people behind bars. Plus, I imagine the money is better on your side of the legal fence."

"Well that depends," he said, considering the statement. "What was your pension plan? I don't even give my guys a 401(k). I'd urge you to consider that before you commit to anything crazy."

Her face flushed, and she smiled. "If today was your definition of 'crazy,' then count me in. I'm ready for a change."

He shook her hand. "Welcome to the team."

"Think you can convince the other two?"

"Have a little faith. Let me go call them—I'll get you when they're arriving."

"Well what am I supposed to do, sit here and wait for you to return?"

"You're in a bright red dress and your face is all over TV. We can't risk you getting spotted."

This logic halted her in place. Sterling started to walk away, then stopped and turned to toss something to Blair with the question, "Know how to use one of these?"

She caught the object midair. It was the same taser he'd used on the bank guard.

"Really, Sterling?" She gestured to her cocktail dress. "Where exactly am I supposed to put this?"

Smiling at her, he shrugged. "I don't know. Use your imagination. I'll be right back."

Turning, he jogged toward the pedestrian exit and disappeared down the footpath.

Shaking her head, Blair went to set the taser atop the BMW. Thinking better of it, she slid it into her left boot, which had been selected for its ability to cover her ankle bracelet. She'd hated wearing that shackle. But now, the plastic surface of the taser occupying the same space felt oddly reassuring against her skin.

Then she felt a chill run up the length of her spine. Blair glanced around the darkened garage, trying to shake the inexplicable feeling that she was being watched.

52

JIM

Jim pulled off the street, cruising past the entrance to the parking garage where he and Blair had met for their workday rendezvous.

The sight of the entrance made something twinge deep in his belly, a pang of emotion striking when he saw the surveillance camera and the twin signs warning prosecution for trespassers. He'd just been here earlier today to recover his throw-down piece; this time, however, the setting felt entirely different. This time, there was a chance of seeing Blair.

Focus, he told himself.

Parking his SUV outside, Jim turned off the engine. Then he pulled out his duty phone, staring at the screen in a last-minute deliberation on whether to call for backup.

Jim was a good liar, and trusted he could think up some reason for suspecting the garage. But if Blair was inside, and if she said something to the other officers before he could explain the possibility of Wycroft redeeming her, she could incriminate him. He wanted to speak to her alone first.

Besides, he'd already hesitated once today on the 23rd floor of Geering Plaza. He'd been expecting to encounter three armed men near the elevator bank, and those extra few seconds of waiting had cost him the lone advantage he'd had, which was his ability to anticipate the crew's actions before anyone else. Jim wouldn't hesitate a second time.

But most of all, he wanted the glory. If he could pull off a one-man hostage rescue...well, that'd make him a Bureau legend.

Jim placed his phone on silent mode so an incoming call wouldn't betray his presence in the tunnel he was about to enter. He repeated the process with his burner phone, then reached into his console, withdrew a pouch with a set of handcuffs, and clipped it to his belt.

Then he exited the truck, hearing the wail of police sirens as he set foot on wet pavement. He eased his door shut, letting it click in place, and appraised his surroundings. Uncountable sirens cried out from the streets of El Segundo now, with every available unit responding to find the missing BMW. He looked at the building's exterior. Nothing seemed out of place, but why would it?

Jim lifted the right side of his navy FBI jacket and drew his service issue 9mm semi-automatic pistol. He cursed himself for leaving his borrowed 12-gauge and body armor with the FBI support team. Truth be told, pistols were next to useless as anything other than a concealed piece or secondary weapon. But only one bad guy would be inside, if there were any at all. Jim could get the drop on one robber, blow him away before anyone knew he was there. He knew the garage interior inside and out. And under the miniscule chances that the thief wasn't armed, Jim had the comforting weight of his throw-down piece strapped to his left ankle.

He entered the tunnel with his weapon at the high ready. Then he looked down, trying to ascertain whether anyone had entered here before him.

Yes, wet vehicle tracks led through the tunnel. Had the building finally sold? Jim gave a momentary thought to how ridiculous he'd feel if he cleared the final corner to find a pair of teenagers parking, or some kid with a can of spray paint creating his own personal masterpiece on the interior walls.

But something assured him that his hunch would pay off. His intuition had rarely steered him wrong, and if there was ever a day he needed it, it was today.

And this was where he felt natural. Where he *belonged*. In a way he longed for his SWAT days, would have felt no regret at trading in all his rank and achievement to be back with his old team, kicking in doors to serve high-risk warrants with a weapon in hand.

With the rush of exhilaration flooding into his system, Jim had to force himself to move slowly, stealthily, as he walked forward into the darkness.

53

BLAIR

Rotating slowly in place, Blair took in the dank garage. It smelled of dusty concrete, like some forgotten basement—yet Blair had returned here repeatedly for Jim, like some love-drunk teenager. She'd slept with her own boss here despite the fact that he was married, and that wasn't close to the worst part.

This was also the location where she'd agreed to Jim's plan of lying on her surveillance report. And that, in itself, was probably the darkest hour of her soul. Not the act of lying itself, and not even her prison cell, no matter how much it reminded her of this tiny parking lot at times.

Instead, agreeing to lie for him was worse than anything she'd ever done. She'd compromised her integrity, sold her soul for the promise of a better future with Jim. And that fateful day, when Jim had proposed his plan and Blair had shamefully agreed to it, was the last time Blair had ever set foot in this garage.

She almost shuddered at the thought. Now it felt cold and strange, every detail a reminder of the worst things she'd done in her life. She wanted to leave so badly, considered following Sterling up the footpath regardless of his instructions. If she'd had time to think about it earlier, she probably would never have suggested coming here.

Blair made a move to follow Sterling, and then stopped abruptly.

She thought she heard a scuffling sound behind her, the slightest whisper of movement against concrete.

Could the police have found them already? It was certainly possible, though they'd have no need for sneaking around. They'd be swooping in with sirens blaring, blocking off all avenues of escape.

Maybe it was just a rat.

And then Jim stepped into view.

Yes, she thought, that's exactly what it was.

Blair released a gasp. "God, you scared me."

Jim didn't lower his pistol at first, taking a sidestep into the parking area to visually clear for anyone else.

"Relax," Blair said. "I'm alone." She tried to sound calm and confident, but in reality knew she was trapped, felt her heart thudding dully in her chest. This was how it would end. At least Sterling could still get away clean. One loud scream from her, the slightest indication that anything was wrong, and Sterling would be a ghost.

Wouldn't he?

Jim lowered the pistol at last, but he didn't holster it.

She asked, "So, are you here to arrest me?"

He flinched at the question. "Arrest you? Blair, I'm not here to take you in. I'm here to redeem you—I thought you understood that from my speech to the media."

"Redeem...me?" She felt her body flushing with heat, her pulse speeding at his mention of the press conference.

"I talked to Wycroft. He's agreed to represent you, already informed the LAPD and the Bureau—"

"Oh, *now* you talked to Wycroft? Because that would have been immensely useful to me *before* I went to prison."

Jim gave her a stern look. "Don't negate your role in this, Blair. You did falsify an official report."

"I lied, yes. Then I was betrayed, imprisoned, released to a run-down apartment, and barely got work as a waitress. I get taken hostage and dragged into a bank robbery, and your response is to have your little press conference—"

"Blair, that was a mistake."

"There he is!" she yelled. "Jim, my knight in shining armor! With the audacity to call me a criminal mastermind after I went to prison without mentioning your name. Do you know how many times OPR offered me a deal to testify against you?"

"I can't change the past. But I can do this for you now. You can get your life back."

"Whether I'm a fed or not, there's no going back to the woman I was."

"Blair," Jim hissed, looking around as if to make sure no one could hear them. "These people are *criminals*."

"So are you, Jim. So am I."

"Blair, you need to listen to me. You've got Stockholm syndrome. I'm telling you there's a chance of getting your *pension* back. You're not thinking clearly."

"Jim, right now I'm thinking clearly for the first time in my life. And I'm never going back."

His face grew dark, and when he spoke again his tone was ominous.

"I played my golden ticket with Wycroft...for you," he hissed, "and you're telling me you don't want to go back?"

Blair couldn't believe what was happening to her—but unwillingly, even impossibly, she felt a smile playing at her lips.

Jim was silent after that, and she began nodding knowingly.

"I see what's happening," Blair said. "I see the wheels turning inside your head. You're realizing I won't go back with you, and wondering how to parlay this into some political victory for your career. Have you thought of it yet?"

"You can no longer claim I coerced you to lie. Not after your involvement in a bank robbery. No jury would believe you."

"No jury at all."

"You can sing all you want, but I'll have a better story every step of the way."

"Of that, I have no doubt. Which leaves you with what?"

"Arrest. I bring you in."

"Or?"

"Or I kill you."

"Very good, Jim. Now you just have to decide which option is more appetizing for you."

"You think so little of me?"

"Call me a cynic."

After a moment's hesitation, he took a resolute breath.

Then he aimed his pistol at her chest.

"Blair Morgan, you are under arrest."

Blair exhaled, pinching her eyes shut.

"Put your hands up, turn away from me, and get on your knees."

She opened her eyes and looked at him—shirt and tie under the FBI jacket, two-handed shooting stance squared off at her. Just like back at the Academy.

Then Blair took a relaxed breath and said, "No."

"Blair, I'm placing you under arrest. If you resist, you'll just add one more charge to the long list of things for which you will now stand trial."

"You want me, Jim, you come and get me. Or you could just execute me, and see how that works out."

Jim released one hand from the pistol, pulling the phone from his pocket.

"There's no reception in here, remember?" Blair said. "The FBI isn't here to help you, and neither is your mentor. You want to shoot me or arrest me? You're going to have to do it yourself. Or," she taunted, "you could walk out of here and risk me fleeing the other way."

She saw his eyes deaden, some emotional switch being flipped within him.

But he calmly put the phone away and holstered his pistol, looking up at her with both hands empty.

"You. Ungrateful. Little. Whore."

Blair felt a spike of adrenaline, her muscles quivering with rage. "What did you just say to me, you—"

Jim closed the distance between them and slapped her hard across the jaw.

Blair's vision burst into bright splotches of color as her head recoiled from the blow. She swung a punch at his face, but Jim caught her arm and violently threw her backward against the BMW.

He was pressing against her before she could retreat, shoving his left forearm into her throat and pinning her against the car. His right hand drew his pistol once more, and he pressed the barrel against her temple as she struggled to breathe.

Jim's eyes were wild now, ablaze with fury.

Blair's first thought was, *I have to warn Sterling.*

She'd warn him, all right. A gunshot would do the trick, and she'd rather die than return to the prison state of Jim's control.

Now he was pressing the gun tighter against her temple. "You could've left this with your badge," he growled. "Now you'll be leaving in cuffs or a body bag—choose."

54

STERLING

Sterling finally made it down the pedestrian footpath, stepping outside into the murky sunlight trying to fight its way out of the clouds. All around him were the distant cries of sirens, and the throaty groan of the police helicopter circling over El Segundo.

He dialed Alec and Marco from his cell.

Alec answered on the first ring. "You forget about us, buddy?"

"I lost radio."

"Told you that BMW was a piece of—"

"Radio, not the car. We need pickup, where you guys at?"

"We're loitering on North Douglas, trying not to get hit by cops. It's a hornet's nest out here. You guys are real popular on the news right now."

"Yeah, I figured. Head to the northwest intersection of Parker and Northrop. Pull next to a..." He glanced behind him. "Red dumpster. Me and Blair will break cover and load."

"You and...Blair?"

"Are you on your way?"

"Yeah, about seven minutes out. But let's think about bringing the dame. The only way this is going to work is if she—"

"Joins us?"

"Yeah. We can't take her back to the bat cave unless she's staying for good."

"I know. She's in."

"You sure about this?"

"I dragged her into this mess, and she just dragged me out. Without her I'd be in cuffs right now. We came in this job three strong. We're coming out of it with a fourth."

"But think about the great heist films, man. There's never been a woman on the crew. The dynamic, remember?"

"Just get here, Alec."

"All right, but we're discussing this when—"

Sterling ended the call and pocketed his phone. It took more effort than it should have—his hand was trembling slightly. Adrenaline hangover and emotional fatigue, he knew. Wouldn't be the last time. But he had to see his people out of this first.

He started to turn toward the building when a gunshot rang out.

Sterling spun in place, looking at the pedestrian entrance. The noise had been hard to distinguish over the helicopter and the sirens. It couldn't have been... had he misheard?

But the sound of the gunshot now echoed unmistakably inside the doorway, and Sterling moved toward Blair at a dead sprint.

55

BLAIR

Blair gasped for breath, Jim's forearm tight against her throat as he pressed her against the car.

His words hung in the air between them, drifting below the barrel of the gun he held to her head.

You could've left this with your badge. Now you'll be leaving in cuffs or a body bag—choose.

Blair had to throw him off his game. If she didn't, she was dead... or worse.

She croaked, "You missed this, didn't you?"

Jim released some of the pressure from her trachea, keeping his forearm in place but allowing her to breathe. His eyes darted between hers, his brow furrowing in bewilderment. And there it was, Blair thought—he still wanted her. Probably had, all this time.

She saw his eyelids growing heavy, his breathing shallow.

Then he whispered, "Didn't you?"

And at that, it all came rushing back to Blair. Her sexual liaisons with Jim in this dank, fetid space, a symbol of how much she was violating her body and his marriage. Being so dominated by the man that she lied for him, believed his assurances. The horrors of prison and her degradation in the aftermath.

It was now or never, she decided. Sterling was either going to hear her scream, or hear a gunshot—either way, he wasn't going to prison today.

And neither was she.

"Jim, I let you have my body, my heart, and my integrity." She swallowed against the pressure from his forearm. "Prison took my spirit. Now that I've gotten all of them back, you're not taking my freedom."

Bracing her back against the BMW, she drove the heel of one hand into his chin as hard as she could.

With the other, she struck his elbow, knocking his forearm off her throat.

The strikes hit near-simultaneously, dislodging Jim's powerful hold and causing him to stumble backward a half step.

She expected his gun to fire, ducking her head out of the way—but it didn't, and Blair utilized the newfound space to slam her forearm into his exposed throat.

The blow was devastating, delivered with enough force to potentially crush his trachea.

Reeling from the impact, Jim loosened his grip on the pistol. It tumbled from his grasp, cartwheeling noisily onto the concrete surface.

Blair tried to sidestep away from him and create distance. He was nearly doubled over, but as she lunged he sprang up and slapped her so hard across the face that her ears burst into loud ringing with the impact.

Before she could recover, Jim had clenched a hand on her throat and forced her back against the BMW.

She felt all the air cut off, and as she gasped for breath, Jim's fury-stricken eyes seemed to soften. Then his face suddenly regained its expression of fury, and Jim used both arms to throw her sideways.

Blair flew through the air, landing hard on her side and skidding to a halt on the filthy concrete. She looked up to see Jim spinning away from her.

He was moving to recover his gun.

Scrambling to her feet, Blair launched forward onto Jim's back, knocking him down. They fell to the concrete together, Jim's body absorbing the impact as Blair tried to route a slender arm around his throat to choke him from behind.

But Jim merely rolled on his side and threw an elbow backward, catching Blair's temple in a painful strike that caused her to lose her grip on him.

Then Jim began crawling forward on his elbows, reaching for the pistol so he could finish this battle forever.

Blair clutched his jacket with one hand, and with the other reached into her left boot.

She withdrew the taser, holding it up to his leg and squeezing the trigger. The dart-like twin probes speared through his pants and into his upper leg, and Blair held the trigger down. She heard the chattering sequence of clicks as the electrical charge ran through the conducting wires and between probes, but Jim kept crawling forward, his hand closing with the pistol.

Blair realized that her near-point-blank firing hadn't allowed the probes to spread from one another in flight, and without enough distance between them, the electrical charge wasn't sufficient to incapacitate him.

She wrenched his jacket back, buying herself an extra fleeting moment. But it wasn't enough—Jim's hand was inches from the gun, descending on it with an open palm.

With all the strength she could muster, Blair made a final lunging thrust to pull herself forward atop him.

Then she drove the front of her taser into his upper back, directly between the shoulder blades.

Jim's entire body turned into a rigid, seizing mass of muscle and bone, his hand frozen open in a state of paralysis. Blair kept the trigger on her taser depressed, sending the electrical current surging through Jim's upper body for long seconds of total incapacitation. Almost in disbelief that he was subdued, Blair dropped the taser and clambered over Jim to clutch the pistol sideways in her grasp.

Then she scrambled forward and away, rising to her feet before spinning to aim Jim's gun at him.

He'd recovered in seconds, and was now trying to push himself to his feet.

Blair yelled, "STOP!"

He froze in place, kneeling and looking up to see Blair standing over him. His eyes registered the pistol leveled at his face as she continued, "I want you to think very hard about what you do next."

"Okay," he conceded, gasping for breath. Then, exhausted, he lowered himself to the ground, leaning backward until he was resting against the side of the BMW. "I'm sorry, Blair." He swallowed dryly, yanking the taser probes out of his legs and tossing them aside. "But we've still got to work this out."

"I thought we just did."

Jim nodded, panting, collecting his knees under his elbows as if trying to gather his thoughts.

Blair sensed intuitively that something was wrong; Jim didn't give up this easily, didn't know how to and never would.

And that's when she saw it.

As his pant cuffs slid up, she caught a glimpse of the ankle holster above his left shoe.

"You packed a throw-down piece for me?"

His hand, which had been moving toward it, stopped when she said, "I wouldn't do that if I were you."

Upon hearing the conviction in her voice, he switched tack.

"I'm a federal agent," he said in an authoritative tone. "Put down the gun and turn yourself in."

"Or what—you'll send me to jail?"

"I can still testify that you cooperated—"

"Really? Like you helped me the first time I went to prison? You buried me, Jim. Nine months in solitary confinement. And I came out of my sentence with nothing left to return to."

"It's not too late. Wycroft has already agreed. You can get a fresh start."

"I've already been through one of your 'fresh starts,' Jim. So now I'm making my own. I didn't choose to be a part of this heist. But I am now."

"Then do it for your country. For the Bureau."

"No, Jim," Blair said slowly. "This time, I'm doing it for me. And there's one thing you should have considered before having an affair with a surveillance expert: I have recordings of you admitting to crimes so you could close a case. And telling me to lie. That evidence is tucked away somewhere safe. Keep that in mind, because I'm done protecting you. The next time you try to take me down will be your last."

He recoiled at this comment, his eyes fixed on hers, staring her down. Jim's next words made her blood run cold.

"You wouldn't dare shoot a federal agent." His hand lunged toward the pistol in his ankle holster.

Blair diverted her aim and fired.

The bullet ripped past Jim's ear, punching a hole in the car door beside his head.

"Jesus, woman!" Jim shouted, curling into the fetal position. "Are you *crazy*?"

Blair coolly pointed the gun back to Jim's face.

"Goodbye, Jim," she said quietly. "Go home to your wife."

Then she stepped forward and swung a kick to the side of his head.

Her boot connected with his temple with a crack, and Jim slumped, unconscious, to the concrete floor.

56

STERLING

Sterling skidded to a halt, bewildered at the sight before him.

A silver-haired man in a navy FBI jacket was sprawled beside the getaway car, which was now marred with a single bullet hole. Beside him on the ground was the taser, clearly discharged in subduing the agent.

Blair was crouched over the man, handcuffing his limp wrist to the spokes of a rear wheel.

She looked up at Sterling as he gasped, "Are you okay?"

Blair stood, giving him a weary half-smile.

"I'm okay." She nodded toward the unconscious man. "Meet ASAC Jacobson. Head of the task force in charge of hunting you."

"No," Sterling replied. "He's the head of the task force in charge of hunting *us*. That is," he quickly added, "if you still want to come with. Because if not, this is your last chance to part ways for some time."

Blair looked around the garage, the site where she'd had her private encounters with the man who'd just tried to kill her. "Oh, I am parting ways." She looked to Sterling. "But not with you guys."

"As you wish, Blair Morgan." He walked around her to open the trunk and sling the bag of cash over his shoulder. Then he slammed the trunk shut, produced the BMW's key fob, and prepared to press a button.

"Wait!" Blair said. "What about Jim?"

"What about him?"

"Are you about to set the car on fire?"

"No—why does everyone assume that? There'd be a beacon of smoke for the cops. And with the extra fuel cells in the trunk...it wouldn't be civilized, Blair."

The real solution was much simpler. Most classes of amateur and professional racing required their vehicles to be outfitted with a fire suppression system. At the push of a button, these systems would fill the cabin, trunk, and engine compartment with an extinguishing agent. Sterling had simply installed a dual suppression system that exceeded most European racing certifications, with a dozen nozzles installed to deliver the contents of two separate tanks of aqueous foam.

He'd only needed to make one small addition to further adapt the system for the hasty destruction of forensic evidence.

With the press of a button on the key fob, the BMW's interior emitted a continuous hissing sound. Within seconds, the windows clouded with high expansion foam that looked like an overflowing bubble bath. A stream of foam drizzled out the bullet hole in the car door, bringing with it the faint smell of sulfuric acid that would eradicate any DNA.

"I'm going to miss that car," Sterling said mournfully. Then he cocked an elbow to the side. "Shall we?"

Blair nodded, approaching him to slide a hand around his arm like a prom date. Together they walked down the pedestrian footpath.

She looked down to see her red dress, now soaked, torn, and filthy. Then she cast her gaze to Sterling and said, "You're paying for a new dress, you know."

He raised his eyebrows as if considering the request, then shrugged and hoisted the bag of cash on his back. "Well now I can afford it."

57

THE CREW

They emerged into the sunshine amidst the distant wailing of sirens and helicopters.

Blair looked upward, blinking.

The clouds had parted further, revealing the first swaths of deep blue sky. Radiant sunshine bathed the city, the residual moisture from the storm rising in hazy waves. The air smelled of fresh rain, like the world had been baptized and reborn anew after the storm.

Before she could reflect further, the white turbo wagon pulled up and screeched to a stop in front of them. She saw Marco at the wheel, and Alec leaping out of the passenger seat to scramble around the car and open the back door for her.

"Your Majesty," he said with a regal bow.

Sterling shook his head as he threw his bag into the back of the wagon and moved to the opposite side.

Blair slipped into the backseat beside Sterling, and Alec closed the door behind her before jogging back to the passenger seat.

Marco drove the wagon forward to the corner, stopping for a police car to speed past, siren wailing.

Then the wagon's blinker clicked on before it took a right turn into the street and accelerated away from the parking garage.

Alec turned around and exclaimed, "Well, guys, nothing like a getaway in the wet!"

"Please stop," Blair muttered. Alec, looking dejected, turned back around.

She continued, "So how good was my theory? How many of those high-level heists are you three responsible for?"

Another police car roared past in the opposite direction.

"Well," Marco called from behind the wheel, "kind of a lot. The best ones, to be sure."

Sterling interrupted, "But first things first. Today's game ball goes to...Blair."

He pulled a hot-pink thumb drive out of his pocket and handed it to her.

"What's this?"

"Your first bonus—Gordon's crypto. 183K. Before you get too excited, half of everything we earn goes to anonymous donations. A majority of the rest is re-invested into planning and executing future heists. Our take-home is five percent split equally, so if you were expecting a lavish lifestyle you've got the wrong crew. But at least your waitressing days are over. And having seen your service firsthand... I think we're doing the city of LA a favor."

Alec offered, "I cracked Gordon's safe for you, Blair. You're welcome. But we've got bigger problems than who deserves the credit—I foundationally oppose bringing a woman onto a heist crew. If having a dame was a good idea, Hollywood would've thought of it by now."

Marco thought for a moment. "But James Cagney had a girl in *White Heat*. Virginia Mayo, remember?"

"She was a doll. She didn't go on the scores."

"What about Marilyn Monroe in *The Asphalt Jungle*?"

Alec lowered his head mournfully. "Again, Marco, she didn't go on scores. If anything, she was a representation of chauvinistic mitigation of the fairer gender. Does Blair look like a ditzy mastermind's girlfriend to you? Does she act like it?"

Sterling snapped his fingers. "*To Catch a Thief*. Brigitte Auber."

"That was really more of a mystery than heist genre. And there was no technical sophistication in the thefts—they just kind of waltzed around rooftops."

"I got it," Marco announced. "*The Italian Job.*"

"Mrs. Beckerman? She didn't rob anything, she just handed over a ready-made heist plan. Kind of a crude plot device, when you think about it."

Sterling shook his head. "Not the 1969 original. He's talking about the 2003 remake, with Charlize Theron. Did you see it?"

"Of course I saw it."

"Do you remember it?"

"Charlize may have supported the score, but I don't think she played a direct role in the heist."

"She drove a car, Alec. She cracked the safe."

"Really—cracked the safe?"

"Yeah, man."

"Huh." Alec was dumbfounded for a moment, and then looked to Blair. "Well, welcome aboard."

"Thanks," Blair said, turning over the thumb drive in her hands. "But I still don't understand why you guys did a bank robbery in the first place." She nodded to the three bags of cash in the back. "That haul is almost pocket change considering what you three have pulled off in the past few years."

Sterling answered, "The 34th floor of Geering Plaza hosts the physical server linking trades between four different financial firms. All of them make a killing on subprime mortgages. All of them transfer more money in a day than that bank does in a week. Marco needed an hour's worth of access to plant a stay-behind device on the server. Now it's pulling...Marco?"

Marco diverted his attention from the road for a moment's glance at the digital readout of a phone in the cup holder. "$523,000 so far, all in skimming transactions below the threshold for reporting. Our estimated yield is $3.2 million every twenty-four hours until it's found."

Blair shook her head. "Why not just break in and install it quietly?"

"The physical server is manned 24/7 unless there's an actual emergency —we couldn't just pull the fire alarm, and we couldn't do a B&E while the station was occupied."

Alec added, "If anyone knew a technically proficient heist crew entered that building, they'd expect the worst and search until they found what we were there for. But a bunch of gunslingers rolling in on a takeover robbery with hostages? Nobody suspects high levels of sophistication. It's a spider heist."

"What's that?" Blair asked.

Sterling answered her.

"A spider heist—everyone sees the spider, and nobody notices the web. And this was a practice run compared to the jobs we have coming up. So," he asked, "are you still in?"

Blair looked forward, watching the city of Los Angeles streaking past beyond the window. She tucked a tendril of hair behind one ear, adjusted the strap of her torn dress.

And then she smiled.

THE SKY THIEVES: SPIDER HEIST THRILLERS #2

Blair Morgan has embraced her second career—as an elite thief.

Her heist crew has set their sights on their latest target: the Sierra Diamond, an 872-carat stone worth $27.3 million. It will be encased in a new vault known as the Sky Safe, a revolutionary strong room built into the side of a Los Angeles high rise.

The FBI says the Sky Safe is impenetrable. Naturally, Blair and her crew think otherwise...and if they succeed, it will be the greatest heist ever pulled.

But Blair's corrupt former boss at the FBI has other plans. He knows Blair will be coming for the diamond and intends to catch her in the act...along with her entire team.

As a dangerous game of cat-and-mouse unfolds over the streets of downtown LA, Blair must go head-to-head against the most cunning adversary from her past—or see herself and her crew imprisoned forever.

Get your copy today at
severnriverbooks.com/series/the-spider-heist-thrillers

ACKNOWLEDGMENTS

I've never relied so heavily on so many people to write a book as I did for *The Spider Heist*.

In roughly chronological order, here they are. As you'll quickly discover, all requests for anonymity were honored with a pseudonym of the contributor's choice.

When I first conceived of this story, I racked my brain for ideas about what Blair's background could be. There was no solution in sight when Mrs. Christina, my daughter's day care teacher, casually mentioned that she used to be a police officer. As a slow learner, I thought nothing of this—until exactly three days later, when I suddenly had a eureka moment. From that moment on, Blair's past was in law enforcement.

As a friend, long-time Los Angeles native, and former deputy sheriff, James Sexton was instrumental in educating me on more aspects of this book than I'd care to admit. He remained a primary technical advisor for the entire time it took me to write and refine the manuscript, patiently advising me every step of the way. Without his help, my fictional robbers would have been stuck in traffic and arrested on the 405 after I planned the worst initial getaway route possible.

Several current and former law enforcement and military advisors put aside their innate aversion to let the "bad guys" win in this book, and patiently answered my many questions.

From the FBI, Sheridan and the Angry Leprechaun educated me on their organization and the structure of a federal task force despite the fact that my book, quote, "murdered the integrity of [their] chosen profession." I plead no contest.

From the State Police, Howie Ryan served as forensic consultant as he has with my previous books. His colleague 3664 answered my every inquiry with his particular brand of Jersey lexicon, casually informing me (without once using the word "arrested") how a "milk toast" member of a federal task force could find themselves "clipped," "pinched," or otherwise have their "pension killed."

From the 75th Ranger Regiment, B87 provided the specifics of three-dimensional LIDAR data that would be used to prove the falsity of an official report.

Fellow thriller author, former detective, and current drinking buddy Brian Shea not only taught me the ins and outs of incapacitation by taser, but read the entire manuscript to provide a promotional blurb. Next time we meet, the first round is on me.

As a former race car driver and instructor, Mark Hutchins was the car chase technical advisor that every author dreams of. He schooled me in the finer points of bootleg turns (AKA forward 180s), J-turns (AKA reverse 180s), ramming, understeer, oversteer, weight transfer, brake bias, line theory, and a lot more in staggering levels of detail. The credit for any accuracies of the chase scene belongs to him alone, and I'm pleased to say that he gave me more ideas than I could pack into this story—so I've got a few tucked away for future books in this series.

Dr. Richard Addison from New South Wales, a special operations mountaineering enthusiast of impeccable credentials, ensured that the rappel scene conformed with actual climbing techniques and use of equipment.

Once the story was complete, Randall served as developmental editor. He provided an incredible amount of detailed feedback and suggestions that greatly elevated the flow, continuity, and pacing of the finished manuscript far beyond what I could have (or did) conceive of by myself. Thank you, Randall—you saved this train wreck.

My pre-beta readers Codename: Duchess, JT, and Julie were extremely generous with their time and helped me revise my rough draft into a streamlined book. As is his custom, Codename: Duchess tolerated my multiple follow-up calls to clarify his opinions and brainstorm solutions to story problems.

Twenty-seven beta readers reviewed the book next, weighing in on possible improvements and helping me steer the rewriting process in the right direction. I owe them all my greatest thanks for their time and patience.

Cara Quinlan performed line and copy editing, as well as a final proofread. I was exceedingly lucky to discover Cara three years ago when seeking an editor for my debut novel, and ever since I wouldn't dream of using anyone else. As always, her notes and corrections resulted in the return of a far better book than I gave her to edit.

Finally, thank you to my beautiful and long-suffering wife, Amy. Her endless support has allowed me to pursue the job of my dreams, with the woman of my dreams. For that and much more, I am forever thankful.

ABOUT THE AUTHOR

Jason Kasper is the USA Today bestselling author of the Spider Heist, American Mercenary, and Shadow Strike thriller series. Before his writing career he served in the US Army, beginning as a Ranger private and ending as a Green Beret captain. Jason is a West Point graduate and a veteran of the Afghanistan and Iraq wars, and was an avid ultramarathon runner, skydiver, and BASE jumper, all of which inspire his fiction.

Sign up for Jason Kasper's reader list at
severnriverbooks.com/authors/jason-kasper

jasonkasper@severnriverbooks.com

Printed in the United States
by Baker & Taylor Publisher Services